W9-BPJ-112

"If I'm scared, I face it so I can move forward. When following leads, I make note of every single detail in hopes that one of them will go somewhere. Because all I need is one. And the emotional detachment… I fight every natural urge."

"Does it work?"

The question hung between them, weighted and dangerous. Sam knew that if he answered with a reference to his past, he'd be giving something away. If he answered in the moment… Well. He might give away even more.

"Not always," he said, carefully neutral.

Meredith didn't let him get away with it. "And what would happen if it didn't work?"

"It would make the job harder. Riskier. Because hearts are at stake as well as lives."

"Has it happened to you?"

Those green eyes of hers held him, and he knew he couldn't lie, even if he wanted to. "Once before." He reached up to smooth back a strand of her blond hair. "And now once again."

A blush crept up her throat. "Is it worth it? Risking your heart?"

"You tell me."

* * *

Dear Reader,

The inspiration for the opening scene of *Worth the Risk* came from my own life. I was lying in bed, not quite awake—on one of those rare mornings when my kids let me sleep past 7:00 a.m.—when a knock came on my front door. I debated whether or not to answer it, mostly because I dreaded getting out of my cozy blankets. Of course, in the end, I couldn't ignore it. I worried that it might be something or someone important. I answered, and it was just a kid from a local business, dropping off flyers.

As I crawled back into bed after, my imagination started building an alternate scenario for who *could* have been at the door. A mysterious figure? The bearer of bad news? And from that, private investigator Samuel Potter was born...

I hope you enjoy the twists of *Worth the Risk*, which all starts with an unexpected knock on Meredith Jamison's front door.

Melinda

WORTH THE RISK

Melinda Di Lorenzo

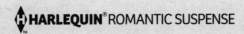

HARLEQUIN®ROMANTIC SUSPENSE

Recycling programs
for this product may
not exist in your area.

ISBN-13: 978-0-373-28200-5

Worth the Risk

Copyright © 2016 by Melinda A. Di Lorenzo

This edition published by arrangement with Harlequin Books S.A.

For questions and comments about the quality of this book,
please contact us at CustomerService@Harlequin.com.

® and TM are trademarks of Harlequin Enterprises Limited or its
corporate affiliates. Trademarks indicated with ® are registered in the
United States Patent and Trademark Office, the Canadian Intellectual
Property Office and in other countries.

Printed in U.S.A.

www.Harlequin.com

Amazon bestselling author **Melinda Di Lorenzo** writes in her spare time—at soccer practices, when she should be doing laundry and in place of sleep. She lives on the beautiful west coast of British Columbia, Canada, with her handsome husband and her noisy kids. When she's not writing, she can be found curled up with (someone else's) good book.

Books by Melinda Di Lorenzo

Harlequin Romantic Suspense

Worth the Risk

Harlequin Intrigue

Trusting a Stranger

Harlequin Intrigue Noir

Deceptions and Desires
Pinups and Possibilities

To my family, who accompany me
on every journey.

Chapter 1

*B*uzz.

Buzz.

Buzz-buzz-buzz.

The insistent vibration so closely matched the one in Meredith Jamison's head that she didn't immediately recognize that the two things were separate.

"Ugh," she groaned and rolled over on the couch.

The couch.

Why was she sleeping there? She had a perfectly comfortable mattress just one room away.

Right, she remembered. *Wine.*

The market research company where she temped had just landed a big client and she'd let herself be talked into celebrating. The third glass had led to a cab home, which led to the couch. Then the dull throb in her head. Thank God her tiny apartment in Bowerville, Washington—a small city outside of Seattle—didn't have an east-facing window. Sunlight would've killed her.

"Ugh," Meredith said again.

She worked to extract herself from sleep mode, but it still took her a few more seconds to clue in that the incessant buzzing wasn't random. It was her phone, lodged somewhere between her uncooperative body and the lumpy cushions. She longed to block out the sound with a pillow. But there was no pillow. Because she wasn't in her bed.

Dammit.

Meredith eased herself to a sitting position, shoved the lingering vestiges of her hangover to the back of her foggy mind and pushed a hand into the couch. Several forceful digs put the phone within reach. She closed her fingers on the noisy little device and yanked it out, shooting it a dirty look as it stopped buzzing before she could answer it.

Her irritation only lasted as long as it took to scroll to the missed call.

Tamara.

Seeing her sister's name on the little screen made her heart hurt as much as her head. Meredith genuinely couldn't recall the last time she'd spoken with her. Which was worse than being able to pinpoint an exact split in their close relationship. Not so long ago, they'd spoken every day. Then every week. Finally, that dissolved into a monthly lunch. And now…the rift seemed impossibly wide. So wide that Meredith hesitated to call her back.

Taking a minute to think about it, she closed her eyes, mentally preparing herself for whatever lecture Tamara undoubtedly wanted to deliver. Though younger by two years, the woman was always brimming with advice. Or criticism thinly disguised as advice, as the case often happened to be.

Meredith had never been sure if that particular dynamic—advisor and advisee—was the result of her sister's wildly successful marriage counseling program, or if it was the other way around. Either way, Tamara was never at a loss for telling Meredith what she *ought* to be doing. But they were still family, and as crazy as Tamara made her, Meredith couldn't ignore her. With a sigh, she pressed her thumb onto the call-back button, then lifted the phone her ear. It rang three times, stopped abruptly, clicked a few times and went dead.

Meredith pulled her cell away from her face and stared at it. She wouldn't have been all that surprised if Tamara sent her straight to voice mail, but the quick hang-up was a little much.

Besides which, she's the one who called me.

Annoyed, Meredith hit redial. This time, it rang once before her sister's breathy voice came through.

"Hello?"

"Tam—"

"Merri? Is that you?" The abrupt reply was barely louder than a whisper.

Even more than the hushed tone and the tremor in the question, the nickname worried Meredith. It was an old one. One that Tamara used when they were partners in crime, united against whatever trouble they were causing at any given moment in childhood. And she hadn't used it for fifteen years or more. Hearing it now ate away at any irritation Meredith had felt just moments earlier.

"What's wrong?" she asked.

"Oh, thank God." Her sister's voice shook. "I need your help. I snuck the phone out, but—"

There was a click, and the line was silent again.

Help?

Worry tickled every part of Meredith's body.

Had Tamara *ever* asked her for help in a desperate tone like that? She doubted it. Her sister was a type-A go-getter. If she did request assistance, it was because she wanted it, not needed it. And very likely, she thought she would be doing *Meredith* a favor by accepting whatever her sister offered.

Meredith shoved aside the thoughts and the questions, knowing the only way to get answers was to ask. She dialed Tamara's number again.

Voice mail. Damn.

She tried one more time with the same result.

Double damn.

"What's your deal, Tamara?" she said to the silent phone.

She'd automatically assumed that whatever Tamara needed had to do with her internet-based business. Everything did. The all-consuming world of Tamara's business—Get Better with Billing—never ceased to amaze Meredith. And not in a good way. Tamara had legions of followers and a whole host of haters. Hate mail and stalker fans. A gated house and money to burn. Every part of the marriage-counseling business impacted every part of her existence. Which, as it so happened, often extended to Meredith. The second someone found out Tamara was her sister, nothing else mattered.

Tamara Billing, celebrity counselor.

Meredith Jamison, celebrity counselor's sister.

It was clear who played the role of help*er* and who played the role of help*ee*.

Concern crept into her heart, and she tried to dismiss it. Wouldn't her sister have called her sooner if something was wrong? *Really* wrong? And why was Tamara sneaking around with her own phone? The emotional distance between them wasn't so great that Tamara would think she couldn't reach out if she was in some kind of trouble. At least not as far as Meredith thought.

She cursed the fact that her sister had done away with her home phone in favor of her cell and scrolled reluctantly through her address book again until she found her brother-in-law's name and office phone number. She'd do just about anything to avoid calling the man. The animosity was mutual, and likely—*no, not just likely, definitely*—the biggest source of discord in this sisterly relationship. But if anyone would know what was wrong with Tamara, it would be Nick. The one thing she couldn't fault him for was his unwavering love for her sister.

With gritted teeth, Meredith dialed.

A crisp, feminine voice answered halfway through the first ring. "Johnson, Johnson and Levi."

Meredith recognized the woman's voice—Hettie had been Nick's office assistant for years—but in an attempt to keep things impersonal, she replied in an equally professional tone. "Nicholas Billing, please."

There was a pause. "I'm sorry, but Mr. Billing isn't currently with us."

For a heartbeat, Meredith thought the woman was announcing Nick's death. Then she clued in. "He doesn't work there anymore?"

"Meredith? Is that you?"

She cringed as she realized that in her surprise, she'd given herself away. "Yes, it's me."

"Nick didn't tell you he left?"

"Nick doesn't tell me much nowadays."

This time the pause was more than a little awkward. "Oh. Right. You know…we still miss you working around here."

Meredith bit back an urge to remind the woman it had been five years, and instead asked, "Why did Nick leave?"

"I wish I knew. He said he was taking a trip. But he cleared out his desk and cut off his cell, too. Said he'd be getting a new number. When I made a joke about wondering if it was a *permanent* vacation, he didn't seem amused. I don't think anyone else even noticed. But a week's gone by and he hasn't come back— Oh, hang on."

Hold music filled the earpiece and Meredith tapped her short, unpolished nails on the couch cushion beside her. Her brother-in-law's departure from the law firm surprised her. He'd been working there for a decade—straight out of law school, in fact—and had to be close to making partner. Had he quit? She couldn't imagine he'd been fired.

"Miss?" Hettie's voice came back on the line, and it had become clipped once more. "I'm afraid I don't have another number for Mr. Billing."

Meredith frowned. "Is someone listening?"

"Yes, that's right. I'm afraid I can't give you any more details, but Mr. Howard has been assigned all of Mr. Billing's cases, if you'd like to speak to him instead?"

The other woman didn't wait for a reply and the *hold* music drifted through again. Meredith waited impatiently, and when Hettie came back on, it was in a much quieter, far more muffled voice.

"Sorry. The police just got here. And it's kind of weird... they just asked about Nick, too."

Meredith's worry came back with a vengeance. She beat it back and reminded herself that Nick's specialty as a defense attorney was white-collar fraud. He was considered an expert in the field, and though the police hated having to go up against him, they often used him as a consultant for their side. Or at least they had, back in the days when she worked with Nick. Still...

"Are they there for a case?" she asked, trying to sound casual.

"I don't know. I don't have them booked in for anything. But maybe. You know Nick. He likes to keep the balance. I'm sorry, Meredith. I have to hang up. I hope everything's okay."

The line went dead, leaving Meredith staring down at the phone.

The police are looking for Nick, right at the same second Tamara comes asking for help? A coincidence?

Possibly. But if not, it added a whole new level of concern. Of course, if Tamara needed help with something Nick-related, Meredith was the last person she'd call. So that brought her right back to Tamara's counseling business. And try as she might, Meredith couldn't quite shake the feeling that something wasn't right. She let out another sigh and decided that the best thing to do was to swallow her pride and make the three-bus trip across town to her sister's mini-mansion. Before she could change her mind, she slipped into some jeans, ran a brush over her hair, brushed her teeth, then snapped up her purse and made her way the door. She swung it open, then froze.

On the other side, blocking the exit, stood a man. A stranger. Who, in spite of his slightly slumped stance, had to be well over six feet tall. At just a hair's breadth over five foot ten, Meredith found it impossible *not* to notice when a man was that tall.

Even in heels, she thought, *I'd need to look up at him.*

And standing across from him like this, she felt damn near petite. Especially factoring in the wide cut of his shoulders and the way he took up the entire door frame.

He cleared his throat and slid his sunglasses up—which were entirely unnecessary anyway—from his face to sit on his dark, near-black hair, showing off the clearest blue eyes she'd ever seen.

An unexpected tingle of attraction swept through Meredith, temporarily overriding the ache in her head and filling it with dizziness instead.

Definitely too much wine.

Except his gaze raked over her, too, moving from her messy ponytail to her plain but fitted T-shirt to her slim-cut jeans. It was an appreciative look. One that said the immediate attraction wasn't one-sided.

But there was also something about the way he took in every detail of her appearance that made Meredith think he never missed a thing. Which finally reminded her that as much as she was enjoying ogling him, she had no idea who he was or what he was doing on her doorstep.

Probably got the wrong apartment number.

The neighborhood where she lived wasn't fantastic, but the one thing her building did have going for it was the glorified bouncer of a doorman. He wouldn't let in a stranger, not without buzzing him up.

Meredith took a breath, cleared her throat and—sounding far too awkward considering it was *her* house and *he* was the one who didn't belong—asked, "Um. Can I, um, help you? With something?"

His reply was a rumble that matched the day-old growth of beard on his ruddy cheeks. "Depends."

She stared at him. "On?"

"On whether or not you're Tamara Billing's sister."

And just like that, the vague worry that something was wrong swelled to a crescendo. The man standing in front of her was either a cop bearing bad news, or he was the source of the bad news himself. What she needed to do was find out which one applied.

Private investigator Samuel Potter watched the changing expressions on the blonde's face with interest. Puzzlement. Irritation. Fear. Resolve. Then schooled blankness.

Mesmerizing.

The word popped into his mind, then stuck.

He hadn't been expecting her to be so pretty. Or for her to have a soft, feminine voice that wrapped around him like silk and held him hostage. He hadn't thought too much about her at all, actually. Except in terms of being a starting point for his missing-persons investigation, of course.

The second she opened the door, though, he'd been unable to stop himself from dragging his eyes over the length of those oh-so-long, trim legs, then up to her slim waist—visible even under that plain shirt—then across the swell of her breasts to that tied-up pile of hair.

Sam ground his teeth together.

Finding the target was his goal. Finding the target's sister attractive…was not.

Focus.

He'd already lost the element of surprise, which was so key in getting people to answer questions honestly. Not that he assumed Meredith Jamison would be a liar, but he knew from experience that the more time people had to prepare, the more hesitant their replies became.

"Are you?" he persisted.

He was already sure of the answer. Her initial reaction had given it away. But Sam needed her to confirm it anyway. Thoroughness. A necessary part of his investigation.

"Am I what?" she replied.

Sam fought an unprofessional eye roll. "Are you Tamara's sister?"

She bristled visibly.

She doesn't like *being the sister of an internet celebrity.*

Sam noted that fact and automatically stored it in the back of his mind; it was the kind of thing that might come in handy later. His business was all about the details—reading people and using their "tells" to get to the truth.

"I do have a name." Her tone was just shy of defiant, and Sam noted that, too.

"Which I'm hoping is Meredith Jamison," he said drily.

"Why?"

"Why what?"

"Why are you hoping my name is Meredith Jamison?"

Sam blinked. He wasn't used to be challenged. Just his physical presence—six foot three, two hundred and ten pounds and perpetually scowling—made people back down. The attractive woman in front of him showed no sign of budging. If anything, her face grew more stubborn by the second.

Great.

"Well?" she prompted.

Sam suppressed a groan. What he needed to do was come up with a way of convincing Meredith it would be in her best interest to help him out. Which it was, of course. Her sister was missing, even if she didn't know it yet, and Sam was her best bet at finding her.

He tried to relax his body, to make himself appear as open as possible. He even managed to lift one corner of his mouth in a smile.

"Assuming you're Ms. Jamison… I just have a few questions about your sister. Easy-peasy. Then I'll get out of your way."

"What kind of questions?" She clearly didn't buy his feigned pleasantness in the least.

"When was the last time you saw or spoke to Tamara?"

"Why?"

Sam clamped his jaw down tightly for a frustrated second, then released it. "Do you always need to know the *why* of things?"

"I do when those things involve a man showing up on my doorstep asking about my sister."

Sam couldn't blame her for her defensiveness or for the fear that lay underneath it. But he also couldn't go into detail about his investigation. The confidentiality clause requested by his client prohibited him from disclosing more than the vaguest details. It tied his hands and made his job that much harder.

"There's no cause for alarm, Ms. Jamison," Sam ventured. "I'm just trying to get in touch with Tamara."

"Fine. I'm guessing you have some ID to go along with the rest of those questions, then?"

"ID?" he repeated.

"A wallet? A badge, maybe?"

She definitely knows something. And she thinks you're a cop. Sam examined her face for a moment, then amended the thought. *No, not quite. She knows something and she's trying to* figure out *whether or not you're a cop.*

He just wasn't sure which answer she wanted. The truth—that he'd once been an officer, but wasn't any longer—certainly wouldn't do.

"Do I need ID to ask questions?" He kept his tone as friendly as he could manage.

Meredith stepped backward, and he knew his window of opportunity was about to close.

And so was the door. Literally.

He realized it with about a second to spare. Sam lifted his hand, intending to close his fingers on the door so he could hold it open. Instead, they landed on Meredith's wrist. They closed on her silken skin. The unexpected feel of it under Sam's rough hand sent his pulse skyrocketing. Desire jolted through him, sucking the air from his lungs.

Slowly, he brought his gaze up to Meredith's face. Her eyes were wide with a surprise that matched his own, and they were as pretty as the rest of her. A liquid green that reminded Sam of the ocean at midnight. Drown-in-me dangerous.

As Sam watched, she drew in a breath and the tip of her pink tongue came out to lick the edge of her bottom lip. Then she whipped her arm from his loose grasp and slammed the door in his face.

For a long second after it happened, Sam stood frozen to the spot, processing. He'd just violated about a half a dozen of his own on-the-job policies, and the result was an epic failure. He hadn't solicited a single piece of information or acquired the slightest hint as to where to go to next. The only thing that would make it worse was if the girl panicked and contacted the local authorities. There was nothing Sam hated more than cutting forcibly through red tape in order to get the job done. Especially the most basic of jobs, like this one.

He took a breath, counted to thirteen—because ten wasn't quite enough—and reminded himself that Meredith was currently his one and only lead. Even if he put that aside, he'd also taken a hefty advance payment from his client. He would work as hard as he could to trace the target. So he couldn't walk away, even if he wanted to.

Is that what you want to do? Just walk away?

He flexed his hand. It still tingled from the brief contact. It screamed of a precarious road ahead, should he choose to pursue his investigation via Meredith Jamison. He *should* want to walk away, just for that reason alone. But he didn't want to.

His eyes sought the closed door.

To knock, or not to knock, that is the—

The thought cut off abruptly as one noisy crash, then a second, echoed through the door. Silence followed the bangs.

What the hell was that?

Every protective instinct Sam had roared to life.

"Ms. Jamison!" he called as his fist hit the door.

No answer.

He thumped again. "Ms. Jamison! Meredith!"

Still nothing. He rattled the handle. Locked. He shook the knob harder.

"Meredith!"

Break down the door!

With a heave, Sam obeyed the self-issued command, slamming himself into the wood. The frame rattled, but held. He took several steps back, then ran at the door, shoulder first, his full body weight behind the second attempt. This time, his effort paid off. The wood buckled then cracked, and at the same time, the hinges ripped from the wall. For a moment, Sam and the door stayed suspended in place. Then they both crashed inward.

Ignoring the sharp ache in his shoulder, Sam pushed himself to his feet and put his hand on his sidearm. Caution and subtlety were already a write-off. He moved through the apartment quickly, room to room, calling her name as he searched.

Bedroom. Empty.

Bathroom. Empty.

Kitchen, closets, living room. Empty, empty, empty.

Then he spotted a shattered vase on the floor beside the patio door. He moved toward it quickly, found the latch undone and slid open the glass. With a careful look up and down, then side to side, Sam stepped outside. A large potted plant had fallen over, its contents spilling onto the deck. Another lay in pieces, red clay littering the ground.

For a panicked second, he thought Meredith had been taken forcibly, but his brain argued against it, pointing out the details. Aside from the plants and the vase, nothing indicated a struggle. There had been no screams. And an intruder wouldn't have taken the time to shut the patio door.

She'd made a run for it.

Chapter 2

Meredith clung to the emergency escape ladder and told herself she wasn't a total idiot for running. She was simply protecting herself and her sister.

The man at her door had no authority over her—the only thing he did have was that demanding stare. And those wide shoulders.

Shut up, she told herself. *Wide shoulders are irrelevant.*

He could be anyone, or anything, and whatever he was or did, he hadn't exactly been forthcoming. The fact that he'd turned up right when Tamara seemed to have gone AWOL couldn't possibly be a coincidence. It didn't make her want to stick around. Not that he gave her a bad vibe. Just the opposite, if she was being honest. That one, brief touch had made her warm from the outside in, then back again. It made her want to melt. Which was dangerous all on its own, regardless as to whatever his intentions were.

"Honesty's overrated," she grumbled as she grabbed another rung and propelled herself up.

Because she *really* wasn't a total idiot. She knew if she just headed straight down, there was a good chance the stubborn, blue-eyed stranger would follow her. She could tell already he wasn't a quitter. So instead of heading to the ground, she was climbing the two stories to the roof. Once there, she'd cross to the vine-covered rear of the building and make her way down, then follow through with her original plan to get to Tamara's house and figure out exactly what was going on.

Meredith reached the top rung of the last ladder and pulled herself over the lip of the roof. She landed on the gravelly surface with a grunt, then sat there for a minute, staring up at the cloudy sky. She was unpleasantly sweaty and panting and her body hurt from the exertion. And she still had the residual wine-induced headache, too.

"I swear to God, Tami," she said to the air, "if that guy down there is your secret lover and you were calling me to help you with him… I'm going to shave your head in your sleep."

But her gut twisted a little. An affair—even one with a man who made Meredith's own heart pound inexplicably—would be preferable to the other things running through her mind.

Don't dwell, and don't assume, she told herself as she stood and brushed off the dirt from her knees. *Just get to Tamara and get some answers.*

She wiped her forehead, shouldered her purse, strode to the other end of the roof and swung a determined foot over the side.

Sam slammed open the front door of the apartment building, ignoring the startled look on the gorilla-sized doorman's face as he barreled by. He'd slipped the guy fifty bucks to get in; he sure as hell didn't owe him an explanation for his mode of exit.

Without looking back, Sam rounded the building with the intention of positioning himself in the bushes just below Meredith's apartment. Out of sight, but not out of reach. But as he approached his intended hiding spot, a flash of movement made him stop short. He spun to follow it, and the hair on the back of his neck stood up as every alarm bell in his well-seasoned body went off.

What the hell?

A man stood on the edge of the yard, binoculars pressed to his face and pointed straight up at Meredith's apartment. At Sam's sudden appearance, he dropped the binoculars to his chest and spun. In the heartbeat he had to do it, Sam catalogued the other man's features. Red hair. Craggy skin. Thick stubble covering his cheeks and chin. Unkempt clothes.

Bad news.

Then the other man took off at a run. Automatically, Sam followed. They tore around the building in a back alley, where a nondescript sedan sat waiting. Before Sam could catch up, the redhead leaped into a vehicle and peeled out.

Sam's PI instincts battled with his protective ones, the former demanding he run to his Bronco and follow the car and its surly-looking driver, the latter insisting he stay behind and make sure Meredith Jamison was all right. He didn't get a chance to find out which part of himself would've won the internal battle. A snap from above sent his gaze heavenward, and what he saw made him still.

"I'll be damned." He craned his neck up as far as it would go.

Right above him, just in view, was Meredith Jamison. Sam's body tensed.

For the love of all that is holy. If she falls, I'll...

His thought trailed off as his eyes landed on her curved, jeans-covered rear end, reminding him of why he'd found her so distracting in the first place. For a minute, protectiveness took a backseat to desire. Her form-fitting T-shirt rose up, exposing a tantalizing amount of creamy skin.

She placed her feet on an elaborate piece of vine-covered metalwork on the side of the building. He couldn't tear his eyes away. Not even when he acknowledged she'd risked her life just to avoid talking to him. He even had to admit to a grudging amount of admiration for her temerity.

Beauty, brains and guts. A deadly, tempting combination.

A little squeal from above brought Sam's attention back to the truly dangerous situation she'd put herself in. She was halfway down the six-story building now, and one of her Converse-clad feet had come loose.

Sam's gut churned.

He stepped to position himself under Meredith. He figured that, best-case scenario, she made it down and landed—probably angrily, definitely reluctantly—at his feet. Worst-case scenario, she came *crashing* down and he took the brunt of the fall. Maybe he'd break a bone or two, but at least she'd be safe.

She grumbled something loud but incomprehensible as her foot regained its hold, then she began to inch down again.

Sam kept his gaze on her, thankful for each yard that brought her closer to him and to safety. He wondered what, specifically, had prompted the rooftop escape attempt. Had she got ahold of her sister? Or was she just that opposed to speaking to Sam? Either way, he was going to get his hands on her and tell her how insane she was for putting herself at risk simply to avoid him and his questions.

She'd reached the one-story mark now, and she finally paused. She was close enough that Sam could hear her labored breathing and see that she was shaking with effort.

Almost there. Don't stop now.

Meredith still hadn't looked down, and Sam tensed as her head tipped in his direction. She looked back up quickly, though, and started moving again.

Good.

She hit the home stretch, and just as Sam was about to reach up and grab one of her ankles, she lost her grip on the metalwork and tumbled backward. Heading straight for Sam.

A shriek escaped from Meredith's lips as she fell, then the sound died abruptly as her back smacked against something that was just the right amount of firm.

Not something, her mind corrected. *Someone. A good-smelling, solidly* male *someone.*

Vaguely, Meredith thought she should be embarrassed about falling into some poor passerby's arms. But she didn't have time. The impact sent whoever it was stumbling backward, and as her savior tried to keep himself on his feet, he propelled them both forward instead. Hard.

Too hard.

Together, they flew toward the wall. The man slipped one hand to her waist and slammed the other out in front of them, just barely stopping their momentum before they hit.

Meredith inhaled a shaky breath, and as her rescuer loosened his hold, she turned to face him.

"Thank you!" she gasped. "I thought I was going to—"

She cut herself off. Too-blue eyes—mildly amused but no less intense than they had been when he'd darkened her door frame—stared down at her.

Dammit. I should've known.

"You thought you were going to what?" he asked almost teasingly. "Get away? Fall to your doom? Don't worry, sweetheart, I'm glad to stop you from doing either."

"I'm sure you are," Meredith retorted.

She feinted to the left and ducked to the right, trying

to slip away, but the dark-haired stranger shot out an arm, stopping her movement. She moved in the other direction, and once again, he blocked her in. No part of him touched her, but she could somehow still feel every bit of him. The rise and fall of his chest. The corded muscles of his forearms. All of it made her tingle. She took a breath. It only made things worse. She could smell his light, masculine scent, and it begged her to drink it in even more.

"Let me go." Her command came out as a whisper.

"Not until you answer my questions."

"I'll scream."

"I'll find a way to keep you quiet," he countered.

Involuntarily, her gaze landed on his lips. "You wouldn't dare."

"There isn't much I won't do to get the job done."

He leaned forward, and his mouth was so close Meredith could practically taste him. And she almost wanted to.

Almost?

She shoved aside the accusing thought and forced herself to speak in a strong voice. "You proud of yourself, Mr. All-Or-Nothing? Capturing a defenseless girl like me?"

The blue-eyed man, who definitely wasn't a cop, pulled away. Just enough to let her breathe safely. But he looked like he was trying to cover a smile.

"Most people call me Sam," he told her. "And I'm not convinced you're defenseless at all. But I'd hardly call this capturing anyway. After all, I *did* just save you from landing on your—"

This time, she cut *him* off. "On my *what*?"

He raised an eyebrow. "Head."

"I don't believe for a second that's what you were thinking."

"Do you want me to tell you what was *really* going through my mind as you *fell* into my arms?"

"Actually, I have *zero* interest in knowing what you think," she stated.

"I'm going to tell you anyway."

"Of course you are."

"I think that you owe me one."

"Owe you one what?"

"One rescue from certain death."

"You didn't save my life!"

"Are you deliberately picking a fight with me?"

She felt her face heat up. "Of course not!"

"Oh. So this was your way of saying thank you?"

"This is my way of avoiding men with stalkerish tendencies."

"By climbing down an entire building like some kind of deranged superhero?"

"A deranged— Ugh! If you weren't following me, I wouldn't have *had* to take the roof."

"That. Or you're hiding something. Did you talk to Tamara?"

"No."

It wasn't quite a lie. She hadn't spoken to her sister *again*. He seemed to sense the deception anyway.

"If you tell me what she said, I might be able to help you," he offered softly.

For several seconds, she considered it.

Maybe he could shed some light on what was going on.

She shoved aside the idea firmly. She wouldn't risk it. Not unless he became her only option. What she needed to do now was to get away so she could figure out what to do next. She didn't need a complication. Especially not a good-looking one who made her knees a little weak. Besides that, he'd made it clear that he didn't know where Tamara was himself. He was asking questions, not giving answers.

"Will helping me help *you* get the job done?" Her voice was loaded with sarcasm.

"I somehow doubt it."

"Good."

"Good?"

"That means I don't have to feel quite so bad about *this*."

And with that tiny warning, she lifted one of her Converse sneakers and slammed it onto his foot, then went running up the alley.

Chapter 3

I hope he's okay.

Meredith had run two hard blocks without looking back when the unexpected thought popped into her head and just about made her trip over her own feet.

Why did she care if he was okay?

He'd sat outside her house, waited for her to come out, too, then jumped on her the second he could. What she needed to care about was putting some distance between herself and those eyes of his. To get to a place where she could stop and breathe.

That's right. Because you sure can't breathe when he's nearby. Or stop thinking about his eyes.

This time she *did* trip. One sneaker caught on a rock and she toppled forward, barely managing to get her palms out in front of her body before she hit the ground. They scraped along the asphalt painfully, but Meredith pushed herself up and forced her legs to move again, this time at a slower jog.

Okay. Acknowledge the attraction before thinking about him leads to a broken arm or something. Then maybe you can get over it.

And it gave her something to consider other than the burning reminder in her lungs that she'd been neglecting her cardio.

The guy—Sam—got to her. There was no denying how her body had reacted to his, how she'd felt every pore come alive as they pressed together.

Well. He did save you from landing head-first on the pavement.

Not that Meredith would admit that to him. Or that she normally went for the hero type. She had no interest in playing the damsel in distress to some man's misplaced sense of knighthood. So maybe the attraction was fueled by adrenaline. After all, it wasn't every day she climbed down the side of a building to avoid a guy, then stepped on said guy's toe and ran off into the streets like a crazy person.

But she'd been attracted to him before that, hadn't she?

Yes, definitely.

The wide shoulders, the impressive height. The way he looked at her, assessing and intelligent, but appreciative, too. Then there was his quick wit…

"Write a song about him, why don't you?" she grumbled.

Truthfully, it'd been a long time since she'd even noticed a man. Longer still since she'd been in one's arms. Her unintentional, chest-to-chest, utterly heart-thumping moment with Sam had been as close as she'd come in years. Literally years. Because being the sister of the woman who created the perfect system for snagging and keeping a husband made dating problematic. Some men went running in the other direction the second they found out. A few went the *other* other direction and were ready to propose by the second date. Meredith had learned to be cautious.

So, yeah. Being this attracted to someone she just met—wondering what that five o'clock shadow of his would feel like pressed to her cheek or if his lips were as firm as they looked—was unusual.

And stupid.

"That, too," she agreed out loud.

She had more important things to worry about. Like what her next move was going to be now that she'd escaped Sam and his crooked half smile.

Dammit.

His smile hadn't even been on her radar until right that second. Now, though… Yep. Right up there with eyes.

Meredith shook her head and spoke her sister's name aloud as a reminder of her priorities. "Tamara."

And saying the name made her think maybe she should call her again. Meredith reached for her purse and then groaned. It wasn't on her shoulder where it should be.

Must've dropped it when I tried to do that head plant.

Which meant that Sam probably had it.

"Great."

What was the man's deal, anyway? Something in her gut told her he wasn't there to hurt her. But if he was so interested in Tamara, why didn't he just go after her directly? Or contact someone who'd spoken to her recently. Her publicist or the host of tech people who helped run her internet business. Meredith's sister didn't exactly maintain a low public profile, and she had plenty of peripheral friends who practically qualified as an entourage. Not so long ago, her house had even been featured in some kind of home-and-garden magazine. Tamara's life was accessible in many ways, but coming through Meredith wasn't one of them.

Just the opposite.

Meredith swallowed, a guilty lump building in her throat. The rift between them might not be something they advertised, but anyone who took a second would see she wasn't involved in her sister's life. Sam's intelligent gaze told her *he* should have figured all of that out. So why was he still so hell-bent on following Meredith?

Unless he tried all that other stuff and still couldn't find her. Maybe his questions and his persistence had to do with that very fact. Tamara was missing. Meredith almost tripped again.

Missing? That's a leap. Isn't it?

She had no real reason to believe Tamara was anywhere but in the middle of a too-relaxed-to-answer-the-phone spa day. Except she *had* answered the phone, Meredith reminded herself. And she'd asked for help. Not typically needed for a pedicure.

She stopped short in her jog as a sudden, dark sense of foreboding shook her, sending a shiver up her spine. The terrible sensation grew even worse when she looked around and realized her haphazard flight had taken her from her own slightly rough neighborhood to the edge of an area that was downright seedy.

The run-down buildings that lined the street and the litter-crowded sidewalk between them made her wish she'd taken her chances with Sam and his questionable motives. Instead, she was sweaty and tired and stuck with no ID, no cash and no phone.

And no choice to do anything but go home.

She'd be lucky if the blue-eyed man turned over any of her stuff without a fight. She could easily picture him handing over each item, piece by piece, in exchange for whatever it was he felt like asking.

If he'd even bothered to stick around.

As Meredith resigned herself to the fact that she didn't have another option and turned to head back, she spotted a navy sedan. It was on the next street over, but she could see it perfectly through the sparse trees, and something about it gave her pause. Maybe its general out-of-place-ness.

Maybe it's Sam. And your purse.

She cut across the road to the median, then took five steps toward the car before she got a good view of the driver. It wasn't Sam at all. It was a redheaded man with a cigarette hanging from one corner of his thin lips. And if Meredith had felt a chill before, it was nothing compared to what she experienced now. There was something deeply disturbing about the way his gaze fixed on her, and if he cared at all that she was staring back at him, he didn't show it.

He kept his eyes on her, butted his cigarette against the dash, then tossed it out the barely cracked window. She swallowed nervously and took a step backward.

The sedan inched forward.

Uh-oh.

Another step, another few inches.

Whoever he was, he was going to round the curb and come at her.

You need to run!

The urgent internal suggestion was different than the one that made her choose to avoid Sam. This one was pure fear.

But when Meredith turned to go back up the street she'd just come from, she spotted a small group of men at the end of the road, and the paranoid part of her brain was sure that every one of them looked as dangerous as the driver in the car.

Meredith spun back again. The sedan had reached the curved part of the median now, and the driver's head had turned sideways as he worked to keep her in view.

Run!

This time, the suggestion came as a scream. And Meredith had no choice but to obey.

She slammed down one foot in front of the other, but made it only a half a block before an old, rusted-out truck came flying down the wrong side of the road and screeched to a stop in front of her. The driver's-side door squeaked open and a masculine hand dropped out at eye level.

Meredith knew without even looking who was attached to that hand.

"Get in!" Sam barked.

"Wh—"

"Now!"

Meredith took a breath, placed her hand in his and let herself be yanked straight into Sam's lap.

Sam gritted his teeth.

He seemed to be doing that a lot since meeting Meredith Jamison.

Right that second, it seemed impossible to do anything else. He tried to unclench his jaw and failed.

When she'd stomped on his foot, he'd chased after her for all of ten feet before realizing he didn't stand a chance of catching up. Not in a neighborhood she knew and he didn't, and not with the ache in his toes.

He'd limped back to his Bronco, irritated as all hell, and tried to come up with a plan. He'd barely made it into the driver's seat before the navy sedan whipped by. He didn't question why he knew it, or even stop to ask himself *how* the man in the car was tracking her, but he was one-hundred-percent sure following that sedan would lead him to Meredith. His gut told him it was true, and his gut was rarely wrong. This time was no exception.

Minutes after his careful pursuit of the car started, he spotted Meredith. And as the ginger-haired driver started toward her, Sam's gut hadn't been content to just be right. It had pushed him to intervene. Quickly.

Now Meredith was lying flat across his lap, her rear end

stuck under the steering wheel, her chest pressed against the outer edge of his thigh and her legs still dangling out the door as he attempted to make a getaway. As awkward as the position was, she still felt good pushed into him like that. Very good.

Sam put the truck into Reverse and pressed the gas pedal as hard as he dared and *gritted his damned teeth*. He spun the wheel—ignoring the little yelp from Meredith as it raked over her backside—and repositioned his vehicle so it faced in the right direction.

Then he heard the squeal of rubber on asphalt, and his teeth were forgotten as he glanced in the rearview mirror. The sedan picked up speed on the other side of the median, the driver struggling to beat him to the curve ahead.

Let him beat me. Then I can give him a little of what he deserves. See if his car can handle being slammed into by the Bronco.

The vicious thought struck Sam by surprise. Typically, he avoided confrontation. He'd fight if he was backed into a corner, but violence was a defensive, last-minute maneuver.

He just wanted the wannabe stalker to pay for... For what? Chasing down some girl he barely knew—*less* than barely knew—and scaring her? Because he thought she was *pretty*?

Yeah, maybe, Sam admitted.

Annoyed at himself, he slammed down on the brakes and came to a full stop.

"What are you doing?" Meredith's voice was breathless and muffled by the truck seat.

More teeth-gritting. "You're seriously questioning me *now*?"

"You stopped."

"For a good reason."

Sam put his hands on Meredith's hips and pulled her up, then shoved her sideways, forcing her to the passenger seat. She flailed for a second before righting herself and shooting him a dirty look.

"You might want to put on your seat belt," Sam offered before she could speak.

He yanked his door shut and did a cursory shoulder check. The sedan had rounded the median completely now. In the not-too-far distance a siren roared to life, and Sam knew someone had called the police.

Super.

He had no interest in explaining himself to the local PD.

With a silent growl and another glance in his rearview, he hit the gas. He spun the wheel and took the Bronco up and over the median. The abrupt move sent Meredith skidding across the seat and back into Sam's lap.

Well, I did tell her to buckle up.

With another pull on the wheel, Sam turned the truck on a diagonal across the road.

"Brace yourself," he said.

Meredith's face filled with panic, and at last she clicked the seat belt into place. Just in time. Sam accelerated again. His Bronco flew along the pavement, careened over a lawn and turned. He revved the engine and kept going. Up one street, down another, looking in the rearview every few seconds. So far, the sedan hadn't caught up. The sirens, though, were getting closer.

Maybe they'd scared off the redheaded driver.

Hopefully.

Sam took the Bronco up another street and scanned for a place to hide the vehicle. He spied a narrow alleyway behind them.

Good enough.

He shifted to Reverse, but Meredith's soft hand landed on his wrist. The contact made his pulse jump even higher than the increasingly loud sirens. It also made him pause. Which, judging by her next statement, was her intention.

"Not that alley."

"No time to be choosy, sweetheart."

Meredith rolled her eyes and released his arm to point at a sign. "It's a dead end. We'll get stuck."

"Fine. A *little* time to be choosy." Sam put the truck back into Drive and sped past the next two buildings, then stopped in front of another alley. "This one meet your needs?"

"*Our* needs," she amended. "Unless you suddenly stopped wanting to get away from that creep. And yes. It'll work. Sweetheart."

Sam fought an unexpected grin as he made the turn, pulled the truck out of street view and cut the engine. He closed his eyes for one second, but before he could take a single, calming breath, he heard the telltale squeak of one of his rusty doors.

Seriously?

His eyes flew open just as Meredith's door slammed into the building beside them. She sent a guilty look his way, then slipped toward the narrow opening.

Sam smacked open his seat belt and reached out a hand, which found purchase in the waistband of Meredith's jeans. She pulled forward, exposing skin and lace. Sam pulled and his knuckles brushed both. With the contact, a jolt of heat shot up his arm, and he let go, startled by the force of it.

Holy hell.

He barely managed to recover in time to see Meredith fall forward. Her legs slid to the ground with a thump, while her upper body stayed in the car. Sam continued to watch for a minute as she wiggled futilely.

At last she turned and glared at him. "Little assistance?"

He raised an eyebrow. "You want me to pull you back *in* or push you *out*?"

"Are you giving me a choice?"

"Not really."

"Then why bother to offer?"

"I didn't." He couldn't cover a grin. "You asked for help, remember, sweetheart?"

"Can we call a truce?" she replied with an eye roll. "And can you stop calling me 'sweetheart'?"

"Hmm. Let me see. No to the second part. And maybe to the first part."

"Sam!"

He liked the way his name sounded on her lips. Even when she said it in such an exasperated way.

"Yes, sweetheart?"

"Are you going to help me?"

"I will. If you agree to stop stomping on my feet and running away."

"You're chasing me!"

"I'm just trying get some information on Tamara's whereabouts."

"Why?"

"I don't suppose if I tell you it's confidential you'll accept that as an answer?"

"My day looks like this so far. A mild wine hangover. A weird—bordering on scary—call from my sister, who hasn't talked to me in *months*. You, on my doorstep. And now a crazy man chasing me down with a car."

"You spoke to Tamara? Today?"

"Yes. Briefly. But that's not my point," Meredith replied. *She's alive.*

The confirmation filled Sam with relief. He itched to know more about the conversation, but he doubted Meredith would tell him a damn thing. Not until they established some trust. Which wasn't going to be easy. He still had to try.

"Look," he said. "Would you be willing to give me the benefit of the doubt? At least until I get you unstuck?"

She wrinkled her nose. "Fine. Just…pull me back in. Please?"

For a second, he considered leaving her there, just to prove a point. Then he reminded himself that he needed her help, if he wanted to solve his case. If Meredith had a good side, he should be making more of an effort to get on it. Or at least try to get off the bad one.

"Only because you asked so nicely," he said. "Put your hands out."

With an exaggerated eye roll, Meredith stretched her arms in the vehicle. Sam took a deep breath and prepared himself for the electricity he knew would be coming, then clamped his fingers down on her forearms. Want hit him hard. He couldn't shove it aside, so he tried to harness the energy instead, to channel it to help pull her into the vehicle. In typical fashion, he overdid it. He yanked too hard and Meredith came flying into the Bronco, knocking him to his back and landing on top of him.

He expected her to leap off. Instead, she wriggled a little, then stayed where she was, her green-eyed gaze fixed on his face. Her lithe form remained pressed against him, her breasts rubbing against his chest, her hands positioned above his shoulders, holding her face above his. He could feel every one of her inhales and exhales. Her lips were so close that if he moved, even a little, they'd land on his mouth. And if he'd had any doubt about his attraction to her, it slipped away right that second. Meredith's body was a perfect fit for his.

"You all right?" he asked, desire making his voice husky.

"I'm okay." She paused. "Sam?"

Yeah, he definitely liked it when she said his name. It sent all the blood in his body straight to his groin.

"Sam?" she said again.

He swallowed. "Yes, Meredith?"

"I think my jeans are stuck to your belt."

"Oh."

At the one-word reply, she lifted a perfect eyebrow. "Do

you think you could, um, *un*stick it? Or does that fall outside the realm of your expertise?"

"Let me see what I can do."

He slid a hand between them, stifling a groan as the backs of his fingers brushed the skin of her stomach. She wiggled a little more, like she was trying to give him some space to work.

"Not helping," he said.

"Sorry."

She moved again anyway.

"Seriously. Could you hold still?" Sam asked.

"I'm trying."

His teeth gritted together again, though this time for a different reason entirely. He dug his hand down, desperate to find his belt buckle before he went crazy. Finally, his fingers closed on the warm metal. Sure enough, the button from Meredith's jeans was lodged under the frame. With a firm tug, Sam set it free, then dragged his hand out regretfully.

"You're all set," he told Meredith.

She righted herself. "Thank you."

"So that's what it takes to earn your gratitude? Third time's the charm?"

"Third time?"

"First, I saved you from becoming a pancake. Then, I saved you from our friend in the sedan. And now, I saved you from yourself."

"Ha. I think you only get a half a point for the second one since I had to navigate you into the correct alley."

"No, I definitely think you owe me three."

Meredith answered him, but Sam barely heard a word. Because a necklace slipped out from under her T-shirt and caught his eye, and suddenly, he was pretty damn sure that the redheaded thug was tracking her.

Chapter 4

Before Meredith could comment, Sam reached over, closed his hand around the pendant charm hanging from her neck and pulled it close to his face. And since she was attached to the necklace, Meredith had little choice but to follow. Which drew her near enough to Sam that she could smell his clean scent once again.

After a second, Meredith cleared her throat. "You a big fan of gaudy jewelry?"

"Not particularly. Where'd you get this piece?"

"Why?"

He sighed. "Can you answer *any* question without a long, drawn-out explanation?"

Meredith resisted an urge to stick out her tongue. "Depends on who's asking. Can I have my necklace back?"

"Nope. I just hope you didn't have that anywhere near your shower."

For the second time that day, a blush crept up Meredith's cheeks. "What?"

"Bedroom?"

The color in her cheeks deepened. "It was still in the box it came in. Until yesterday, anyway. Why does it matter?"

Sam's brows went up. "Still in the box? Did you buy it for yourself?"

"No. It was a gift."

"From?"

Meredith bit back another of her own questions. "Tamara. But you're not telling me—"

"She gave you a gift?" he interrupted. "Recently?"

"Two days ago. Like I said, we hadn't spoken in months and then this box turned up…" She trailed off with a shrug.

"You haven't spoken in months, but she sent you a necklace out of the blue and you didn't think to question it?"

"She's my sister and it was my birthday, okay? And…"

"And what?"

She shook her head. She had to admit, she'd been a little surprised to receive the necklace. It wasn't her style. And more importantly, it wasn't *Tamara's* style. Meredith had considered calling her sister when the necklace arrived but never got around to it. Now she really wished she had.

"Meredith?" Sam persisted.

"Nothing. Has anyone ever told you, you sound like a cop?"

"A few people," he replied drily.

She frowned. "Speaking of cops…"

"No."

"*No* what?"

"We can't wait for them or assume they'll get to us before the guy in the sedan does."

"Does that mean you're going to tell me why you're following me around and asking me questions about Tamara?"

He smiled grimly, and with a quick yank that burned Meredith's skin a little, Sam tore the pendant clean off.

"Hey! You can't do that!"

But any further protest died in Meredith's throat as the blue-eyed man set the necklace on his knee and pulled a Swiss Army knife from his boot, then used it to dig in behind the large, black stone that formed the charm's focal point. One sharp push and the stone flew off. And underneath it sat a microcamera.

"What the hell!" Meredith exclaimed.

"What the hell, indeed," he murmured, then met her eyes. "I think we can agree that Tamara didn't send you this."

Meredith swallowed. "Yes."

"Does your sister have any enemies?"

"Enemies? Lots of people don't like her program, but enemies?" She shook her head. "What's going on, Sam?"

In reply, he held the necklace up for a second, examined the camera once more, then placed it on the dashboard and smashed it with the handle of his knife.

"What's going on is that I need to get you out of here." He shoved the damaged piece of equipment into his pocket. "Quickly."

"You think I'm leaving with you without more of an explanation of who you are and how you knew someone was *spying* on me?" Meredith knew her fear was making her defensive, but she couldn't seem to stop herself.

"Do you see a better option?"

"No, but—"

"It doesn't matter anyway. I'm not giving you a choice, and I don't have time to give you an explanation."

"What're you going to do? Drag me by my hair?"

He eyed her hair like he was seriously considering it, then shook his head. He barely managed to open his mouth, though, before a ping echoed through the air, followed by a sharp crack. Sam's eyes flew to the windshield, and Meredith followed his gaze with wide-eyed horror. A flattened piece of metal had buried itself in the glass directly in line with Sam's head.

It only took a second for Meredith to figure out what it was.

A bullet.

Sam confirmed it a moment later. "The glass is only bulletproof-ish, apparently. I should probably ask for a refund."

He was making *jokes*? While someone *shot* at them? Was he completely insane? But when Meredith met his eyes, she saw that his face was deadly serious. And under that, he was worried. She could see it in the pinch in the corner of his eyes.

He was trying to reassure me, she realized.

For a weird second, she appreciated the gesture. It even helped her—a little—to recover from the fear making her heart thump against her rib cage. Then a second ping rang out, and this time the side mirror located to Meredith's right exploded, and any semblance of bravery went out the window. She dove into Sam's side and clung to his arm.

"Listen to me," he said into her hair, apparently unperturbed by how she held on to him. "We can't stay in the truck. And I know you have no real reason to trust that I'm telling the truth, but I promise you, I'll get you somewhere safe, then I'll tell you what I can. Can we agree to do that?"

Her mouth was too dry to answer, so she just nodded into his chest.

"Good. You can go back to fighting with me as soon as we're in the clear."

Sam reached over her to pop open the glove box, and Meredith sucked in a breath as she caught sight of what was inside.

A gun.

No, wait.

Two guns.

Sam pulled both out, then leaned forward to tuck one into the holster under his jacket. The other, he held out, butt-end first, to Meredith. She didn't reach for it.

"Take it," Sam urged.

She shook her head. "I can't shoot."

Why did she feel bad about the admission? Firing a gun wasn't something she'd never even considered doing before that second.

"It's easy." He pointed at the trigger. "Aim. Click."

Meredith took it cautiously. "I don't know if I can."

"You won't have to."

Meredith wanted to ask why, if she wasn't going to have to fire it, he was so insistent that she carry it. But he didn't give her a chance. He reached down to her feet, snapped up the purse she'd dropped back at her building and handed it to her.

"We're going out my side," he told her. "And all I want you to do is stay as close to me as possible."

Then he flung the door open, threaded his fingers through Meredith's and dragged her into the street.

Sam was absolutely sure of two things. One, he was in over his head, and two, he needed to get Meredith out of whatever this was, alive and unscathed. Especially if his suspicions about the origin of that camera turned out to be true.

No. Don't focus on that. Concentrate on the moment.

He held his body in front of Meredith's as they snaked along the side of the Bronco. His flesh might be an ineffective shield from a bullet, but at least he could make her feel secure. They reached the edge of the truck unharmed, and he scouted for the next point of safety.

"What do you do for work, Meredith?" he asked as he scanned the area.

She replied in a shaky voice, "What?"

"Work. What do you do?"

"I'm, uh, at a temp agency. So right now, I'm at a market research place. Internet survey stuff, mostly. Compiling data."

He spotted a potential spot for cover, about fifteen feet away. It was an easy dash. One that would build confidence for the next, undoubtedly longer run.

"Can you see that building sign over there?" He inclined his head.

"The one that says Brookside Apartments?"

"That's the one."

"Yes, I see it. Why?"

"In a few seconds, we're going to run toward its south side. Whoever is firing is coming from the north, and I don't think they know exactly where we are or they would've shot again already. Okay?"

A pause, followed by an audible inhale. "Okay."

Sam counted to ten silently, then tightened his grip on her hand. "Go!"

At full speed, they hit the pavement, propelling themselves away from the Bronco, and in seconds they reached the sign, unharmed.

"Do you think they're gone?" Meredith whispered.

"No. They wouldn't give up that easily."

"Then why aren't they firing?"

"Probably waiting for a clear shot," Sam replied. "But we're not going to give them one. How well do you know this area?"

"Not very."

"Could you navigate our way out?"

"I think so. You want to go somewhere specific?"

Sam had an idea, but he didn't want to get ahead of himself. "For now, let's just get away from this neighborhood—and let's stay away from yours, too. If you can do that, I can get us somewhere safe."

"All right," Meredith agreed.

"Which direction takes us out?"

"We can stick to the south side, if you think it's safer?"

"Sounds like a plan."

Sam eyed the urban terrain again. "Do you like what you're doing for work?"

"Not really."

"Why are you doing it, then?"

"It's complicated."

"Try me."

"Well, I'd planned to study law eventually, so I took the paralegal program to tide me over. But…" She trailed off and didn't pick up the statement again.

And Sam hadn't yet found a viable option for their next point. The lampposts were too narrow, the nearest car too far.

"But what?"

Meredith sighed. "I never found the time, I guess. Maybe it sounds funny, but having a semifamous sister limits your options. People expect things."

"People expect things? Or you expect things from yourself?"

He felt her eyes on his back. "Why are you asking me about this now?"

Sam shrugged. "Getting to know you."

"Getting to know me? Or trying to distract me from the fact that we're running for our lives?"

"Maybe both." Then he spotted it. "Central mailbox."

"I see it."

"You ready?"

"As I can be."

"Good enough."

He snapped up her hand once more, and they moved together. As they reached the mailbox, a shot finally rang out, pinging against the ground and tearing a hole in the concrete a few feet from where they crouched. Meredith let out a barely audible whimper. Sam pulled her closer.

"We're okay," he said. "But we can't wait here long. Can you keep going?"

He expected Meredith to protest, or to ask for more time, but she squeezed his hand and said, "Ten feet behind us, there's a pickup truck, and five feet from that, there's a sandwich board. If we can make it there, we can get to an alley, and I think I can find a way out from that point."

Sam nodded, impressed by her fortitude. "On three, then."

She met his eyes. "One."

"Two," he replied.

She opened her mouth, but *three* never made it out because a not-too-far-off shout and the pounding of feet on pavement announced they'd run out of time. Sam moved to pull away from the mailbox, but this time, Meredith was quicker. She held fast to his fingers, dragging him along as she shot out into the street. Sam let her lead, marking their stops.

Pickup truck. Check.

Bizarrely large sandwich board. Check.

One alley. Two alleys. Then three. Triple check.

At the end of the fourth one, they burst out of the apartment-lined streets and into a lower-density area. Duplexes and one-story homes. Tidier lawns. Evidence of children in the form of bikes and colorful sprinklers. They paused for just a moment at the end of a pebbled driveway, breathing heavily, but Meredith wasn't done pulling him along.

"C'mon," she urged.

Sam complied, placing his trust in her ability to guide them out. The flash of her Converse sneakers—black-white, black-white, black-white—kept him moving, and her soft hand in his kept him motivated. She led him through the neighborhood at a barely manageable jog, not stopping until they'd put even more distance between themselves and their pursuers.

"Just a bit farther," she gasped. "And you'll owe *me* one."

"Are we keeping tabs?"

"Definitely."

"Then we're three to one."

"One to two and half."

Sam managed a smile. "All right. I can compromise."

They pushed onward, and in a matter of blocks, they reached an area devoid of broken-down cars and replete with uniformly emerald lawns.

"Here," Meredith said at last. "In this area, one gunshot here will bring out every neighbor and six police cars." Then she let out a laugh. "Who knows? Maybe they'll see *us* and call the cops."

Not if I can help it. Sam felt his pocket to confirm the camera was still there.

Out loud, he agreed, his own voice ragged with exertion, "Perfect."

"What now?"

"We call my friend and ask for some help. But first…"

"But first what?"

"This."

Sam took a breath and took a chance because he might never get another opportunity. He broke his number-one rule—never get personally involved in with an investigation—and grabbed Meredith by the waist. Her green eyes widened, then shut as he dragged her body against his own and closed his mouth on her lush lips.

Chapter 5

Coherent thought flew from Meredith's brain as Sam kissed her. His exploration was almost tentative at first. Gentle. But as soon as she lifted her arms to his shoulders, welcoming the attention, the kiss deepened, and Sam's exploration grew more demanding. He tasted the corners of her mouth with his tongue, probing firmly.

Then his hand lifted to the small of her back, and Meredith gasped at the contact. He took advantage, delving between her lips. And each time his tongue found a new spot, Meredith's desire spiraled higher. In mere moments, a fan of heat radiated through her. It was hottest at the points where Sam's body touched hers directly. Their mouths. The tips of his fingers under the back of her T-shirt. The brush of his cheek on her chin. But where it was most distracting was at the points where she *wanted* to be touched.

Everywhere, she thought. *I want him to touch me everywhere.*

Except he was already pulling away, already giving

her lip a final, light tug and putting a few inches of space between them.

"Meredith…" He spoke her name in a low, sexy rumble and ran his thumb along her jaw. "I'm not going to apologize for that."

Apologize?

She stared at him wordlessly. She seemed to be having a hard time catching her breath. And it had nothing to do with their frantic escape. Not that she would fully trust her voice anyway. She'd never, not in all her twenty-seven years, been kissed like that. Never felt such a strong attraction to a man after such a short time. Maybe never at all. She didn't know if the adrenaline really was heightening things, or if it was just Sam. All she knew was that the last thing she wanted was an apology. But she couldn't make the words come.

After a silent minute, Sam sighed and pulled a slim black phone from his pocket. He keyed in a set of numbers, then carried on a monosyllabic conversation before turning his attention back to Meredith.

"Worm's on his way."

She finally found her voice. "Worm?"

"A guy I trust when I can't trust anyone else."

"Why can't you trust anyone?" Meredith's forehead creased with worry.

He met her eyes. "The less I tell you, the safer you are."

"Then I must be the safest person on the planet, because you haven't told me anything."

"Meredith." His voice was flat. Totally at odds with the kiss he'd just given her.

Fine. We can both do that.

"Tell me why you showed up at my door this morning," Meredith said, just as evenly. "And tell me why you're looking for Tamara. I think I've been patient for long enough."

A smile tipped up one corner of Sam's mouth. "This is you being patient?"

Meredith narrowed her eyes. She wasn't going to let herself be charmed.

"Tell me, or I swear I won't go another step with you. I'll walk up to one of these big houses and knock on the front door and tell them I need to call 911," she warned.

He shot her a glare, but when she took a step toward the closest driveway, he relented.

"I'm a private investigator, Meredith. Someone—a client of your sister's—hired me to look in on Tamara."

"Why?"

"I'm breaking the terms of my contract by telling you anything, you realize that?"

"And I'm breaking the terms of my *life* by running through the streets while someone tries to kill me."

He let out another sigh. "Fine. The client showed up for an online session, and your sister wasn't there. I guess that's pretty unusual."

"The business is everything to Tamara," Meredith stated. "She'd never abandon a client."

"Which is what she said. So when Tamara missed a second session that week, she started to get worried," he explained. "The client didn't want her identity compromised and she didn't want to involve the police, so she called me."

She sensed there was more. "And?"

"I haven't been able to locate Tamara. And now this."

"Do you think—" Her voice caught. "Do you think someone took her?"

"I try not to get ahead of myself."

"But you won't call the police?"

Sam's face darkened. "I can't."

Worry spiked at his unwillingness to involve the authorities. Then she thought about the police at Nick's office. Was it something she should tell Sam? It seemed more and more relevant. But aside from his skills as a lifesaver and as an incredible kisser, what did she really know about the man in front of her? She had no clue if his reluctance stemmed from a lack of trust in cops, or if it was something darker. Meredith opened her mouth to ask—or maybe just to insist that the situation was far too dangerous to not call for help—but an oversize truck whipped around the corner, cutting her off. It barreled toward them, then jammed to a stop a few feet away. A big, fully bearded man with a curly ponytail stuck his head out the window.

He tossed a suspicious look at Meredith. "Who's that?"

"The target's sister," Sam replied. "Meredith, this is Worm."

"Why's she here?"

Sam put an arm around Meredith's shoulders. "Because she is."

Surprise registered on the big man's face for a second before he recovered. "Let's see it."

Sam stepped away from Meredith, reached into his pocket and pulled out the smashed camera.

"What the hell did you do to it?" Worm reached out and snatched it away.

"Disabled it. I hope," Sam replied drily.

"Possibly. Sure as hell didn't give the serial number a fighting chance."

"It's there," Sam assured him.

Worm ducked back into the truck and, over the engine, Meredith swore she could hear the sound of a keyboard clacking. A minute later, the bearded man leaned out the window again, drew back his hand and tossed the camera through the air.

"You were right," he said. "Police-issue."

Meredith gasped. "The *police* planted the camera?"

Well. At least now his paranoia about the local authorities made sense.

"Still want to call 911, sweetheart?" Sam teased grimly, then looked up at Worm. "Can you give us a hand, my friend?"

"I'm here, aren't I?" the big man replied. "Hop in."

As Sam helped boost her into the truck, Meredith's mind alternated between wanting to go numb and wanting to race wildly. What had Tamara done? Fixed the wrong marriage? Or *not* fixed it? Or was it Nick? Had he crossed the wrong client? She still had a hard time believing her sister would call *her* in an attempt to help *him*. And what about the police involvement? She didn't have an answer for any of the questions bogging her down, and she was left staring out the window blankly, wondering just how she and Sam would figure it out.

She and Sam.

From the backseat, she stole a glance at him. His held his head tipped to the side, his striking profile on display. He was on the phone, talking in a low voice, attempting to leave a message for the client who hired him to track down Tamara. When he hung up and shot her a reassuring smile, Meredith's heart gave a surprising lurch.

A half a dozen other questions surfaced. What would have happened to her if he hadn't shown up when he did? Would the gun-wielding man in the sedan have kidnapped her? Killed her? And what about Tamara? Would her sister have stood a chance if the local PD had been put in charge?

"You okay?" Sam's voice cut through her worried thoughts.

"Should I be?" she replied.

"Probably not," he admitted. "But I'm working on it. And we're here."

"We're where?"

"My place," Worm said and cut the engine.

Belatedly, Meredith realized the big truck had come to a halt in front of a squat bungalow.

"You can rest up," Sam told her. "Maybe eat something,

if you want. Though from what I remember, Worm's cooking skills consist of takeout and toaster waffles."

"I've had worse," Meredith said and she let Sam help her from the truck.

Her body ached, and as weird as it seemed, her stomach rumbled the second she thought of food. But as soon as they'd settled into Worm's living room, and Sam started to lay out his plan, hunger and exhaustion quickly took a backseat to her concern.

"I need to get my notes from my apartment," Sam said. "Once I have them, Worm'll use his super tech skills to track Tamara's movements. I won't be gone long."

"You don't really expect me to agree to being left here, do you?" Meredith asked.

Sam shot Worm a look, and the big man glanced from one of them to the other, muttered something about making coffee, then disappeared up the hall.

"Sending him away isn't going to change my mind," Meredith said. "You're my only lifeline to my sister. If something happens to you while you're out there getting your notes…"

At the end, her voice almost broke. Because it suddenly struck her that it was true. The man standing over her was the only one she could count on right that second. He was the only other person who knew Tamara was missing and quite possibly the only other person searching for her. The police couldn't be trusted. Nicholas was nowhere to be found. Not that she exactly trusted him, either. Meredith also couldn't put any of her friends in danger by telling them what was going on. And if the media got involved, the situation would turn into a circus and Tamara's life would be at risk. If it wasn't already.

Oh, God. What if she's— Meredith shut down the thought before it could even finish. She refused to consider that her sister was anything but alive.

Sam sat beside her on the couch, and she lifted her hand to stop him from getting any closer. She knew if he touched her, that zap of attraction would floor her again, and she'd be in a bad position to say no to whatever he asked. And she wasn't backing down. But as her arm raised, so did his, and before she could draw away, his fingers closed on her wrist. He pulled her palm to his chest in a gesture that was both strangely intimate and comforting at the same time.

"I promise I'm doing what I think is best to help Tamara," he told her gently. "And nothing's going to happen to me while I'm doing that. It's my job."

"If you really believed that, you wouldn't be asking me to stay here." Meredith shook her head. "And this might be just a job to you, Sam, but to me, it's my sister's life."

"I didn't say this was *just* a job," he amended. "I said it *is* my job."

"I don't see the difference."

He finally let her wrist go.

"I get paid, but I'm not in it for the money. My goal is always the same—to help people. Because I know how it feels to—" He cut himself off abruptly, cleared his throat, then started again. "I've seen how my clients feel when someone they love can't be located, and I wouldn't wish that on anyone. I only take on missing-persons cases, nothing else. My closure rate has been one hundred percent since I started doing this. So the difference is, Meredith, it's *never* just a job for me."

At the end of his short but impassioned speech, Meredith stared at him. What had he been about to say before he stopped himself? And why did she get the feeling that, whatever it was he did before he became a PI, his success rate *wasn't* a hundred percent and that made him unhappy?

So many more questions. And no time to ask them.

"If all of that's true," she said, "then you know I can't just sit around waiting."

"Let's say I agreed to let you come with me. What if something *did* happen? How much worse would it be if you were there? How much worse would it be if I couldn't protect you?"

"How can you protect me at all if I'm here and you're somewhere else?"

He said her name in a frustrated growl. "Meredith…"

"Just because you don't want me to be right doesn't mean I'm not."

Sam lifted a hand to his hair, which he tugged, then released. "The car."

"What?"

"You're going to wait inside of it. You're going to hold my phone with Worm's number set to go. If a single thing goes wrong, you call him. You don't follow me, you don't call the cops. Just Worm."

And Meredith nodded her head quickly, afraid if she spoke, he'd change his mind.

Sam kept his mouth shut and his eyes on the road as he maneuvered the borrowed hatchback—another of Worm's vehicles, but a far less obtrusive one than his truck— through the streets. He hated that Meredith had talked him in to letting her come along. He hated that it still seemed better than the alternative of leaving her behind. She was right, though. He couldn't keep her safe if she wasn't in sight.

Is that the real reason you want her here? asked an irritating voice in his head. *Or is it something more?*

Her safety was definitely a factor, no question. The problem was what was making that safety so important to Sam.

He cast a quick look at Meredith. She'd closed her eyes, her long lashes dipping down to caress her skin. Sam was ridiculously envious of that motion. When was the last time he'd felt an attraction like this one? Had he ever? The jolt each time they touched was definitely unique. Even now, his fingers itched to reach across and trace the ridge of her cheekbone to her delicate jaw. He longed to feel her lips again.

That kiss.

He'd told her he wouldn't apologize for it, and he wouldn't. It might've been a mistake, but that didn't mean he was sorry. If anything, he was glad. Life was fragile; sometimes moments *had* to be seized in case they never came again.

No one knew that better than Sam. His heart squeezed. He'd almost told Meredith how well he knew it. That was far more significant than any kind of physical attraction.

He tightened his hands on the steering wheel. Sam didn't talk about his past. He didn't discuss the reasons he'd left the police force or the motivation for his devotion to his business. With Meredith, he'd almost slipped up. Another thing he never did.

What was it about her that made him so careless? What made him want to dredge up things better left buried, lay them bare and share them with her?

He shook his head mentally. She didn't need to know. It would only scare her, make her doubt his abilities.

"Sam?" Her voice cut through his brooding.

"Yes?"

"I can practically *hear* you thinking."

"What, are you psychic now?" His tone was far lighter than his mood.

"Hardly. I think every person in a five-mile radius can feel the gloomy musings rolling off you."

In spite of himself, he smiled. "Gloomy musings. That's a new one."

"Thanks. I was rather proud of it, too."

She paused, and Sam swore that now *he* could hear *her* thinking.

"Do you want to talk about it?" she asked.

The question was hesitant, but somehow open. Like her offer to listen was a genuine one, and once again, Sam felt the maddening urge to answer her candidly. He actually had to force himself to do the opposite.

"Talk about what?" he replied flatly, his eyes staring straight ahead. "My gloomy musings? I think I'll keep those to myself, thanks."

Meredith's hand landed overtop of his. The immediate, magnetic desire hit him. But this time, there was something else lying just underneath it. The satisfying feeling of receiving comfort after needing it.

"My sister might be the official counselor, but I'm not a bad listener, either," Meredith said, her voice as soft and tempting as her touch.

Sam made the final turn onto his street, pulled over and put the car into Park before turning to answer her. "The quicker I go in and grab my notes, the quicker I get back, and the quicker Worm can help us figure out where Tamara is."

"Is it cliché to tell you to be careful?"

"Only if you don't mean it."

There was no hesitation. "I definitely mean it."

"Good." He pointed to a well-worn building on the other side of the street. "See those apartments?"

"Yes."

"I live on the sixth floor in the corner unit."

"You're parking this far away? How am I even supposed to know you've made it inside?"

"Because when I get to my living room, I'm going to turn on a light, flick open the curtain and wave from that window just above the big evergreen." He reached into his pocket, pulled out his phone and punched in Worm's number, then placed it on the dashboard.

"And if that doesn't happen?"

"On the very slim chance that something goes wrong,"

he said, "all you have to do is hit Send. I'll leave the keys in the ignition and the gun is in the glove box."

"All right." She met his eyes. "Sam?"

"Yeah?"

"Seriously. Be careful."

"Always am, sweetheart."

He swung open the door, then climbed out. Before he slammed it shut behind himself, though, he stopped and bent down.

"My musings weren't all gloomy," he said.

"They weren't?"

He shook his head and met her eyes. "Nope. Part of them included thinking about you and when I might get to kiss you again."

He let himself stare into her eyes for a moment, enjoying the way they widened in surprise at his declaration. As he closed the car door, he realized the teasing statement was true. The idea of another kiss had been creeping around his otherwise worried mind with greater and greater frequency. Her soft lips. The way she melted under his touch. Yeah, Sam definitely wanted round two. Soon. So much that he had to fight an urge to turn back and get it that second.

Good motivation to come back in one piece, he told himself. *And good motivation to focus on the task at hand.*

Firmly, he shoved aside thoughts of Meredith's mouth and shifted his brain into work mode. His eyes scanned the street, searching for anything out of the ordinary. An unusual car or an out-of-place individual. His caution was habitual, honed by his years as a cop, and the mental inventory was almost soothing.

No one suspicious in sight. Good.

A peal of laughter in the distance. Excellent.

Door to the apartment building intact. Perfect.

Still, something made Sam pause. Nothing he could see—just something he could feel. Quickly, he weighed intuition versus fact and picked the former. He trusted his gut. Besides that, he *had* promised Meredith he'd be extra careful. So at the last second, he veered to the side and lifted a hand in a backward wave, sure she would understand the signal. He walked past his own building and the next, then turned up a dead-end path. He made his way to the end, stared up at the fence there for a second, then hoisted himself right over it. Finally, he pushed his way through the tangle of overgrown bushes and made his way back toward his building.

It surprised him to find it as unguarded as the front. He'd fully expected the uncomfortable tingle along his spine to play out into something concrete.

Overactive intuition, apparently, he chastised himself.

It didn't stop him from taking another slow look around. The rear of the apartment complex was dim and gray and silent. There were no patios off the back, and all the windows appeared closed and covered. Nothing worth looking at.

He fingered the solitary key in his pocket. Pilfered long ago from the building manager, it would open any exterior door, including his chosen point of entry—the emergency door on the side of the building. He turned his attention there now. Even though the few stairs leading up to it were clear and there was nowhere in their vicinity to hide, the hair on the back of his neck still refused to lie flat. It made him want to move slowly. To be careful enough to please even Meredith.

But thinking of her actually spurred him to speed up. The more time he took to get up to his apartment, the more likely she was to panic and dial Worm's number. And the longer she was alone, the less Sam could protect her directly.

He inhaled, brushed aside his worry, and made his way toward the door. No one jumped out at him. No one fired a shot. In less than a minute, he'd unlocked the door and stepped into the dimly lit staircase. He inhaled again and started up the steps, counting them off silently in twos.

Four, six, eight—crrrrick!

It only took Sam a heartbeat to recognize the noise for what it was. The cock of a gun, amplified by the hollowness of the stairwell. He threw his back to the wall just as a silencer-muffled shot whizzed by and smashed into the cement at his feet.

Sam's training and experience took hold immediately.

Offense, at the ready.

He whipped out his own weapon.

Locate the shooter.

He eased forward, and another bullet came flying at his toe. From above. Good to know.

Open the communication.

At that, his target beat him to the punch.

"Put down your weapon!" called a gruff voice. "And no one gets hurt."

"Might've tried to sell that line *before* you fired at me. Twice." Sam inched along the wall as he spoke, wondering how far he could get before the other man noticed.

There was a pause. "Good point."

Sam stifled a snort. He was at the edge of the stair now, and he closed his eyes for a second, trying to recall how the stairs were configured. Every eighth step, like the one where he stood now, was a wide one. Then a turn. Every sixteenth step ended in a landing at a new floor. If Sam had to guess, he'd say the shooter was on the second-floor landing. There was no way to come at the other man without getting shot first. He'd proven that already.

I need to get myself some kind of advantage.

"How about *you* put down *your* weapon and no one will get hurt—for real?" he called, opening his eyes and scanning the limited area.

"Forgive me if I don't believe you, either."

"The thing is, unlike you bad guys…we good guys ask questions first and shoot later."

"Hilarious," the shooter responded.

"What can I say? The art of conversation is underrated."

Sam spotted the exposed bulb on the wall. Right. One of those hung at every eighth step, too.

All right, then.

He lifted his weapon, aimed it, then thought better of it. The man above him could fire at will because no one would be the wiser. Sam's own weapon was far from silenced and would alert every person on the block.

Thinking quickly, he holstered his gun and reached to his boot. He pulled out his knife, then drew back his arm and took aim again. With a practiced flick of his wrist, Sam released it.

The light shattered. Shards of glass flew in every direction, and a curse echoed from above. Sam made his move before the surprise could wear off. He leaped up the stairs. Just as he expected, he found the shooter on the next landing. The man's gun was on the floor, clearly dropped in the mad attempt to brush off the exploded glass that had already dotted his face with flecks of blood. The second he spotted Sam, he stopped flailing and dove. Not for the weapon, but straight at Sam himself.

Instinctively, Sam sidestepped the attack. But his balance had already been thrown, and instead of moving smoothly out of the way, he stumbled. He reached for the wall and he caught himself. Barely and briefly. For a breath, he hung at an angle, one foot on a stair, one hand on the wall. Then he tumbled sideways and followed the shooter down the stairs.

Chapter 6

As Meredith stared out the window, waiting for Sam's signal, she frowned. A flash made her squint her eyes and take them off the curtained window. She couldn't see a change in the scenery. She breathed in irritably, chastising herself for getting distracted. But her inhale brought a whiff of something. She drew in another breath. Yes, there it was again.

Cigarette smoke.

But there was no one in sight.

Meredith scanned the shrubs on the edge of the apartments a little more carefully. And paused. There, just behind a particularly shabby tree, a tiny ribbon of gray swirled up. She brought her eyes down to the bottom of the foliage. She could see the edge of a thick black boot. Her heart thumped.

It could be anyone. A resident. A visitor. A—

Her thoughts cut off as a cigarette butt flicked up, then landed on the ground, and the booted foot followed it. She got a second-long glance at the person wearing the boot. And that second was all she needed to recognize him. It was the redheaded man who'd chased her down with his sedan.

Oh, crap.

Why was the man outside Sam's apartment? Was he going in? Standing guard? Was it already too late?

In a panic, Meredith reached for the phone, and in that same panic, she dropped it.

Get it together!

The silent, self-directed command could only help so much. She was too frazzled. Too worried about Sam's safety.

And when she did manage to retrieve the phone, it only got worse. Worm's number had disappeared off the screen. Quickly, she scrolled through in search of an address book. It came up blank.

"You've got to be kidding me," she muttered.

She eyed the keys hanging from the ignition. But she knew she wouldn't use them. No way would she leave Sam alone.

She popped open the glove box and retrieved the gun Sam had left behind. She grabbed a ball cap that had been stuffed in beside it, too, and shoved it down low on her head. Then she snapped up a wrinkly jacket from the backseat and draped it over her shoulders. She eyed herself in the rearview mirror. A shoddy disguise, but the best she could do.

As she climbed from the vehicle, Meredith decided to take a direct approach. They—whoever *they* were—would be expecting a subtle entry. A sneak attack. She'd draw less attention if she acted like she belonged there.

Unless they've all got your face on their radar.

Meredith shoved aside the frightening thought and pulled her hat even lower. She commanded her feet not to slow as she neared the glass doors at the front of Sam's building. Just inside, she could see a man in a police officer's uniform. Her pulse quickened.

Keep calm. Like you're just coming home from a coffee date with a friend and there isn't a shiny weapon stuck in your belt.

She reached the door and lifted her hand. And before she could even fake dropping her key like she planned, the cop was there, swinging it open.

"Miss," he said, his voice full of overblown authority. "The building's on a lockdown."

Uh-huh, Meredith thought, remembering all too readily that the little spy camera in her necklace had been police-issue. *If it's on lockdown, why are you* un*locking it?*

What she said aloud was *"No hablo Inglés."*

The cop blinked. "You. Can. Not. Come. In. *Comprende?*"

"No hablo Inglés," Meredith repeated and moved to sidle past him.

One of his meaty hands shot out and landed on her shoulder. "Stop."

"Qué?"

"Seriously?" the cop grumbled. "Sit tight, all right? Just…stay."

He stepped back, turned away from Meredith and pressed down on his two-way radio.

"I've got some chick down here," he said. "Yeah, no. That's not happening. She doesn't understand English."

When the door had almost closed, Meredith scooted her foot to the edge of the door and propped it open, just an inch. She held her breath, waiting for the cop to notice. But he just continued to speak into his radio, growing more agitated with each sentence.

"No, man. Spanish!" A pause. "It's not funny."

Meredith wiggled her foot, widening the opening. The

officer still didn't turn, so she pushed the door even farther. And the moment it was big enough to slip through,
she took a breath and slid into the lobby. Then, as quickly
as she could, she moved along the wall, turned up the hall
and waited for the policeman to notice she was gone.

After a moment, she heard him say, "You know what?
Never mind. She must've given up. No, of course not! See
where she went? What the—"

Not bothering to listen to another word or to verify
that the cop was actually going to check outside for her
presence, Meredith moved again. She hurried past a series of first-floor apartments and eased open the door to
the stairs. And froze. A man, leaned over at an awkward
angle, blocked her way.

She took a step back, then froze a second time as the
man shifted and she saw why he stood the way he did.

He held Sam beneath him, throat in hand.

And Sam wasn't moving.

With fear making her heart bang, Meredith drew the
gun from her waistband. She shoved aside the doubtful
voice in her head that reminded her she had no clue how
to use the damn thing. Because she wasn't going to fire it.
She was going to improvise. She turned the weapon sideways, gripped it tightly, lifted it over her head and swung
with all her might.

The gun slammed into the side of the stranger's skull
with a thump that jarred Meredith's arm. As the man's head
whipped to the left, his body wobbled, too. His arms shot
out, but the momentum was already too great. He toppled
over. The other side of his head smashed into the stairs.
Then he rolled the rest of the way over onto his back and
went still.

Ignoring the way her whole body shook, Meredith turned
her attention to Sam. One eye was swollen, and above that

was a laceration. She could see a bit of red on his neck, and his breaths came shallowly, but at least they came.

She smoothed his hair back gently. "Sam?"

"Meredith?"

She practically swooned with relief. "Oh, thank God."

His cleared his throat and opened his eyes. "Did you just clock that guy over the head with a gun, or was that a hallucination brought on by lack of oxygen?"

"Are you cracking jokes? Now?"

"Why? Is now a bad time?"

"I thought he was going to kill you, Sam."

"Just trying to converse with me. In an extrapersuasive way."

"This really isn't funny."

"I know it isn't."

Meredith opened her mouth to tell him he had a weird way of showing it, but before she could get out a word, Sam pushed himself to a sitting position, then dragged her close. And she was too startled to pull away. His lips—a little dry and a little rough—pressed against hers.

She knew the timing was terrible. The situation was precarious. Dangerous. Not to mention the unconscious man on the floor just a few feet away. But the moment Sam's tongue flicked out to part her lips, it all seemed unimportant. And when he slid his hands to her waist, pulled them both to their feet and pushed her to the wall, everything outside of the two of them slipped away. She forgot the waning adrenaline that made her shake. She forgot her fear. She forgot everything but the sizzling heat between them.

Meredith let herself sink into the kiss, impressed by the thoroughness of Sam's exploration and startled by her own reaction to it. And react she did. Delicious explosions filled her mouth. They sent warmth down her throat and into her chest, where it bloomed into something fantastic and inviting. Something that forced out one little moan, then another.

Sam deepened the kiss. His hands dug into her hair and his chest pressed to hers. And the contact was no longer just dazzling; it was consuming. The kind of kiss that could go on for an hour, just the way it was, or lead to something more.

Something more.

Meredith's body sang at the prospect. Tendrils of desire moved through her, settled in and took hold. And when Sam pulled away, she felt the loss acutely.

He cupped her cheek in his palm. "Well. That was even better than the one that I imagined while Mr. Unconscious and I were chatting." He let her face go and moved his gaze to the man on the floor. "Speaking of which… We should go before he wakes up."

Abruptly, Sam moved toward the man on the floor. He stared down for a long moment, and when he looked up, a deep frown clouded his features. And Meredith saw immediately why his attention had shifted so quickly. The rough-faced assailant's coat had dropped open, and a shiny badge peeked out from an inside pocket.

As Sam bent down to grab the other man's identification, a deep sense of foreboding made him draw in a shallow breath. The air sucked roughly against the ache in his throat, thickening it, and it only worsened as he confirmed what he already knew.

The man who'd fired at him—who'd seemed to enjoy delivering more than a few blows while he demanded information about Meredith's sister—was a cop, no doubt about it. And not *just* a cop. A detective. He read the name on the shield.

Brody Boyd.

"Don't know him," Sam muttered, not even realizing he'd spoken aloud until Meredith answered him.

"Were you expecting to?"

"No." Sam paused, then decided he owed her a bit of disclosure. "But I thought his name might ring a bell. I used to do his job. Same department, too."

"You were a detective?"

"I was. But I left the force years ago. Personal reasons." He nodded toward the door. "We should move while we talk."

"We can't go out the front," she told him. "There was another cop out there."

Sam grimaced and studied the man on the floor again for a second. How far up did the corruption go? How many of them were involved? And what the hell did they want with Tamara Billing? Too many questions and far too few answers.

"We need to get my notes," he said decisively.

"Your apartment is probably a little…occupied," Meredith pointed out.

He nodded. "That's why we're going to do it indirectly."

"Indirectly?"

"Can we extend that bit of trust again?"

She looked like she wanted to argue, but after a second, she shrugged. "Sure. But just so we're clear, I did just knock a guy out for you, so now you owe me two."

Sam smiled and pulled her toward the stairs. "I'm still ahead by a half. And didn't you tell me it wasn't funny?"

"Laugh or cry, right?"

Her words were flippant, but her voice was serious, and Sam had to fight to keep himself from stopping to comfort her. It bothered him that Meredith was in pain. That she was in this situation at all. He knew, logically, that it wasn't his fault. That didn't mean he didn't feel responsible. Or that he didn't wish he could somehow soothe away her bad feelings. And as they got closer to their destination—the fifth floor, right below Sam's own apartment—even more worry crept in.

You should've forced her to stay with Worm, he told himself.

Except Meredith wasn't the kind of woman who could be forced to do anything. She'd made that abundantly clear.

Besides that, if she had *stayed behind, you'd probably be dead.*

Sam acknowledged the truth of the mental reminder. He did owe her his life, and though he wasn't overly fond of being indebted to anyone, he was sure as hell thankful for her stubbornness at that moment. Thankful enough to kiss her. Again. And again.

As they reached the fifth-floor landing, Sam ordered his libido to calm down and lifted a finger to his lips to indicate to Meredith that they needed silence. He eased open the heavy fire door and peered through the crack. The hallway appeared vacant. Still and quiet. It made Sam a little uneasy, but his intuition didn't rear its head, so he pushed the door open wider and led Meredith past three doors. At the fourth one, he stopped.

"Just follow my lead," he said.

"What do you mean?"

Before Sam could answer her, the door swung open and a well-wizened woman greeted them with a shake of her finger.

"If this isn't your girlfriend, Sammy, I'm shutting the door right now," she said.

In spite of her words and her shrewd expression, Sam grinned a genuinely affectionate grin. "Eileen, this is Meredith. And yes, she belongs to me."

"Hmph. Does *she* know that?"

Sam squeezed Meredith's hand again, this time in a silent prod.

"Oh, I know all right," she said quickly. "Sam's making sure of that."

Eileen laughed. "Come in, then. Have some tea. Tell me what happened to your face and I'll tell you why I think this building lockdown is bull."

Sam bit back his need for urgency and allowed his elderly neighbor to take her time. He knew she'd only stall further if he pressured her. Or ask questions he'd prefer not to answer. So in spite of the fact that the more time that went on, the more likely it was that his stairwell assailant would wake or be found, Sam simply sat back and let her prepare the tea and cookies. He interlocked his fingers with Meredith's, just as much for his own pleasure as for show, and listened to Eileen complain about the service at their local grocery store. Finally, when they'd eaten enough to satisfy her, she turned the conversation to their present concerns all on her own.

"Damned fake cops showed up about an hour ago," she said. "Told us all to stay in our apartments because there's some kind of criminal in our building."

Sam kept his face smooth. "Fake cops?"

Eileen snorted. "You think real cops come door-to-door, hands on their guns, and *tell* the residents they're arresting someone in the building? Or that they cut the telephone lines and demand that people hand over their cell phones? Threaten them when they refuse? I thought that gang-type fellow down the hall was going to get capped when he didn't want to give them his phone."

Sam couldn't suppress a chuckle. "What I think is that you've been watching too much TV."

"So it's just a coincidence that you show up at my door, all beaten up and ex-*real*-cop-like?" Eileen lifted a nonexistent eyebrow and turned her attention to Meredith. "He tell you he used to be a cop?"

As Meredith nodded her reply, Sam was glad he *had* told her.

Eileen crossed her arms. "Hmm. Well. I'm guessing whatever's going on in the building has something to do with you, and I'm guessing you want a favor without telling me a damned thing, too."

"Pretty much," Sam agreed.

His neighbor sighed. "All right. What is it?"

"Just a few minutes in your bathroom to clean myself up."

"And?"

Sam forced his body to stay relaxed. The woman had a nose for a lie, and he didn't want her to pick up on the bit of deception he was about to toss her way.

"And we'd really appreciate it if you'd let us climb down your emergency ladder."

Eileen stared at him for a moment, then sighed for a second time and waved her hand toward the hall. "You know where it is. But don't think for a single second that I don't suspect you're up to something else, Sammy Potter. Don't make me check your pockets for my good soap on the way out."

He let out a breath as he stood. "I'll try to keep my kleptomaniac habits to a minimum." He bent to kiss Meredith's cheek and whispered in her ear, "Sorry, sweetheart. Ten minutes and I'll have the files and we'll be back to finding your sister. I promise."

She gave him a nod, and he slipped up the hall. In spite of his tension, Sam smiled to himself as he heard Eileen open up the conversation with the declaration that she was a little bit psychic. The woman was as nutty as a candy bar, and nowhere near as sweet. He could only imagine what she'd said to the "fake" cops who'd come banging on her door. But she liked Sam, and at that moment, he was pretty damn glad they were friendly.

Months earlier, an investigation into the disappearance of a young woman being stalked by her ex-boyfriend had gone south. The ex in question discovered Sam's involvement in the location efforts and turned his attention to Sam directly. In an attempt to shut down the investigation, the stalker had robbed him, taking every note, every lead, every detail, straight out of his apartment. As a result, he'd gone digital and sought a secure but accessible hiding place for his things. And that spot was the shared space between his own bathroom floor and Eileen's bathroom ceiling.

So all Sam had to do now to retrieve his notes on the Billing file was to go in from the bottom. And as he locked the door, he looked up and spotted a means of doing it.

Quickly, he turned on the shower, made sure it was beating down loud enough to block out anything else, then ignored the stream of water. He lifted a leg, placed his knee on the tub's edge and hoisted himself onto the countertop. He steadied himself, then reached up to press in the sides of the ceiling fan together, forcing the clasps loose, then pulled off the lid. He reached inside and after just a few seconds of feeling around, his hand brushed the right beam and he clasped the familiar little black box. He opened and stared down triumphantly at the three objects inside—a USB stick, a wallet and an even smaller black box.

But his triumph gave him pause. Because it stemmed not from the retrieval itself or even from the fact that he now had the information and resources to move on with his case. It came almost entirely from the fact that it would help him fulfill his obligation to Meredith.

Chapter 7

Meredith frowned at Sam as he came back into the room. He'd definitely been in the bathroom long enough to shower. And the water had run the whole time. But his hair was barely damp and his face looked like it had been wiped off, not thoroughly cleaned.

Suspicious, but not surprising, Meredith thought.

From the moment he disappeared up the hall, she—like Eileen—was sure he'd been up to something else. So Sam's not-so-freshly-washed appearance wasn't the reason her eyebrows knit together. Instead, it was the way he paused and stared at her with an unnerving intensity. She didn't know what his expression meant. But something about the look made her want to both blush and shiver at the same time.

Then, abruptly, his face relaxed and he stepped fully into the room and cleared his throat. "I take it you had a nice chat?"

"Lovely," Eileen said.

Meredith wasn't sure she'd describe being grilled about her life and being told to find some direction as *lovely*. She definitely could've done away with the two-minute safe-sex talk and inquiry into her genetic history. And those topics were the *most* comfortable parts of the so-called chat. Not to mention that every second heartbeat she spent was another second away from figuring out what had happened to her sister. And in between *those* heartbeats, she'd been worrying about Sam. He seemed fine. But was he more seriously injured than he let on?

She fought a head-shake. Lovely? No. Not so much.

"Meredith?" Sam prompted.

"Yes. Perfect." She didn't sound *quite* like she was choking.

Sam's eyes twinkled for a moment anyway. "Ready to go then, sweetheart?"

"If you are," Meredith replied as indifferently as she could manage.

She swore she heard him chuckle under his breath, but she didn't dare comment on it.

And seconds later—with an appropriate amount of gratitude from Sam and a promise to think about everything Eileen had said from Meredith—they were moving down the ladder that extended from the woman's tiny balcony. Meredith knew why Sam thought this particular escape route was a good idea. The wide evergreen tree that stopped just short of Sam's own apartment provided cover from the street view. Its thick branches blocked them in from anyone who might happen to be on the ground as well. With who knew how many corrupt cops in and around the building, there was no safer way to make their exit.

But Meredith kept her lips zipped until they hit the bottom. She kept them sealed as they moved stealthily from the building back up the street to the car. She even stayed silent until they'd both buckled their seat belts and Sam had put the car into Drive and pulled out onto the road. Then she couldn't hold it in anymore.

"I want you to promise me you won't leave me alone ever again!" she blurted, then colored as she realized how it sounded. "Not like that."

Sam's mouth was turned up on one side. "Like what then?"

Meredith refused to give in to that sexily crooked smile.

"I'm serious. This is *my* sister we're looking for. From now on, whatever you're doing, I want to be there. And before you say it's not safe, let me remind you that *you're* the one who just about got killed and I was the one who saved you. Then, to top it off, you left me alone with a crazy woman, who—" She cut herself off abruptly.

"Who what?"

"Nothing."

His smile grew wider. "Eileen isn't so bad. She's not nearly unpleasant enough that it's fair to compare her to being shot at, beaten and partially strangled."

Meredith's throat constricted at the remembered fear that Sam was dead or dying. It had been a terrifying few moments. But she knew he was using it to try and distract her.

"You wouldn't be so amused if you knew what she'd said to me."

At her tone, Sam's cool blue gaze slipped to her for an appraising second before turning back to the road. "What did she say?"

"Never mind."

"But now I'm intrigued."

"We have more important things to talk about. Like what you were doing in the bathroom."

Sam's gaze found her again. Dammit. Why did he have to have that stare down to an art? The one that said, *I'll figure it out anyway, so you might as well just tell me now.*

And he was so damn efficient with it that his eyes were already back on the road.

Probably a cop thing, Meredith thought.

But that didn't mean she had to like it.

When she didn't reply, Sam raised an eyebrow, lifted a hand from the steering wheel, reached into his pocket and pulled out a memory stick. He held it out for a moment, then shoved it back into his pocket.

"I can't do anything with this until we get back to Worm and his little slice of tech heaven. And I think you have time between here and there to divulge a few of Eileen's words of wisdom," he said.

Meredith tossed her gaze to the roof of the car. Why hadn't she kept her mouth shut?

"You aren't going to let it go, are you?" she asked.

"Nope."

"Fine. She said that by the end of today, you'd have put a ring on my finger."

The car jerked underneath them, giving away Sam's re-action, even though his face remained impassive and his gaze stayed on the road. And Meredith had to admit she'd felt just about the same way when Eileen had said it. The old woman had sounded utterly confident that she was cor-rect. Okay, maybe it couldn't be compared to Sam's ordeal, but that didn't mean it hadn't scared the heck out of Mer-edith. In fact, *both* things scared her. Nearly as much as not knowing what Tamara had gotten herself involved in.

"So I guess your request is a little redundant anyway, then," Sam stated, interrupting the remarkably thick si-lence.

Meredith frowned. "What?"

"If I'm putting a ring on your finger today, it's prob-ably fair to say that I *won't* ever be leaving you again. I think I'd be a very dedicated husband. Although I might demand a third kiss before I decide for sure."

An immediate lick of desire danced through Meredith. He was kidding. He had to be. But his tone was serious. And the thought of kissing him again gave her an all-over tingle. And hearing him use the word *husband* made her heart do a peculiar flop in her chest. She was so busy listening to the erratic thud that she almost missed Sam's next question.

"Have you ever been married before?"

Meredith shook her head. "No."

"Engaged?"

"No. And before you ask, no serious boyfriends, either."

"How come?"

Briefly, Meredith wondered if he was doing the same thing he'd done earlier—asking personal questions to distract her. But a quick examination of his face told her he was at the very least curious. And for some reason, she wanted to tell him.

"When I was younger, I didn't have time. When Tamara was twelve and I was fourteen, my mom got sick. Her cancer consumed her. And my dad, too. By the time she was sixteen and I was eighteen, we were on our own completely. I worked two jobs to make ends meet and went to school at night. Then it just seemed hard to meet someone. I didn't do clubbing or much after-work socializing. And once Tamara finished school and started her virtual counseling service and it went crazy..." Meredith shrugged.

"And now?"

"Now? I'm sitting in a car with a man who thinks he'd be a good husband because he has excellent stalking skills."

Sam laughed. "So you're hopeless."

"Pretty much," she agreed. "What about you?"

"No. I definitely have hope." He shot a look her way that left no doubt about where his hope lay.

Meredith felt her face go pink again. "I meant have you ever been married?"

"Nope. Same story as you. Family. Work."

She got the feeling he was being intentionally vague. It stung in a surprisingly forceful way. What was he holding back? And why? She opened her mouth to point out that she'd been honest about her own past, but the words didn't make it out.

Because Sam's face had gone from relaxed to tense. And before Meredith could speak, he spun the steering wheel hard, veered the car into a driveway that *wasn't* Worm's and slammed on the brakes. With lightning quickness, he undid his seat belt, then hers.

"Get down!" he ordered.

And his voice was gruff enough that Meredith didn't even hesitate.

Sam had been so involved in listening to her talk about how *un*attached she was that he almost hadn't noticed the warning left behind by Worm. He'd nearly driven right past to the now familiar, dark-colored sedan up the street.

He reached across the console, threaded his fingers through Meredith's and gave them a squeeze. "You okay?"

"*I* am. But are *you*?"

"Worm's garage was half-open."

"Is that supposed to mean something?"

"He's got thousands of dollars' worth of electronic equipment in there. Half-open tells me he ran into some trouble, but got out okay," Sam explained. "And I think our redheaded friend—the one who tried to run you down—is parked on the corner."

Meredith groaned. "Crap. I almost forgot. That guy was at your apartment, too. I saw him outside and that's why I went after you in the first place. Do you think he's a cop?"

Sam shook his head. "I think he's their muscle. Someone who doesn't have a reputation to maintain and can do their dirtiest work."

She sucked in her bottom lip nervously. "What do we do?"

"We wait. At least long enough to be sure he didn't see us. And we hope that whoever lives in the house where we're parked doesn't confront us or call the police. Then we find somewhere else to set up."

He felt a slight tremor in her hand, and Sam's protective instincts kicked in. He wanted to reassure her. To ease the fear she clearly felt but stoically held in. He wished he was better at offering comfort, but it had been years since he'd allowed himself enough emotional attachment to anyone to even want to try to reach out. So long since he'd felt a connection. Or even wanted to. Surprisingly, Meredith stirred that need in him. But in order to follow through on that, he would have to share more of himself than he had in a very long time.

Meredith adjusted a little, and Sam spied the pinch between her brows and the worry in her eyes. He knew that feeling personally, and seeing it on her face tugged at his heart. He could at least try.

He squeezed her hand again. "What I said earlier about my story being the same as yours, I meant that literally."

"Which part?"

"All of it, really. A younger sibling, relying on me to provide for her. I was twenty-two when our parents died in a car accident, but my sister was only fourteen. I was busy working my way up through the ranks, keeping a crazy schedule and trying to keep her in check at the same time." Sam smiled, trying to ease the seriousness of his disclosure. "Anyway. You wouldn't believe how hard it is for a man with a dangerous job and a needy little sister to convince a girl to settle down."

"Oh, yeah," Meredith said. "Sexy cop with a family attitude. Sounds like a really tough sell."

"I'm not a cop anymore," Sam pointed out, then added, "And did you just call me sexy?"

He knew she was fighting a blush. "Maybe. But it was an accident."

"Accidentally calling someone sexy. That's gotta be a new one."

"Cut me some slack. I'm under a lot of stress here."

He let her hand go, then reached over to touch her face. "I know you are. But I'll take a compliment anyway I can get it. Accidentally. Backhandedly. You name it."

She leaned into his palm and offered him a small smile, but when she spoke, her tone had turned serious again. "I'm scared, Sam. And I really wish I knew what Tamara's gotten herself into."

"We'll figure it out together." He placed a soft kiss on her lips—a gentle touch that felt as natural as it did right. "And not just because you're making me promise to never leave you alone, either." He eased away again, then turned the key in the ignition. "I think we're safe to move. If our redheaded friend had seen us, he would've come after us or called in some help. You can stay low until we're out of sight, though."

Careful to keep one eye on the navy sedan, Sam guided the hatchback down the driveway. He pulled the car onto the street and said a silent prayer of thanks when a second vehicle pulled out just a few houses up. It blocked the sedan from view, which was perfect. He let out a breath, turned his attention to the road and drove out of the neighborhood in silence.

Less than two blocks later, Meredith was buckled in again, and Sam had come up with a tentative plan.

"Hey, sweetheart?"

"Yes?"

"Assuming it gives us chance to go through my files, would you fight me on a hot shower and a nice meal in a five-star hotel?"

"What's the catch?"

"No catch."

He caught her narrow-eyed stare as he did a quick shoulder check and changed lanes, but Sam didn't elaborate. Not right away. Mostly because he wasn't sure whether or not what he was about to suggest could be accurately described as a *catch*. He maneuvered the car out of the residential neighborhood, silent once again. Meredith didn't say anything, either, but when they reached the highway turnoff, she finally did speak—it was just two words.

"Gloomy. Musings."

Sam laughed. "You can feel them rolling off me again?"

"Like a thunderstorm."

He let out a sigh. "I want us to make noise."

"I'm not going to pretend to know what that means."

"They're going to be expecting us to hide. To try to evade their search. And clearly they're employing considerable, fruitful resources. They found your apartment and mine. They tracked us to Worm's. So I think we should do the opposite of what's expected. Make ourselves obvious wherever we go. Be people who are remembered. But not as *us*."

"You want us to wear disguises?"

"More or less."

Meredith paused, stared out the windshield for a second, then said, "And now the catch."

Sam didn't argue. "They'll be looking for a woman and a man. Together, but separate."

"Not a couple," Meredith observed.

"Exactly."

Sam let go of the steering wheel then and reached into the pocket that didn't hold the USB stick. He pulled out the small black box and set it on the dashboard. He watched from the corner of his eye as Meredith reached for it slowly. She flicked open the box, then drew out the modest diamond ring. As she held it up, her expression was one part admiration and one part curiousity, and Sam's heart lurched in his chest as the deepening moonlight caught in the stone and flickered through the car. It had been years since he'd seen the setting. A hundred memories fought to resurface, and Sam fought right back. He needed to stay focused on the present.

He cleared his throat. "My mom left the ring for my sister, but things didn't work out the way they should have. I don't even know why I held on to it."

Meredith continued to pinch it between her thumb and forefinger. Right in Sam's view. He had to admit that seeing it against her skin made it even prettier than he remembered.

He suddenly wanted her to put it on. And not because it helped him with his plan.

Sap, Sam chastised himself. "What do you think?"

"It's perfect."

At her agreement, he couldn't hold in his surprise. "It is?"

He'd been expecting her to argue. Or at least to ask him if he wasn't being a little over-the-top. But she was nodding.

"Yes, definitely. A newly engaged couple would make some noise. Champagne-and-strawberries kinda noise. And we just met, so who would suspect *this* as a cover?" She smiled. "Besides Eileen with her psychic predictions, I mean."

Sam groaned. "I hate it when she's right."

Meredith held the ring up one more time. "If it makes you feel any better, I think she had a more bended-knee ring in mind."

"Makes me feel worse, actually. Put it back in the box."

"What?"

"If I expect other people to believe we're champagne-and-strawberries in love, the least I should do is provide a convincing fake proposal."

He tugged on the steering wheel and dragged the car across three lanes. Ignoring the loud honks that followed, he swerved onto the shoulder of the road and flung open his door, then bolted around the vehicle to open the passenger-side door, too. He dropped to his knees and met Meredith's stare with a grin.

Chapter 8

Meredith's heart thudded in her chest.

This is just a game, she reminded herself. *A ruse to help you find Tamara.*

But something in Sam's blue stare made it seem real enough that her pulse thrummed.

"What are you doing?" The question came out in an embarrassing squeak.

"Bear with me. I'm not very good with spontaneity. Or romance."

"Umm. Okay." A blush crept up her cheeks.

He nodded toward the ring in her hand. "Didn't I tell you to put that away?"

She was too nervous to point out that she didn't take orders. She just slid the diamond-and-gold band back into the velvet and held it out. Sam took it, winked, then snapped the box open once again.

"Meredith Jamison, will you do me the honor of fake-marrying me?"

For a dizzying second, Meredith could see a world where it was all real. Where a crazy twelve hours together led to a lifetime together. Where going through the scariest emotional time of her life helped her come out on solid ground. The *trip-trip* of her heart became a roar. Then a semitruck rumbled by, its light glaring in the dark, and Meredith came tumbling back to reality.

She forced a smile. "Yes, Sam Potter. I'll fake marry you."

His handsome face lit up, and the balance between real and pretend tottered again. He pulled the ring from the box and slid it onto her finger. It fit perfectly, and for some reason, that didn't surprise Meredith in the least.

She met Sam's eyes. "What now?"

"Now I use this as an excuse to kiss you again."

Meredith braced herself for another onslaught of passion. But when Sam pulled himself up and cupped her cheek, he did it tenderly. The kiss still lingered. It still ignited an explosion of fireworks in her head. But it did more, too. It made her feel warm and safe. It made the two-minute delay worth it.

And when Sam pulled away, his teasing grin was gone. In its place was a slightly overwhelmed look Meredith thought must match her own.

"We ready for this?"

His voice was a little rough, and the question seemed to hold a bigger meaning than Meredith imagined he intended.

She swallowed nervously, trying to figure out what the right answer was. But Sam didn't wait anyway. He just stood, eased the door closed, then made his way back to his own side of the car.

Probably a good thing.

Because Meredith doubted she'd have been able to manage anything more than a nod. And she was *still* struggling as Sam eased the car back onto the highway. Still silent as the lights of the city became visible on the horizon. And every few seconds, the ring on her finger caught her eye and made her mouth dry.

What would Tamara think if she could see it?

At the thought, Meredith smiled, and at last she found something to say. "It really *is* perfect, isn't it? Like, extra-perfect."

Sam glanced her way. "Extra-perfect?"

"Pretending to be married so we can find my sister, the ultimate marriage counselor. It couldn't possibly be more fitting."

She liked the way his mouth curled up in immediate amusement. Even if seeing the extra curve of his lips did make her want to be speechless all over again.

"It'd make Tamara happy," Meredith added.

Sam guided the car onto an exit off the highway. "I can't tell if that makes you happy, too, or if it annoys you."

"Both, probably," Meredith admitted.

She paused, thinking about how to put into words the complicated relationship she had with her sister. But she didn't have to. Sam spoke for her, seeming to understand a lot of what she felt without being told.

"It's a tough one, isn't it?" he said. "You were the grown-up in the relationship for a long time. You're proud of what she's done. But she's your sister, too, and part of you is envious of what she's accomplished."

Meredith studied his profile. "Is that how you feel about your sister, too?"

Sam's smile dipped a little. "Well. She told me it was true, so it must be."

They'd reached the edge of downtown now, and they both went quiet again. But this time, it felt companionable. Like their similar pasts united them even more than their mutual goal of locating Tamara.

Present. Check. *Past.* Check. *But what about the future?* Would she get to put a check there, too?

The diamond on her finger caught a flash from a multicolored sign, and for a second it glittered blue, then red, then blue again. Was it a good omen? Meredith didn't usually believe in them. But what were the chances that the one man who could help her find her sister was also the one man she'd feel a proper connection to? What were the chances that the same man would be carrying a diamond ring in his pocket?

Sam nudged her shoulder. "We're almost there, sweetheart. Prepare for a bit of a show."

"A show?"

Sam pointed to his chest. "Rich jerk." He tapped her knee. "Vapid trophy wife." He pointed out the front windshield. "Fancy hotel."

She followed his finger. Just ahead, she spied a glass-fronted building. It rose ostentatiously into the night air, metallic columns decorating the front. And as they got closer—when Meredith thought they should be slowing down—Sam stepped on the gas. By the time they reached the curved driveway, Meredith had to squeeze her eyes shut. She held on for dear life, sure they were going to crash, but willing herself to trust in Sam's abilities. And just when she thought she couldn't take it anymore, the car screeched to a halt and the smell of burning rubber filled the air. Meredith peeled her lids back in time to see a harried man in a hotel uniform push through the smoke and rap on the driver's-side window.

Sam gave her a final nod, then relaxed his face into a cocky grin. He didn't bother unrolling the window. He just tossed open the door, jumped straight out and held out his key.

"Park it somewhere it's likely to get stolen."

His disparaging tone made him sound completely unlike the man Meredith had been getting to know over the last day. And when the valet didn't take the proffered keys, Sam pushed it a step further. He reached out and tapped the other man's name tag.

"Ian, is it?"

"Yes."

"Well, *Ian*. My wife and I just arrived in Seattle for the first leg of our honeymoon. Our luggage was stolen from our plane. The car rental company gave us *this* instead of the convertible I requested. I'm already guessing that our reservation here will have been lost. So. Instead of standing there like a mindless donkey, *Ian*, take my keys so *I* can do *your* job and open my wife's door. Then drive this pile of rusted-out bolts off the edge of a cliff. Or at least to a place no one will see it and realize I drove it here. Please." Sam paused, then added, "Now."

For a few seconds, the only sound was the hum of the city. Then Ian the valet choked out something unintelligible. He grabbed the keys, promptly dropped them, picked them up, dropped them a second time, mumbled something else and, on the third try, finally managed to hang on to them. And in the time it took him to do it, Sam had made his way to the other side of the car, opened the door and fixed Meredith with an expectant stare.

She stared back. Had he meant to say *wife* instead of *fiancée*? Was it a slip? Or did it mean something?

He looked different. He held his shoulders back, showcasing his full height. He had one eyebrow cocked, one hand outstretched, and his stance gave off a confident, know-it-all attitude. But then he leaned down just a little and tossed her a slow, lazy wink. And just like that, his put-on persona became as attractive as his everyday one.

Did it matter if he said *wife*? And was there any reason Meredith couldn't enjoy this? Any reason she couldn't take one tiny, pleasurable thing away from an otherwise dismal situation?

No.

Meredith shoved aside a tug of guilt, swung her leg from the car and resolved to show Sam just how *noisy* she could be.

Sam couldn't pretend he didn't like the extra effort Meredith was putting into their act. As he guided her into the hotel, she clung to him, her slim form a second skin. She smelled sweet. Enticing. When they reached the concierge desk, she ignored the woman behind the desk, lifted her face and pressed her lips to his in a deep kiss that made Sam want to growl. Or throw aside everything on the counter and toss her onto it.

When she pulled away at last, she released a breathless, out-of-character giggle, then smiled at the concierge. "Oops. Didn't see you there."

"I bet," replied the other woman drily.

Sam suppressed a laugh. He reached into his back pocket and drew out a designer wallet. The stack of cash inside was thick enough to draw attention from anyone close enough to see. Which was the whole point right that second.

Sam pulled a gold-tinted credit card from its slot, grabbed a falsified driver's license as well and placed them on the counter. "Mr. and Mrs. Hall."

As the concierge picked up the cards, Sam felt Meredith's hand creep up under his jacket. It slid to his waistband. Then *under* his waistband. Her fingers caressed the skin on his back, and this time he did give in to the urge to growl.

He bent down to speak right into her ear. "You were one of those little girls who always wanted to be an actress, weren't you?"

She let out another loud giggle, like he'd said the funniest thing in the world, then nibbled the line of his jaw. "Nope. I was one of those little girls who wanted to put away bad guys. Trial lawyer."

"I don't think that's actually a type of little girl."

"Oh, really?"

Sam ran his palms down her arms, then slipped them to the small of her back. "Uh-huh. Princesses. Rock stars. Mommies. But trial lawyers? No way."

She pushed her curves against him and stood on her tiptoes to bite his lip. "Misogynist."

Fierce desire raged through Sam. He wondered if she could tell how quickly this was becoming more than a game. Then he decided she *must* be able to tell. His body wasn't exactly reacting subtly to her closeness. She didn't back away, though. Not even when Sam pulled away and met her eyes and said in a serious voice, "Do you have any idea how sexy you are when you call me names?"

A palpable sizzle shot through the air.

"Name calling does it for you?"

"Not *just* name calling."

"What else?"

"Long walks through bad neighborhoods," he said, his voice still low. "Being chased by bad guys while in the company of a woman who wants to put them away. Saving lives."

"Not trophy wives?"

Meredith made a pouty face and Sam couldn't hold in a chuckle.

She is *sexy. Damned sexy.*

The thought should've been redundant. After all, Sam's attraction to her had been building with each passing moment. Each kiss sent that attraction into locomotive mode. But acknowledging it acted like the flick of a switch, illuminating what had probably been obvious all along. Sam didn't just find Meredith Jamison attractive. He found her more attractive than any woman he'd ever met.

He leaned down, fully intending on putting that realization into action. But the concierge—whom Sam had all but forgotten about—cleared her throat, temporarily breaking the spell.

"Mr. Hall," she said. "We don't appear to have your reservation here."

"Of course you don't." Sam's irritation at being interrupted translated easily into his act.

"I apologize, Mr. Hall. I don't have the honeymoon suite available, either. It's just a—"

"Do you see my name on your preferred guests list?"

The concierge jumped back at his tone. "Yes, and—"

"Is David Turn still the primary operator of this hotel?"

"Yes, but—"

"Dave and I are golfing this week. I'm sure he'd love to hear about my lost reservation and lack of a honeymoon suite. And your wrinkled shirt."

With another little jump, the woman glanced down at her shirt, then bent back to her computer. As she typed away, Meredith's mouth brushed Sam's ear, sending another flood of heat through him.

"You and Dave are buddies?" she asked.

"Dave and Derek Hall are buddies," Sam amended, dusting her forehead with a kiss. "Or at least they are on hotel records."

The concierge cleared her throat again. "All of our premier suites *are* empty, Mr. Hall. Second floor from the top. Any of them is yours for the taking. And we can offer you some complimentary wine and maybe some dinner? Breakfast tomorrow?"

Sam fixed her with a cool glare. "I'm going to need more than that, actually."

"Tell me how we can help." Now she sounded hopeful.

"Better get a pen."

With Meredith still clinging to his side, Sam listed off what he hoped sounded like a reasonable list, blaming baggage theft for the items he needed. A high-end laptop. Changes of clothes for the both of them. He put in a food request, too, and not just because she'd offered. Even thinking the word *steak* set his stomach growling. He hadn't eaten since breakfast, and he anticipated being in for a long night, searching for connections and clues. And if Meredith touched his rear end one more time, a hell of a lot of non-work-related things, too.

By the time he finished with his requests—ending with a warning that all the items had better be upstairs by the time they get to their room—Sam's willpower had reached capacity.

He grabbed Meredith's hand and dragged her across the lobby to the elevators, ignoring the bellhop who struggled to keep up with them. He smacked his knuckle on the up button, pleased when one of the doors signaled its readiness immediately. Before it could even open all the way, he pulled Meredith inside. He pushed her backwards pinned her arms over her head, slid his knee between her thighs and slammed his lips to hers. Hard.

Chapter 9

Meredith's body burned. And not with the flickering, banked kind of fire, but with flames to the ceiling. Searing and soaring. Hot enough to light up a lake. Scorching enough to wipe away the world. *That* was the kind of burn she felt as Sam kissed her against the back of the elevator.

Meredith didn't want the kiss to stop. And Sam started to pull away far too soon. She lifted her arms to his neck, digging her fingers into the hair on the back of his head, trying to prolong it. But he murmured something against her lips and it puzzled her enough that she let him go.

"Hmm?" she mumbled.

"S'getting a free show."

"What?"

"Bellhop."

Sam inclined his head to one side and Meredith gasped. Sure enough, a gangly youth, dressed in the stereotypical uniform—complete with floppy epaulets—had managed to make it into the elevator without her noticing. He now stood to one side, his face turned politely away. But the purple in his cheeks and the bob of his Adam's apple gave away his discomfort. Meredith wasn't sure if she should laugh, apologize, or simply die of embarrassment herself.

And apparently, Sam had his own idea of what she ought to do. "Thank him."

"What? Why?"

"Because, dearest wife, while he doesn't appear to have noticed we don't have any luggage, he *is* the only thing standing between a publicly ravished you and a publicly unravished you."

Sam's statement sent Meredith's heart racing all over again. Was he kidding? Or was he truly tempted to be as roguish as he sounded? But before she could examine his face thoroughly enough to determine which it was, the elevator came to a smooth stop. And when the door slid open and the bellhop all but stumbled out, Meredith heard Sam chuckle under his breath.

"You're terrible." She pushed past him to smile at the bellhop. "Which room is ours?"

The kid cleared his throat, gave her a grateful nod. "You're in 1003. If you come this way, I'll show you to your door."

"Stop, right there," Sam ordered.

He blinked. "Pardon me, sir?"

"Did you say 1003?"

"Yes."

"We're supposed to be in 1006."

Meredith shot him a dirty look. "I don't see why it matters."

Sam lifted a hand. "It's okay, sweetheart. We can tell him."

"Tell him?"

Sam turned back to the kid. "My wife's first husband died on October third. We specifically asked for any room but 1003. The concierge gave us 1006."

The bellhop's eyes widened. "I'm sorry— I didn't— She didn't— I'm sorry."

"Do you have a key for 1006?" Sam asked.

"I have a master key, but I've got you listed as—"

"How about you just get our stuff from 1003, and we don't mention this mistake to the concierge, and everybody stays happy?"

As the kid nodded, then moved down the hall, Meredith clued in to what Sam was doing. Creating a cover. Buying them time in case someone *did* find them.

"Still think I'm terrible?" he asked.

"Yes. Deviously terrible."

"And deviously brilliant?"

"You wish."

The bellhop clanged back into the hall, dragging one cart behind him and pushing another in front of him. "1006?"

Sam grinned and said, "Exactly. Lead away. And don't forget to give us the full sell."

"The— Okay." The kid guided them down the hall, doling out a practiced spiel as they walked. "There are only six rooms on the tenth floor. Each one is a luxurious suite with a separate bedroom, open-plan office space and spa tub."

Showing a little more confidence with each sentence, he slid the key card into the slot, then held the door open and let them enter first. "As you can see, the bedroom boasts French doors, a king-size bed and also has its own bathroom."

Whatever else he said faded into background noise as Meredith's mind paused on just one dangerous phrase.

A king-size bed.

Her eyes sought the offending object. Wooden headboard. Gorgeous linens. Plush pillows.

Meredith swallowed. In minutes, they'd be alone. With

that bed. With the wine that already sat chilling in an ice bucket on one of the carts. Her eyes flicked around the room, and her whole body buzzed with an anticipation so thick she almost didn't notice when her purse started to buzz, too. But the second she pulled out the vibrating phone and glanced down, all her lascivious thoughts flew from her brain and her throat constricted. Because it was her sister's name flashing across the screen. She let out a gasp that stopped the bellhop's speech, midsentence, and drew Sam's attention.

Meredith saw the way his brow furrowed, saw the way his eyes darkened, saw the way his gaze landed on the phone. And she knew what he was about to do.

Acting on instinct, Meredith bolted through the French doors into the bedroom. She slipped past the bed and ran straight for the bathroom. She heard Sam's feet hit the floor behind her. And she slammed the door without checking to see just how close he'd come, then locked it firmly.

As fast as her shaking fingers would allow, she hit the answer button. "Hello?"

A masculine voice on the other end greeted her. "Meredith Jamison?"

Sam pounded on the door and his muffled order carried through the wood. "Dammit, give me that phone!"

Meredith backed away from the holler. She swung open the glass shower door and climbed inside. Then she pushed the phone to one ear and put her hand over the other to block out Sam's continued banging.

"Yes, this is Meredith."

"Good. I need you to do something for me."

"Where's Tamara?"

"She's here."

"I want to talk to her."

"I'm sorry Ms. Jamison, but your wants don't supersede mine in this little scenario."

Meredith took a steadying breath. "They do. At least until you prove that my sister is alive."

There was a grunt. "Hang on."

The thumping on the other side of the bathroom door intensified, the wood shaking so badly Meredith thought it might burst. She pictured Sam throwing his shoulder against it and winced at the mental image. He was going to hurt himself and it would be her fault.

Bigger picture.

Then the thumping stopped, and it was almost worse. Silence all around as Meredith waited for confirmation of her sister's life and wondered what Sam was doing outside the door. Was he looking for another way in? Getting the bellhop to get a manager to break in? She needed him to stay out until she'd spoken to Tamara.

And just a moment later, she got her wish. Tamara's voice came through the line. She sounded small and far-away, but blissfully, thankfully…she was alive.

"Merri?"

"Tami! Thank God. Are you hurt? What the hell is going on?"

"I'm okay. Still in one piece, anyway. I wanted to—"

A shuffle and clatter cut her off, and the masculine voice was back. "Good enough."

Meredith disagreed. Good enough would be her sister sitting across from her, sipping tea and complaining about the weather. But she didn't dare argue.

"What do you need?" she asked.

"The Hamish file." He said it like Meredith should know what he meant, and his next statement confirmed it. "Mrs. Billing told me you were involved in hiding it, so don't tell me you don't know where to find it."

But she had no idea what he was talking about. Was it something to do with one of her sister's clients? But Tamara didn't share their names. She didn't do anything that came close to breaking their confidentiality, and she certainly hadn't ever mentioned a file to Meredith, Hamish or otherwise. So that begged the question…why would her sister feed this man a lie that could jeopardize her own life?

"Ms. Jamison?"

She closed her eyes. "I need time."

"That's a luxury you don't have."

"The Hamish file isn't somewhere accessible," she lied.

There was a long pause on the other end. "Forty-eight hours."

Forty-eight hours?

The deadline seemed both too close and too far away. This man, whoever he was, wanted to hold her sister for another two days. Meredith wanted to see Tamara right that second. To count every hair on her little sister's head. Forty-eight hours would be tortuous. But on the other hand, the man also wanted her to track down some file she'd never even heard of—and for that, two days hardly seemed long enough at all.

But she made herself speak calmly. "Once I have the file, what do you want me to do with it?"

"I'll call you with the instructions. Keep this line open. And one other thing, Ms. Jamison… The present company you're keeping? The ex-cop? Not the best choice under the circumstances."

What did he mean? Once again, Meredith had no idea. And even if she'd wanted to ask, she couldn't. The line clicked, leaving her with a sick feeling in the pit of her stomach.

Sam paced the length of the bedroom.

He'd all but chased out the bellhop, and now that the kid was gone, he kind of wished he hadn't left. It would've given him someone to yell at.

Because Meredith sure as hell wasn't listening.

She was on her damn phone. Her very traceable phone. "Bloody hell."

He paused and stared at the bathroom door. He knew exactly who'd called, too. He didn't even have to ask. He resumed striding back and forth across the room.

"I should be the one asking questions and taking the ransom demand," he muttered.

It was what he did. What he'd lived for as a cop. And besides that…he wanted to be the buffer between Meredith and whoever had her sister. Had to be.

Dammit.

He moved toward the door, fist raised again. Before he could knock once more, it swung open. Meredith stood on the other side, her beautiful face an ashen mess. She looked truly vulnerable for the first time since they'd met.

"Sam," she said. "They have Tamara and I don't think I can do what they need me to do in order to save her."

Wordlessly, he opened his arms. She fell into them, and for several long moments, he held her pressed to his chest, smoothing her hair and offering what comfort he could. He knew *true* comfort wouldn't come until her sister was safe and sound. Which could only happen if they stayed safe themselves.

"Sweetheart, you need to give me the phone," he said.

"I can't."

"You have to. We don't know what kind of tracking abilities they have. If they've got access to police resources—"

"I *can't*. This phone is the one they're going to use to call me back. If I give it to you…"

Sam's jaw stiffened. Whoever had Tamara Billing had effectively handcuffed them, and at the same time given themselves a perfect way to track them. He leaned away from Meredith, prepared to tell her they had no choice. Instead, the utter heartbreak on her face stopped him short.

He knew they'd have to find another way of staying off the radar.

"I feel so helpless," she said. "So responsible."

"This isn't your fault, Meredith."

"You've known me for five seconds, Sam. You have no idea what this feels like."

"Try me."

"It's like you said. I'm proud of her and envious at the same time. More than envious. Crazy jealous. I've always resented everything she's accomplished. So much that the more she succeeded, the more distance I put between us, and now…"

Sam pulled away, this time a bit farther. "Maybe I've known you for five seconds, but I know *exactly* what this feels like. You're scared and guilty and frustrated and questioning every decision you've made for not just the last few hours, but for the last few years."

Meredith's face grew speculative, and Sam wished he hadn't spoken. Or at least not said quite so much.

"You *do* know, don't you?" Meredith's voice was soft. "How?"

"Because…" Sam swallowed. *Because I went through it. Because I lost her.*

He couldn't make the words come. As much as he wanted to, he really couldn't. Not yet.

"We need to focus on the present," he said instead. "On Tamara and how to get her back."

"Okay." Now Meredith's voice was uncertain enough to make Sam's heart ache.

Tell her. He didn't quite shove aside the voice. More like nudged it gently with a promise that he would tell her later. Once they had Tamara, and revealing the details of his past wouldn't shake Meredith's faith in him.

"Why don't you tell me what they want, and I'll pull up my notes and see where we should get started, okay?"

Sam slid his hands down to hers and pulled her gently to the couch and gestured for her to sit down. He dug through his pockets for the USB stick, plugged it into the laptop and positioned himself next to her.

"I'm guessing they wanted something more complicated than money?" he asked as he waited for the menu to load.

"A file," Meredith confirmed. "But not one I've heard of."

"Where is it?"

"I don't have a clue. And what I really don't get is that Tamara told them I would. Why would she endanger her life like that?"

"She must think the file means something to you. They didn't give you any hint what was in it?"

Meredith shook her head. "No. Just the name. The Hamish file."

"It doesn't ring any bells?"

"None."

The password prompt popped up on the screen, and Sam glanced at her before typing. "If you ever need to get into this and I'm not around, the password is 'Kelsey.'"

"Kelsey?"

He forced some lightness into his reply. "My sister's name. No need to be jealous, dearest wife."

"I'm not jealous. But that's not a very secure password."

"That's because it's not so much a secret as it is a reminder." The words were out before Sam could stop them, and he caught Meredith's curious expression.

"A reminder?"

"Of what's important."

He could feel her eyes on him as he opened up his notes, and he knew she wasn't buying it. He pretended he didn't notice and focused on scrolling through the info from the USB stick.

"This is a list of your sister's closest acquaintances.

You. Her husband. A few friends." He pointed at his own annotations. "The friends didn't pan out. They do coffee and wine and not much more. Her husband, I haven't been able to locate. Generally a red flag, but I couldn't find a connection between that and the case. And that's how I wound up at your apartment."

He ran a frustrated hand through his hair. He'd forgotten how little he had to go on.

"What next?" Meredith asked.

"I try to get a hold of a list of her clients."

"How? I don't think she even writes them down. She told me once that she stores it all in her head, just to be safe."

Sam could relate. Paper trails were a private investigator's bread and butter. But to anyone who wanted to maintain a low profile, they were a hazard. Luckily, most people didn't have enough foresight to think about *not* writing things down. Not most honest people, anyway.

A thought occurred to Sam. "Is your sister a career criminal?"

"No, of course not."

"She pays her taxes?"

"As far as I know. Why?"

"Because she gets paid for her counseling work, and somewhere, she tracks those payments."

Hope lit up Meredith's face. "You're right. If we can get a hold of Tamara's bank records, we can see who she's working for. How can we do that? Her accountant isn't going to tell us. Wait! I know where she banks. If I go in and pretend to be Tamara—just to get an account record, not to take any money out or anything—"

Sam shook his head, stopping her midsentence. "No."

"It's a good idea," Meredith insisted.

"It *would* be a good idea. If there weren't God-knows-how-many corrupt cops and their closest friends looking for us."

"But the man on the phone gave us forty-eight hours to get him the file."

"Do you think that means they're going to stop chasing us? Trust me on this one, sweetheart, they won't. They'll only wait for you to find the file if they absolutely have to. Whatever's contained inside…they'd kill for it. If they can get to it faster by taking you and forcing you to give it to them sooner rather than later, that's what they'll do."

At the end of his speech, the hope slipped away from Meredith's eyes. "What do we do, then?"

"I don't know yet." Sam wished he had something more reassuring to tell her. "Get access online somehow, probably. I usually count on Worm to help with that end of things, but who knows where he is or how long he'll take to contact us. Normally, I'd say we wait it out, but…"

He didn't finish the thought, frustrated once again. He needed to think. To come up with some creative solutions. Fast. With a sigh, he set the laptop on the coffee table, leaned back and tried to figure out his next move. He had to do this. He had to succeed. For Tamara's sake, and for Meredith's, but also for his own. He needed to prove that letting himself care wasn't the source of his single, previous failure. That allowing himself some feelings— whatever they turned out to be—for the beautiful woman beside him wouldn't lead down the same path that had led to losing Kelsey.

Because Sam was damn sure he couldn't go through something like that again.

Chapter 10

They sat still, knee-to-knee, Sam lost in his worry, mixed up in his battling emotions and his search for a clear path. Meredith stayed silent, too, but after a few moments, her hand crept to his and she squeezed. Sam squeezed back, glad to take comfort in her touch.

"I'm sorry," he said softly.

He wasn't sure what exactly he was apologizing for. That he should've been the one doling out the reassuring gesture? The way his past interfered with his present? The fact that he didn't have a ready-made solution to their current problem? All of it, probably.

"Whatever it is, Sam, you can tell me."

"I want to, sweetheart. I really do. But it would take longer than we have right now." It sounded like a cop-out.

Because it is.

"If we're just sitting around waiting for Worm, we have nothing *but* time," Meredith reminded him.

"It's not time I want to waste talking about myself."

She pulled her hand away, pained disappointment clouding her eyes. He opened his mouth to try and smooth over his verbal blunder, but Meredith beat him to it.

"It's fine. Just do what you have to do to find my sister." Her expression and tone were both laced with false indifference.

Damn.

Sam sure as hell didn't want to be the source of any more hurt in her life. He grabbed her hand again, brought it to his lips and kissed her palm.

"It's a long story," he said. "One without a happy ending. It's painful to tell, but if you really want to hear it, I'll share it with you. Now, if that's what you need. But my past isn't relevant. It's not going to help us find Tamara, so if you can hold off for a little while, be patient with me…" He trailed off, puzzled by the sudden change in her expression. "What's wrong?"

"What if your past *is* relevant?"

"How could it be?"

"The guy on the phone. He told me that being with *you* wasn't in my best interests."

Meredith's statement gave Sam pause. A missing girl. Corruption on the Bowerville PD. His old stomping grounds. Coincidence? Likely.

Still…

"Did he use my name?"

"No. He just said 'ex-cop.'"

Sam relaxed. "No corrupt cop wants another, clean cop breathing down his neck. Not even if that clean cop happens to be retired."

She studied his face. "How do you do this?"

"Do what?"

"Deal with this kind of man. Not get scared. Follow leads that go nowhere and maintain emotional detachment."

He met her gaze. "Methodically. If I'm scared, I face

it so I can move forward. When following leads, I make note of every single detail in hopes that one of them *will* go somewhere. Because all I need is one. And the emotional detachment… I fight every natural urge."

"Does it work?"

The question hung between them, weighted and dangerous. Sam knew that if he answered with a reference to his past, he'd be giving something away. If he answered in the moment, well… He might give away even more.

"Not always," he said, carefully neutral.

Meredith didn't let him get away with it. "And what would happen if it didn't work?"

"It would make the job harder. Riskier. Because hearts are at stake as well as lives."

"Has it happened to you?"

Those green eyes of hers held him, and he knew he couldn't lie, even if he wanted to. "Once before." He reached up to smooth back a strand of her blond hair. "And now once again."

A blush crept up her throat. "Is it worth it? Risking your heart?"

"You tell me."

Sam lifted his thumb and traced her bottom lip. A soft sigh left her throat, and the sound warmed his blood. He leaned forward, enjoying the way her eyes closed immediately, liking the way she tipped her mouth toward his in anticipation. He took his time with the kiss. He tasted the corners of her lips and the edges of her teeth. Then deepened the contact. As he did, Meredith met his passion with equal fervor. Sam reveled in the feel of her hands running over him. First his hair, then his neck, then down his shoulder blades. Wanting more, Sam slipped his fingers to her waist and drew her into his lap.

She gazed down at him, her pupils large and her cheeks flushed. Then she seemed to find whatever it was she was looking for, and her lids sank shut and her face dipped toward his. Sam tipped up his face to meet her eager mouth. He ran his hands up and up again, pausing just below her bra line, waiting for her to protest, to remind him they'd known each other for less than a day.

He stopped moving.

Less than a day?

How was that possible? It felt like a lifetime. Like he'd been waiting for this explosion between them forever.

"Sam." His name came off her lips in a throaty whisper.

"Yeah, sweetheart?"

"Don't stop. Please."

The invitation brought Sam back to the moment. Back to Meredith and the sweet curve of her lips. He dragged his palm to the bottom of her shirt, then under it. The feel of her skin against his hand was enough to make him release a rumble from somewhere deep in his chest. Her responding gasp heightened his arousal, too. He eased her back against the couch, kissing every exposed bit of her his mouth could find.

Lips.

Throat.

Mouth.

Collarbone.

Throat again.

Each bit of her tasted as good as the last. Sweet and tempting.

"So beautiful," he murmured against her goose-bump-laden skin.

He dug his fingers into her silken hair and tugged on her bottom lip with his teeth. She let out a little cry; one of her knees lifted to his hip, and Sam pushed forward, resentful of the two layers of denim that lay between them. He wanted to get rid of them. Now.

"Stupid clothes," Meredith breathed, echoing his thoughts.

"Mmph," Sam agreed.

He fumbled to reach his jeans zipper—or maybe hers, he wasn't sure—and failed. In an attempt to make it easier, he rolled them over. He overshot, and they tumbled to the ground, sending the coffee table jerking across the carpet and knocking the laptop to the ground. Meredith was on top of him now, her eyes wide, her shirt askew and her blond hair in complete disarray.

Damn, was she beautiful.

Sam smiled up at her. "I knew my timing sucked, but I didn't think my technique was off, too."

Her mouth tipped up at the corners. "Trust me. It's not all that off."

"Oh, really?"

She grabbed his hands and placed them on her waist. "Mmm-hmm. Why don't you keep trying? Maybe you can perfect it."

Slowly, his eyes on her face, Sam slid his fingers under her shirt again. He moved them up, inch by inch, until they hit the lace edge of her bra.

He paused. "How am I doing now?"

"Good," she breathed. "Well, I mean."

"Grammar is important," he teased as he lifted a thumb and ran it over one of her still-covered nipples. "Especially at moments like this."

"Shut up."

"What? My goal is to do well at being bad."

He shifted his hands to her back, but only got as far as touching the clasp of her bra before the bang of the hotel door made him freeze.

"Room service!" called a rough voice.

"Ignore it."

Under other circumstances, he would've obeyed the sexy command without question. Not now.

Sam's eyes darted to the corner of the room. Yes, there

it was. A wheeled cart, silver platters still covered, cutlery still wrapped.

"I don't know who that is, but it sure as hell isn't room service."

He eased to a sitting position, then lifted her to the couch. He stood still for a breath as he worked out a plan in his head. Priority one was Meredith's safety. Sam grabbed her hand and pulled her through the French doors into the bedroom, then to the bathroom.

"I want you to lock the door and stay in here," he ordered.

Meredith shook her head. "I'm not going to hide!"

"It's not hiding, sweetheart. It's keeping safe. For my sake."

"What are *you* going to do?"

"I'm going to get my gun and find out who the hell's pretending to serve us a late-night snack," he said grimly.

She opened her mouth like she was going to protest again, but Sam didn't give her a chance. He leaned forward and kissed her lips, then gave her the tiniest shove backward and closed the door.

Meredith stared at the white-paneled door, fear mixing with irritation.

Sam wanted her to be safe. Well. That was *her* decision. *Her* life. But then he'd thrown in that little bit about doing it for *his* sake, and that made her urge to ignore his order harder.

"Dammit, Sam."

She leaned against the pedestal sink and met her own gaze in the mirror. Worry darkened her eyes. But under that, she saw determination. Sam *had* to know she wasn't just going to stay in the bathroom. Not when there was a good possibility that whoever stood on the other side of the door posed a threat to his life.

Ninety seconds.

That's exactly how long she'd give him to deal with it.

Maybe it wasn't long enough to indulge his protectiveness. But it was as long as she could stand it. And long enough for him to sort out whatever was going on. To gain an advantage. Or to lose one. Though obviously she preferred the idea of the former. The man she'd knocked out in the staircase was already one too many.

"But I'll do it again if I have to," she muttered.

Sixty seconds more.

Of course, it was going to be hard to smack someone in the head with her gun if she didn't know where her gun had gone to. *Her gun.* Just the fact that she'd mentally taken ownership of a weapon of any sort should've been troubling. Instead, all she could think about was the fact that she wished she had it in her hand right at that moment. When had it fallen out? How had she not noticed?

"Maybe it has something to do with the fact that you've never had to keep tabs on a gun before," she told her reflection.

Thirty more seconds.

She released the sink and moved toward the door, then pressed her ear to cool wood. Why couldn't she hear anything on the other side? Meredith was sure there should be the sounds of struggle. Banging. Yelling. Fighting. Something. Concern made her stomach flutter. She couldn't wait anymore.

"Screw the last ten seconds."

She eased the door open, thankful for the well-oiled hinges that made it silent, then inched into the room. Still nothing. She tiptoed toward the French doors, put her hand on the handle, then paused as a metallic flash from under the bed caught her eye.

The gun. Thank God.

Relieved, Meredith let go of the door to retrieve the weapon. But as she kneeled down to grab it, she finally *did* hear something. Sam's voice, dropped in a low laugh.

A laugh?

She had to have misheard.

Slowly, she pulled herself up and stepped back toward the door. The sound came again. And she knew she hadn't misheard. Meredith swung the door open and relief flooded her body.

"Worm!"

At her gasp, the big man spun around and his eyes traveled from her face to her hand, then back again, then moved to settle on Sam, who stood at his side. "Did you give her a gun?"

Sam shrugged. "Seemed prudent at the time."

"Doesn't seem prudent now. Is she going to shoot me?" Worm asked.

Meredith exhaled and set the gun down on a decorative table in the corner. "I'm not going to shoot you. I don't even know how to fire it."

"Good. Because it took quite a bit of effort to get away from those deranged, so-called cops at my house. And even more effort to find you. I came to help you out, but if I'm just going to get shot…"

"I think you're safe," Sam assured him.

Worm sank down into the couch and grabbed the laptop from the floor, muttering about the mistreatment of technology. Meredith barely heard him. Because as the big man's hands closed on the computer, she immediately remembered how it wound up on the floor in the first place, and heat crept up her face. In the excitement of the last few minutes, their shared intimacy had gone out of her head. But seeing the evidence of it laid out in front her—the slightly askew table and the bunched-up carpet and the laptop that Worm was now typing away on—brought it back full force.

Sam's lips. Sam's hands. How they felt all over her. If his friend hadn't shown up when he did, how far would she have let things go?

Let things go? asked a little voice. *You weren't letting things go. You were propelling them along.*

Meredith tried to argue against it, but a warm, already familiar hand landed on the small of her back, rubbing in a reassuring circle. And she knew it was true. She liked Sam. A lot. And whether the urgency of the situation fueled the urgency of her feelings, or maybe the feelings were just that intense all on their own, Meredith couldn't say for sure. But she did know that she had zero interest in slowing things down. She leaned into his touch.

"You okay?" His voice, right in her ear, sent a wave of heat down her spine, where it met with his hand and traveled inward.

"Fine as I can be," Meredith responded after a pause.

"You sure?"

"Yes. Why?"

"Because Worm's asked you to look at the screen three times and you're just kinda staring at the wall."

Whoops.

Meredith turned her attention to the computer, and her embarrassment quickly went by the wayside. A map of Bowerville, peppered with her sister's name and a series of numbers and arrows, dominated the screen. "What is this?"

"Flowchart," Worm stated. "Those are the numeric codes that represent the businesses where she used her credit card over the last two weeks. The arrows just show you the order in which the transactions happened."

Meredith blinked. "This took you five minutes?"

Sam nudged her. "Creepy and impressive, right?"

"It'll be more of both once everything is filled in," Worm said. "It's a shame someone on the other side of this also has some technical know-how. They've disabled the GPS in her phone. Or maybe somehow removed it completely because I can't even gain access."

He clicked a few more times, and a new layer of windows popped up, but Meredith wasn't looking. She just met Sam's eyes, then pulled her own cell from her pocket. She held it out and cleared her throat.

Worm looked up and blinked. "What?"

"Can you do that to mine? Disable its GPS?"

"Sure."

He gave the phone a cursory look, but didn't take it. Instead, he turned back to the computer and tapped away.

"Done," he said after a minute.

"It was that easy?" Meredith asked.

He shrugged. "For me."

"Can it be just as easily undone?"

"No."

"Why not?"

Sam chuckled. "Sorry, man. She's got to know everything."

Worm sighed. "My software—basically a remote-installed app—is a little more sophisticated than that. Instead of blocking the GPS signal, it reroutes it. Gives whoever's tracking it a false signal and sends them to Timbuktu. Good enough?"

Meredith nodded, relieved. "Good enough."

"Let's move on." He angled the computer in her direction.

She sat on the edge of the couch, trying to get a better view. "Those are Tamara's bank records."

"Some of them. The personal ones, mostly. Her business accounts are more secure, but you can still see the basics. She and her husband keep separate accounts. Like, all over the place. Visa and savings and…well, everything. Pretty unusual for a married couple." Worm stopped talking and turned a speculative eye in Meredith's direction.

"You think he has something to do with this?" she asked. "As in, he might be directly responsible for Tamara's kidnapping?"

"You don't?" the ponytailed man responded.

"I just—no. It's not him," she said. "It can't be."

"What makes you so sure?" The question came from Sam, who'd positioned himself behind the couch.

"It's always the husband," Worm added.

Meredith clenched her jaw. "This time, it's not. Nicholas—my brother-in-law—isn't my favorite person, but I know him. And he wouldn't hurt my sister."

"His last purchase was for a ridiculously overpriced luggage set."

"He took a vacation. He told his secretary—" Meredith stopped abruptly as she realized what she'd just revealed.

Sam's jaw tightened. "You contacted him?"

"I tried to. I spoke to his office assistant. She told me Nick went on vacation."

Worm jumped in. "That doesn't raise a giant red flag? Why the hell didn't you mention it earlier?"

"Because I knew you'd jump to conclusions. And trust me. Nicholas is as straight as they come," Meredith said. "Like, pleats-ironed-into-his-pants kind of straight. He won't even jaywalk. He only defends clients who are irrefutably innocent in his books. Since I've known him, he's only made one big mistake. Wherever he is and whatever he bought, I'm sure this has nothing to do with him."

Worm shot her a disbelieving look, but Sam stepped in front of the table and shook his head. "She clearly doesn't like the man, Worm. She's not defending him to be nice."

"You're just taking her word for it?" The big man flicked back his ponytail. "Since when are you so trusting, Potter?"

"Since now."

Worm's expression darkened, but Meredith didn't care. Because Sam's eyes had found her, and they contained something that warmed her heart more than her face. Some *things*. Genuine affection and trust. A hint of promise. Desire. And all of those mattered far more than anything his computer-crazy friend thought.

Chapter 11

Faster than seemed possible for a man of the hacker's size, Worm jumped to his feet.

"Can I see you in the other room?"

Sam tore his gaze away from Meredith and pushed aside the mounting heat between them. "You can. But nothing you say is going to change the fact that I trust Meredith's instincts."

Worm rolled his eyes. "I just want one minute."

"Fine." Sam bent down and dragged a finger along Meredith's jaw, then said emphatically, "You okay here for *one* minute?"

She leaned into his touch, then picked up the laptop. "Sure. I might even last for two. Maybe I'll just see if I can find anything weird in Tamara's time line."

"Sounds like a good idea." Sam kissed her forehead more chastely than he wanted to and followed Worm from the living room to the bedroom, closed the doors, then faced his long-time friend. "I meant what I said out there."

"I know."

"Then why the hell are you pulling me in here?"

"To ask you if you're insane."

"Insane?"

His friend met his eyes. "You're dismissing a prime suspect because that girl said so."

Sam sighed. He had to admit his curiosity about Nicholas Billing was piqued. But if he admitted *that*, then he'd have to admit it wasn't about the case. It was about the way Meredith claimed to know him well. Something in her tone. Sam didn't like it, but it had nothing to do with the case.

"Potter!" Worm urged. "The husband's purchases stop three days before the wife's. The man's a defense lawyer. And I don't care what he told his damned secretary, he hasn't booked a vacation anywhere that I can see. You can't ignore the facts."

"I'm not ignoring the facts. *That girl* is my best and only lead. This is her sister we're talking about. Do you think she'd just pretend her brother-in-law wasn't a suspect if she thought it meant we could save Tamara? I'm not going to let it go if the investigation turns to him, but I haven't been able to locate the man to question him, and aside from his abrupt departure from his office, he hasn't done anything truly suspicious."

"Yet," Worm muttered.

"My number-one priority is locating Tamara Billing. So for now, I'm giving Meredith the benefit of the doubt. I trust her instincts."

"You trust her— Hell. You *are* insane. This case is the most complicated one you've ever asked for my help with. Probably the most dangerous, too. Cops and guns and… every reason you left the Bowerville PD to start out with. Are you sure this is what you want to be involved in? And if you're sure about yourself, then are you sure about the Achilles' heel you're dragging along behind you?"

"What do you mean?"

"Anyone who's in a room with you and that girl for more than thirty seconds is going to see this isn't about her instincts or the benefit of the doubt. You're halfway in love with her."

Sam choked on the breath he'd just drawn in. "In love? I met Meredith Jamison this morning."

"So?"

"People don't fall in love in hours."

Worm shook his head. "People fall in love at first sight."

"You don't believe that."

"Kelsey did."

"And look where that got her."

Worm sighed. "Not my point. You've always been an all-or-nothing guy, Potter. It's what made you a great cop. It's what made you a great brother and what made you the right guy to step in and be her guardian when your parents died. It's what's making you work like a dog to solve this case for that girl out there. Throwing yourself into the middle of things that are the exact opposite of where you've wanted to be for half a decade."

Sam's eyes strayed to the door, then came back to his friend. "You think this is too dangerous and I should cut her loose."

"No. I don't. Just the opposite."

Sam didn't bother to cover his surprise. "So why are we here, having this little chat, then?"

"Because insanity aside, I think you should tell her everything."

"Tell her? That's it?"

Worm nodded. "Tell her and let her decide. No one understands more than you how precarious life is. But I haven't seen you act on that in five years. If you're going to do it now, don't do it blind. And don't let *her* do it blind, either. So, yes. That's it. And that's my condition for helping you out with this, too."

"Your condition?"

"What? You think I've been working for you all this time for the sad bit of money you toss my way now and then? I'm capable of hacking into government computer systems. What you pay me can't keep me in instant noodles, let alone cover my services."

Sam narrowed his eyes. "I always assumed it had something to do with our friendship."

"It does. Which is exactly why I'm making this condition." Worm gestured toward the living room. "And assuming you're agreeing to it, we should probably get back out there and get back to work."

"Assuming you were right about what I was feeling, I would tell her anyway."

Sam closed his fingers around the handle, pulled the door open, then froze as Meredith's almost-still form caught and held his attention. She'd discarded the laptop on the edge of the couch and curled her legs up underneath her body. Her eyes were closed and her chest rose and fell gently. Sound asleep.

And Worm was right.

Sam's heart swelled with the reality of it; he *did* care about her. A lot. Especially considering how little he knew her. Love? Maybe not. Not yet, anyway. He couldn't just chalk it up to lust, either. Yes, he felt a strong physical attraction, but he was already sure there was more to it than that. And his gut told him every passing day would only send him deeper.

"She's kinda in my way, Potter." Worm's statement jerked Sam out of his not-so-gloomy musings.

He bent down and smoothed away a lock of her hair, then started to speak her name, but thought better of it.

She needed a rest. So instead of waking her, Sam slid his arms under her knees and around her back and lifted her from the couch. She shifted and murmured something as she settled against his chest. Sam held still for a moment, just enjoying the feel of her. Then he carried her to the bedroom, where he eased back the covers awkwardly, and tucked them around her.

When he made his way back into the living room, he found Worm already working on the laptop again. Sam tried to speak, but his friend put up a hand, stopping him. He typed away furiously for another couple of minutes, then pushed the laptop onto the table and stood.

"All right," he said. "Here's what I've set up. Automatic tracking on the sister's phone, just in case. Virtual tracking of her credit cards, also just in case. I doubt either of those things will help you, but covering all our bases, right? I'll take all the info we have and use a better equipped location—not my house, and thanks for that, by the way— to get you access to her business accounts. See if I can find anything weird. You guys can fill in the gaps by deciphering the coded locations, then you can get your PI on."

Sam raised an eyebrow. "Get my PI on? You mean put on my fedora, sit on a park bench with a newspaper in front of my face and hope not to look suspicious? That kind of PI stuff?"

"Exactly. Unless you want to back out? Put the case aside?"

"Not even close."

"All right. Your funeral. But I gotta get going. A twenty-minute nap and a crappy apartment are calling my name." Worm stood up, stretched and yawned widely. "Can't say I'm not envious of Mr. Hall and his five-star accommodations."

"You created the man," Sam pointed out. "You could've been him if you'd wanted."

"Nah. I could never pass for some rich jerk. My own alternate identity is a reclusive computer nerd."

"You *are* a reclusive computer nerd."

"I know. It's beautiful, right?" His friend moved toward the door, opened it, then paused and shot a meaningful nod in the direction of the bedroom. "Don't forget our deal."

Sam grunted noncommittally as he shut the door. He *would* tell Meredith his story, but not because Worm told him to. Because he wanted to. And when the time was right.

At the moment, though, he had other things to focus on. Like trying again to get ahold of the client who'd hired him. He had more questions than answers, but that didn't mean he shouldn't check in. He pulled out his cell and dialed the number. It rang and rang and no one picked up on the other end. On the ninth ring, the air just went dead. Sam clicked the off button, then stared down at the phone. No option to leave a message this time.

Weird.

He'd never had someone who hired him become so difficult to reach. Most of them wanted updates. Immediately and often. On the odd occasion they didn't, it usually turned out to be because the case had no merit after all.

So under any other circumstance, the lack of communication would be enough to make Sam put the investigation on hold. Except this circumstance was nowhere near usual. He'd already identified his target, and he knew her life was in danger. He'd taken a very large down payment. And even if *those* things weren't true… Sam's eyes drifted to the French doors.

Meredith.

Money aside, lack of communication aside, there was no way Sam would abandon her. Just thinking about her peaceful form on the other side of the curtain-covered glass warmed his blood. What would happen if he gave in to the nearly overwhelming urge to go to her? What would she do if he slid his body in beside hers and ran his palms up the length of her curves?

He didn't think she'd turn him away. In fact, he thought she would welcome the comfort she'd find in his arms. But as much as he wanted to live in the moment, he knew what Meredith needed wasn't a short-term distraction. What she *did* need was to find her sister.

So Sam forced his gaze away from the bedroom, turned his attention back to the computer and got to work on meeting that need.

Meredith woke slowly. Uncomfortably. Her whole body ached, and her mind protested against consciousness. She tried to open her eyes and failed. Even her face hurt.

Then it all came rushing back to her.

Tamara.

Sam.

The hotel.

She sat bolt upright. And regretted it instantly. The all-over ache became an all-over screech. She let out a groan.

The last thing she remembered clearly was staring down at the blurry laptop screen, trying to make sense of her sister's credit-card habits. The numbers and purchases were a nonsensical mess that seemed totally unrelated to Tamara's kidnapping. And yes, her brain had been tired. But she'd been tingling with worry, too. She had no idea how she'd even managed to fall asleep. Or how long she'd been out. Her eyes sought the alarm clock on the bedside table, but its red glow was nonexistent. And when she swung her feet out from under the blanket and blinked against the dark, she saw why. Someone—Sam, probably—had unplugged the clock. And turned out all the lights, and drawn the curtains, too.

Puzzled, Meredith pushed herself to her feet and moved

across the room, calling his name. But her muscles protested heartily and she only made it two steps before she crashed into an unidentified piece of furniture. With a curse, she stumbled back, scraping her arm on another *something*. Then, without warning, the lights came to life, temporarily blinding her. Meredith pitched forward, swearing again. But as she braced for the inevitable impact, a steadying hand landed on her elbow.

"Whoa. Let's try not to break too much stuff. My rich alter ego only has so much money to burn."

The rumble of Sam's voice—so close to her ear while they were so close to the bed—made her insides warm. And for a second, Meredith forgot her aches and pains and leaned against him gratefully. But when she let him guide her across the room to a cushy chair, her muscles balked again at the movement, and when she eased down her thighs protested the simple action of sitting.

"Apparently, the thing I'm most in danger of breaking is myself," she stated. "I feel like hell."

Sam shot her a teasing grin. "I beg to differ. You feel pretty damned fantastic to me."

"Flattery isn't your friend right now."

"Maybe it could be. If it was accompanied by some mediocre news."

Meredith frowned. "Seriously? Mediocre news? That's what you're offering?"

"Mediocre is better than bad."

She lifted her eyes, and hope bubbled in her chest in spite of Sam's neutral expression. "What've you got?"

"Sit tight for one second and I'll show you."

"Like I can do anything else."

She stifled another self-pitying moan and resolved to take a renewed interest in exercising regularly. Maybe enroll in one of the Pilates classes her sister used to try to talk her into taking. *Her sister*. Meredith squeezed her eyes shut and let the guilt wash over her. Why hadn't she just swallowed her pride and her envy and done the things Tamara wanted her to do? Like that trendy martini bar, just a few months back. She'd lied about having to work to avoid going. Now, she'd give her right arm to be there right that second with her sister. Drinking some awful mix of chocolate and gin. Listening to bad piano music. Just to know Tamara was safe and sound.

"Sweetheart?"

Meredith opened her eyes and found Sam standing in front of her, a room-service cart at his thigh and the laptop under one arm. He set the latter on top of the former, then opened his palm and held out two ibuprofen tablets. Meredith took them gratefully. As she popped them into her mouth, Sam handed her a cup of orange juice, too.

"Breakfast of champions," he said. "My favorite choice after a long day of chasing bad guys followed by a crappy night's sleep."

Meredith just about choked on the liquid in her throat. "Wait. Breakfast? How long was I out?"

"About seven hours."

"How could you let me sleep the whole night away?"

She tried to push herself back up, but Sam put a hand on her shoulder, stopping her. She fought him for a second, but her weak muscles weren't on her side. And even though Sam wasn't exerting much pressure, she didn't stand a chance of winning.

She sagged backward. "I can't believe I wasted seven hours."

"You needed the rest," Sam said firmly. "And now you need something to eat."

"I'll eat and rest when Tamara is safe."

"If you don't eat now, you won't be in any shape to help make her safe. The same goes for the rest."

"I don't see you eating."

"I ate steak dinner last night. Yours and mine. And I promise I didn't let the time go to waste. I said I had news, remember?"

"You also said it was mediocre. And you've yet to tell me anything anyway," Meredith grumbled.

Sam turned away and lifted the lid of the platter on the room service cart, and the scent of food wafted from the plate. Meredith's mouth watered.

Sam held out a forkful of scrambled eggs. "Have a bite, and I'll open the laptop."

"Are you seriously threatening to *not* tell me if I don't eat?"

"Definitely. I'm also threatening to leave you behind if you don't accept the terms of my blackmail. And since you already begged me once not to do that…" He wiggled the fork.

With an annoyed sigh, Meredith opened her mouth. Sam popped in the eggs, and she had to admit the food was more than welcome. She chewed and swallowed, and almost immediately she felt better than she had just moments before.

"More?" Sam offered.

"Mediocre news?" she countered.

He handed her the fork, then wheeled the cart closer. And he waited—stubbornly, Meredith thought—until she'd swallowed two more bites before he opened the laptop, typed in his password, set it up so she could see and positioned himself on the arm of her chair.

He pointed at the screen. "I filled in the blanks. Translated all those location codes Worm gave us, then plugged in the names and addresses of every place your sister's been over the last week. They're all here on the map."

Meredith leaned forward, grabbed a piece of toast and gave the screen a once-over. Most of it looked typical. A nail salon. A couple of high-end restaurants and a boutique clothing store. All of Tamara's favorite places. But something was off.

Sam read her frown perfectly. "Something stand out?"

"Give me a second." Meredith chewed slowly and took a more careful look, following the arrows. "What's this purchase here, the day before the credit-card activity stopped? Somewhere called Bowerville Station."

"That's the bus station."

"Tamara owns two cars and she *hates* transit. I can't picture her getting on a bus. Even if her life literally depended on it."

"So why did she spend sixty dollars there? She obviously bought a ticket of some kind."

"Not one she'd use." Meredith paused, thinking. "Is it crazy to wonder if she was trying to draw attention to the bus station itself?"

"No. That's not crazy. It's genius."

"But how would she even know someone would be looking at this stuff? And if she *did* know they were going to kidnap her, why wouldn't she call me *before* it happened?"

"Probably for the same reason you wouldn't call her, if the roles were reversed."

"To protect me." Guilt tickled at Meredith again, and her eyes drifted back to the computer. "She waited until it was too late and she had no choice but to contact me. Maybe she thought she could fix whatever was wrong."

"Or she thought she could outrun it." Sam leaned back. "I guess there's only one way to know for sure."

"Take a trip to Bowerville Station?"

"Yep. Time to do what Worm said."

"Which is?"

"To get our PI on."

Meredith might've laughed. If Sam hadn't sounded so serious. And if she hadn't been so pleased that he'd said *our* instead of *my*. Like they were a team.

Chapter 12

Sam used the excuse of wanting a coffee refill to give Meredith some space to change clothes. Truthfully, though, he needed the short-term distance himself. He could feel the hopeful vibe taking hold, bubbling outward from Meredith. Threatening to overtake him. He liked that the sparkle was back in her eyes. He wanted to make it even brighter. But what he *wanted* to do and what he *had* to do were two different things. The case needed clarity and objectivity, and at the moment Sam's growing emotional attachment was bogging it down.

So he sipped the hot liquid in his cup, grateful for the way it slid down his throat, burning just a little. It helped him focus. Helped him sort through the puzzle pieces in his mind. To try and figure out what detail it was that nagged at him but he couldn't quite put his finger on.

Was it Tamara's motivation for not calling until it was too late?

No. Not that.

Like he'd told Meredith, he believed Tamara had waited in the name of protection.

So was it something about the credit-card purchases that bugged him? Sam didn't think so. And he agreed with Meredith's conclusion that Tamara had been leaving a clue.

"What then?" he asked the empty room.

He took another healthy slurp of coffee and tapped his fingertips on the closed laptop. Meredith said her sister was by-the-book. Sam thought it was safe to assume she was smart, too. He tapped harder. Then paused.

The police.

Why hadn't Tamara called *them*? Had the kidnappers threatened her MIA husband? Meredith? His rarely wrong gut told him no. Besides which, if they'd made the threat, Tamara would've turned over what they were looking for. So maybe...

"She had to know," Sam murmured.

"Know what?"

He set the mug down, stood and faced Meredith. And was momentarily tongue-tied. She'd tidied her hair and cleaned her face, and the clothes sent up by the concierge fit her perfectly. Skin-tight jeans. A pale pink shirt, short-sleeved and buttoned up, but cut low across her chest. Somehow tough and feminine at the same time.

"You look fantastic," Sam blurted.

Meredith's face went several shades darker than her shirt. "Thank you. But shouldn't I be blending in? Maybe I should put my other stuff back on."

She turned to go, but Sam shot out his hand and stopped her. "Don't."

"Don't?"

"They sent up a sweatshirt, too. Stick it on over your top and you'll—" He paused for a beat because he couldn't possibly imagine her even blending in, then cleared his throat and tried again. "You'll be fine."

"You look good, too, you know." She narrowed her eyes. "Maybe you need a sweatshirt."

"Got it covered." Sam grabbed the hotel-provided hoodies and tossed the smaller of the two her way. "See?"

"Then I'm sure you'll be *fine*, too."

Her eyes slid down his body, then up again. Sam saw the movement and the accompanying appreciation. More importantly, he felt it. An arc of heat that curved with her gaze and made the room sweltering.

Sam cleared his throat again—this time to remind himself that he wasn't supposed to be mentally unbuttoning Meredith's blouse. He was supposed to be helping her.

"Your sister," he said. "I think she knew that the cops were involved in her abduction."

"Because otherwise she would've called them herself."

"To quote you...*exactly*. But it doesn't change our plans. Our best lead is still the bus station. You ready?"

"As ready as a girl can be when she's getting her PI on."

Sam smiled, glad again that Worm had provided him with the colorful phrase. He slipped into his sweatshirt and did it up quickly, then noticed that Meredith's zipper was stuck. He reached over to help her adjust, and she let him pull the soft fabric over her chest, standing still as he worked the zipper from her waist to her throat. When he reached the top, he stopped, but didn't pull away his hands, struck by how intimate the gesture seemed. How it seemed to exemplify an increasing level of trust.

Sam leaned down to brush a kiss over her mouth. She felt so good. So right. Like he'd done it a hundred times rather than half a dozen or so.

Only you would find the perfect girl in the middle of all this, Potter.

He pulled back slowly, met her eyes and ran his thumb over her velvety lips.

"I'm scared as hell, Sam," she said softly, and the admission made his gut clench.

"Listen to me, Meredith," he said. "I don't make outright promises to my clients. Life has no guarantees and I'd hate to make a liar of myself. And even though I know you're not technically my client, I'm doing this as much for you as I am for the person who hired me. Probably more, if I'm being honest. So I'll make an exception and I *will* make you a promise."

"You don't have to do that."

"Yes, I do, sweetheart. I want you to know that you mean something to me. I might not know yet what that something is, but I do know it sure as hell matters. So my promise is this—no matter what happens, I'll protect you. I'll make sure that for every one I owe you, you owe me two. Or three and half, if that's what it takes."

"I—"

The light thump of feet somewhere outside the door, followed by a muffled voice, cut her off. Their gazes locked, and both of them went still. Then, with his finger at his lips, Sam inched toward the door. Before he even reached it, a thunderous bang sounded. He heard Meredith gasp from behind him, but he held steady and lifted an eye to the peephole. Two people stood on the other side, down the hall and directly in front of room 1003. One was the familiar redheaded thug, and the other was a man dressed in a nondescript suit—Sam was sure he was an officer. And his suspicion was confirmed just a moment later. A uniformed hotel employee approached, clearly put off by the noise. He pointed and said something. They exchanged a few words, and the suited man flashed a badge. Then he turned, and Sam realized something worse. It wasn't just a detective. It was the detective Meredith had so unceremoniously knocked out. Brody Boyd.

Dammit.

It got worse. The uniformed man pulled out a key card,

and Sam held his breath as the man shoved it into the lock. Thankfully, the door didn't respond. Sam let out a relieved sigh and watched as the three men's animated discussion carried on for a just another moment. Then the hotel employee disappeared, and the other two men relaxed into a conversation. Boyd even went so far as to lean against the wall.

The idiots thought they were just going to walk in and surprise them. Well, they'd be as displeased as they were surprised when they got in and discovered that "Mr. and Mrs. Hall" weren't where they expected them to be. And it wouldn't take long after that to figure out they'd gone.

Sam leaned back and lifted the slide lock, careful to keep it from rattling. He latched it silently, then backed away from the door and turned back to Meredith.

He spoke in a voice as firm as it was quiet. "We need to get out of here. Fast."

"Cops?" she whispered back.

"Two of our old friends. The redhead and the detective from my apartment. And someone is on their way up with a key card to open 1003."

"Okay. Fast. But thorough, too."

"What?"

"Like this." She moved to the laptop and flipped it open, cleared the browser history, then snapped up the USB stick and held it out. "You want to toss the computer out the window, too?"

Sam took the flash drive from her. "Too noisy and not subtle enough, either."

"Right. Okay. Got it."

She turned from him and hurried across the room to the minibar, where she snagged a small bottle of booze. She carried it back, cracked it open and drizzled half of it over the laptop keyboard. It snapped once, then went black.

Meredith shot him a smile, then sucked back the rest of the liquor. "Now we can go."

"Not yet."

"But you said we needed to—"

Sam reached out, pulled her close and pressed his mouth to hers. He darted his tongue between her lips. *Peach liqueur.* Delicious. He pulled back and answered her smile with one of his own.

"*Now* we can go," he repeated.

He touched her cheek, closed the ruined laptop and strode toward the sliding glass doors that led to the patio. He closed his hands on the lock. He pushed. It didn't budge. He pushed harder. Nothing. Sam looked down. And realized why.

He spun to face Meredith. "The lever's broken. We need to find another way out."

"What way is that?"

"I have absolutely no idea."

Meredith waited for Sam to retract his statement. To say he had a plan. Instead, he just stood staring at the glass.

C'mon, c'mon, Meredith urged silently.

He stayed still. And the seconds were ticking by.

"Sam?"

"They're going to figure out where we are, pretty damned quick," he muttered.

"No kidding."

"We need a fire."

"Hmm?"

"We need to shut down the hotel down. A fire will do that."

"And it'll give us a felony record," Meredith added.

"You want to take our chances with those guys out there instead?"

"No, but—"

"Good. We can fight about it if we get out of here alive."

"No we can't," Meredith grumbled. "They don't have coed prisons."

"I promise my rich-guy persona will pay for the damages."

"I don't know if that makes me feel better or worse."

But he was already on the move again. Collecting any stray piece of fabric he could find. A towel. A blanket. The runner from the room service cart. Even a small rug. Then, with his arms nearly full, he snapped up the laptop and strode to the bedroom.

Meredith started after him for a moment, unable to believe he was really considering lighting it all on fire.

"Meredith?" he called.

She hurried to follow him. By the time she reached him, he'd already fashioned the beginnings of a pyre in the center of the bed. He'd added a pile of toilet paper to the top, too, and held the bedside lamp in one hand.

"Shield your eyes," he ordered.

As Meredith lifted her hand, Sam ripped the shade from the light, then smacked the bulb into the wall.

"Sam!"

"Flick the light on. Quickly."

But her feet seemed frozen to the spot.

"One of us has to hold the lamp," Sam said. "The other needs to create the spark. If we don't do this, sweetheart, they're going to open that door and they're going to see that we're not there. All it's going to take to figure out where we are is one call down to the concierge and one call to our favorite bellhop and we're going to be toast."

And then Meredith swore she could hear the door to 1003 rattling and shaking up the hall. And it spurred her to move. She took three sharp steps and hit the switch. The filaments in the glassless bulb came to life in a single zap. And that was all it took. The toilet paper flamed up in a rapid burn that quickly caught the rest of the flammable material beneath it. But as the orange glow took hold, Sam strode to the bathroom, then returned with a glass of water. He doused the fire and smoke billowed out. It lifted up toward the ceiling, hit the smoke detector and a localized alarm sounded. Then it filled the room, making both of them cough.

From outside in the hall, someone let out a holler. Meredith wondered if they'd seen the smoke, or if they'd simply discovered that room 1003 was empty.

Sam grabbed Meredith's arm. "Let's go."

She let him pull her across the room to the walk-in closet doors, which he flung open, and then he yanked her inside. The second the doors closed behind them, Meredith whipped her elbow free and rounded on Sam. But he beat her to the punch.

"Seven minutes in heaven?" he joked.

"We don't have seven minutes. And this isn't my idea of heaven."

He flicked on the light above their heads. "Two minutes, then."

"You just lit a fire, then all but put it out, and now we're trapped in a closet while two deranged men wait to bust in on us!"

"Speaking of which…" He grabbed a spare blanket from one of the closet shelves, rolled it up and tucked it against the door. "Don't want to die of smoke inhalation."

Meredith stared at him incredulously. "Please. Tell me you have a plan. And then when you're done telling me you have a plan, tell me that plan includes you *not* having lost it."

"I have a plan."

"Which is?"

"Wait for it," he replied calmly.

"Wait for what? My head to explode?"

"Nope. Give it another second."

As if on cue, the in-room alarm was joined by chorus of other shrill sounds. Even from inside the closet, Meredith could tell the noise must be filling the whole floor.

Sam gave her a kiss. "*That* is what you were waiting for."

Meredith sent an eye roll his way. "You did *not* plan that."

"Might as well have."

He lifted both arms over his head and dislodged one of the hanger rails, then dropped to the floor. He drew back the rail and slammed it into the rear wall hard enough to make Meredith yelp. She started to lift her hand to cover her mouth, then stopped. Although the blaring alarms were muffled inside the closet, outside they covered any possible noise. Yelps. Screams. Breaking walls.

And that was Sam's plan, she realized. A distraction. A completely chaotic distraction.

He pulled back and let the wall have it again. Bits of paint and drywall flew out and up, and Sam tossed the rail aside in favor of his foot. He smashed it into the wall. Once. Twice. And on the third time, it gave out. A wide hole opened up and Sam backed away.

"All right," he said. "Use your tiny hands to help me tear away enough wall from the wood that we can fit through."

"I do *not* have tiny hands."

But she bent down beside him anyway, and did as he asked. And in moments, they'd exposed the framing, and through the person-sized hole, Meredith could see an identical closet on the other side.

"Giant-man-handed ladies first," Sam said.

"Such a gentleman."

"Always, sweetheart," he told her seriously, then touched her face. "Now go. Fast. Getting out of here puts us another step closer to Tamara."

Something in the intensity of the statement made Meredith's eyes fill with unwanted tears, and as she slid through the dusty hole, she felt her heart swell with appreciation. This man, whom she hadn't known just twenty-four hours earlier, cared enough about her to go through all of this.

To commit a felony. Just to save her sister—a woman he'd never even met.

Meredith knew she shouldn't feel lucky. She shouldn't be thinking that somehow fate had managed to balance out the toughest moment of her life with the most wonderful. She shouldn't be thinking about herself at all. But when she made it through the hole and pushed to her feet, and Sam followed and his hand landed on the small of her back and his voice filled her ear with a murmured reassurance…she couldn't help it.

"I *am* lucky," she said softly.

Somehow, Sam managed to hear her over the blare of the alarm.

"Lucky?" he queried.

"Anyone else—even another PI, I'm sure—would've run in the other direction by now. You've almost died at least three times in the last twenty-four hours. God know what's going through your head. But you're still here."

"Where else would I be?"

"Anywhere?"

The heat in his eyes made her want to burn up as thoroughly as the bed next door. "There *is* nowhere else, Meredith. I meant what I said about sticking by you. I meant what I said about this not being just a job. There's just you, and me, and taking this step by step so we can get out alive and get to Tamara."

And after that?

Meredith couldn't help but wonder if they'd still take it step by step, just her and him and the chemistry between them.

She swallowed against the thick lump in her throat. "Thank you. But when all this is done…"

"We'll cross that bridge when we get there. But I'm pretty damned certain that I'll still mean it," he told her firmly as he moved across the room to the door to peer out the peephole. "Hallway's empty, sweetheart."

"Do you think it's safe?"

"Probably not," he admitted. "But I don't think they know we switched rooms. In fact, since they cleared the floor so quickly, I'm guessing they *did* get into 1003 and found it empty and don't suspect a damned thing. Not yet, anyway. Come here and have a look."

Meredith stepped to the door and peered out into the hall. It had already filled with smoke. But there was no sign of the men who'd been waiting for them. She eased back, allowing herself a moment of relief.

"Up the hall, out the stairs at the far end," Sam said. "We can avoid the main entrance into the lobby, then head out. We won't be able to stop and grab the car keys from the desk, but we can take public transit. There's a direct line that goes from downtown to Bowerville Station."

He held out his hand, and Meredith took it, glad of its reassuring solidity as he eased open the door and guided them out. They pressed themselves to the wall and moved along slowly. Cautiously. And they had almost reached their goal—the far door—when panic hit Meredith.

No. Oh, no.

She turned on her heel and raced for the room. But when she jammed her key and opened the door, a cloud of loose smoke billowed outward. She tried to push through, but a cough overtook her. And that gave Sam enough time to come in from behind and slam the door shut. He pushed her back to the wall.

"Let me go."

"No."

"Sam!"

"What are you trying to do?" he demanded, sounding more concerned than angry.

Meredith's body sagged and a sob built up in her throat. "My phone. I forgot to grab it. Now Tamara's kidnappers won't be able to reach us and we won't be able to save her."

Chapter 13

Sam reached for Meredith and his pocket at the same time.

"Hey now," he soothed as he wiped away a single, fat tear that had squeezed from her eye to her cheek. "I've got it."

"No, you don't under—" She stopped short as she spied the device in his hand. "You grabbed it?"

"*You* grabbed it first, I grabbed it second," he explained. "It fell out of your pocket when you slid through the closet and all I did was pick it up."

"I dropped it?" Her eyes welled up again. "Oh my God. I'm a mess, aren't I?"

"Stop it." He said it kindly, and he pulled her along the wall toward the door, not wanting to waste a moment. "You're perfect."

She stumbled along beside him. "A perfect mess."

"The situation might be a mess, but you sure as hell aren't."

They reached the exit that led to the stairwell, and

Sam opened the door slowly. Empty. He kept their fingers locked and led Meredith inside.

She was silent as they moved down the stairs. Sam wanted to chalk it up to breathlessness—sure, they'd been climbing down, but it was still ten floors. He'd be hard-pressed to carry on any sort of real conversation himself. But his instincts told him something else occupied her mind. And uncharacteristically, he felt a need to know what it was. He actually found himself wishing he could stop and ask her. Except he didn't have the luxury. They'd already reached the bottom.

He shouldered open the door carefully. The lobby was crowded with guests, employees and emergency personnel. The latter were doing their best to shuffle out the former two, and the whole scene was chaos.

Sam scanned the crowd in search of Boyd and the red-headed thug. He couldn't see them, and he was sure that was a bad thing. Then Meredith's voice, low and worried, guided his attention in the right direction.

"There," she said. "By the front door."

Sam's gaze found them. The redhead stood to the side, his eyes fixed firmly on the entrance to the main stairs. The cop had his jacket pushed aside, showcasing the ID on his belt and looking like he was supposed to be there.

Which he damned well isn't, Sam thought irritably.

He curbed an urge to confront the man. To cross the room and demand some accountability. But he knew what would happen if he followed through on the urge. They'd wind up behind bars, not knowing which members of Bowerville's finest could be trusted and which couldn't. And the jerks in front of them now would get to exactly what they wanted. Meredith.

Not a chance in hell.

He tore his eyes from the men who were targeting them and searched for another way out. He thought he saw a hallway and an exit sign, but he couldn't be sure. Frightened people. Frantic people. They blocked his view. They blurred together.

Which was exactly what *they* needed to do, Sam realized.

"You ready to follow my lead?" he asked.

"The first time you asked me to do that, I wound up your fake girlfriend. The second time, I wound up your fake wife. If you're about to hand me a baby…"

Sam smiled. "I'll take that as a yes."

He draped an arm over Meredith's shoulder, tucked his head down and led her into the group of people. Almost immediately, a firefighter came their way. Sam spouted off a lie about his wife having anxiety, and in seconds, they had an emergency blanket surrounding them, and they were on their way up a hallway and out a side door. The firefighter told them to sit tight, then disappeared back into the building again.

"That was almost too easy."

As soon as the words were out of his mouth, Sam wished he hadn't said them. A glance up told him things were about to get harder. The side door was opening and a flash of red hair was already visible.

Sam pushed off the emergency blanket and grabbed Meredith's hand.

"Run!" he urged in a low voice.

He didn't have to say it twice. In fact, in the heartbeat it took to start moving, she was the one pulling him along. Their feet smacked the ground, thump-thumping against the pavement. When they reached the corner, Sam hazarded a glance over his shoulder. There they were. A few hundred feet behind, but there nonetheless. The redhead in the lead, the detective steps behind.

Sam's gaze flew forward again and he didn't see an option. The street was wide and full of morning commuters, with little to no cover. He swiveled his head. The closest intersection looked impossibly far away. He whipped sideways again.

Maybe there's space between the buildings. Maybe we can—

Meredith tugged his hand. Hard. For a second, Sam thought she was going to drag him straight into oncoming traffic. He braced himself for impact. It didn't come. Instead, a whoosh of air washed over him and he stumbled up.

Up?

The ground jolted under him, and Sam landed on his knees solidly enough to flood his legs with pain and drive his eyes closed.

"How many zones, sir?"

The authoritative voice forced his eyes open again. And it only took a moment to figure out what had happened. Meredith had led them straight onto a bus. A bus that was moving and whose driver kept glancing down at him expectantly.

Sam grabbed the rail and pulled himself up. He flipped his stare to the window. The seconds on the bus had already quadrupled the distance between them and the men chasing them.

Sam sagged against the side of the vehicle and met the driver's now-irritated glare. "What?"

Meredith nudged his shoulder. "I think the man just wants us to pay. Honey."

"Right." He fumbled with his wallet, yanked out a bill without even checking the denomination and shoved it into the payment slot.

"Sir, we don't give ch—"

"Don't care."

"We only go as far as the mall on Fourth Street."

Sam gritted his teeth. "So?"

The driver turned wide eyes his way. "That was a hundred-dollar bill."

"Shouldn't you be paying a little more attention to your driving and a little less to my money?"

The other man jerked his attention back to the windshield, and Sam took Meredith's hand again and led her to the very rear of the bus. He settled her onto an empty seat, then took a look out the back window. He couldn't see their pursuers at all. After a minute of scrutinizing the traffic behind them, he was finally convinced that they'd lost them. At least for the time being.

He let himself sink onto the padded cushion beside Meredith and pulled her into a sideways embrace. "We shouldn't ride for long. Definitely not to wherever the hell the Fourth Street Mall is. It'll be too easy to follow us. But they won't be expecting us to get off just a few stops away from here. If we do that, we can backtrack and figure out which bus actually takes us to Bowerville Station and buy ourselves some time."

She tipped her head and stared up at him. "You're really good at this, aren't you?"

"Bus navigation?" He heard the stiffness in his own reply. "Hardly. I prefer having a little more control over my comings and goings."

"Not the bus, Sam."

He looked away. "I know."

When he didn't add anything more, she tugged her hand away, silent again, and Sam knew he'd simply stalled the inevitable. Again. He stayed quiet anyway, not speaking when he pressed the button to get off at the next stop, and saying nothing as they exited the bus, either. But as they stood in the shelter studying the route map, he couldn't maintain it any longer.

"Ask me," he said without turning around.

She didn't pretend not to understand him. "I keep assuming the bottom is going to drop out. Back there, when those men were that close to catching us… In the hotel… Then those seconds before that bus stopped right in front of us… I thought it *had* dropped out, actually. And when those things happened, all I kept thinking about was you. Not my own safety. Not Tamara. And I felt guilty about that."

Sam's jaw and gut clenched simultaneously. "You don't need to feel guilty. If anything, *I* should feel guilty. I'm the one who—"

"Would you let me finish?"

"Be my guest." He spun to look her in the eye, but his face refused to relax.

"I was worried about you because I thought you'd never get the chance to tell me what really makes you so good at this. That I'd never be able to help you unburden yourself. And I felt guilty about that because you somehow managed to trump my sister. Then I realized how ridiculous it is to feel guilty about caring about someone. You asked me to trust you. And I've been doing that. But the patience part you asked for, too? I don't know. I guess I don't have much to begin with, and even if I did, I don't think we have the *time* to be patient. I know I'm missing something, Sam. The more times the bottom almost drops out, the more I feel it."

Sam hesitated, preparing himself to take a leap in what he hoped was in the right direction. No. What he *knew* was the right direction. But before he could speak, a big blue bus turned the corner and came rumbling up the road. It stopped in front of them, and the bright number on the front—351—announced that it was *their* bus. The one that would take them to Bowerville Station. Sam knew there was another scheduled to arrive in just thirty minutes. But even the idea of a minor delay following through on their only lead made him blanch.

It didn't matter anyway. Sam wouldn't ask Meredith

to wait. He'd far rather sacrifice his own emotional well-being than risk Tamara Billing's life.

Or you'll just finding another excuse.

He shoved aside the accusatory voice and gestured for Meredith to step into the waiting bus. She obliged, but stopped on the top stair and looked down at him.

"If you really can't tell me now, then maybe you can't tell me at all. But I need to know which it is so I don't keep wondering if you're going to leave it too late. Because if that happens, I'll be left with nothing. Not you. Not my sister. Nothing."

Her voice broke at the end, and she spun away and moved to the rear of the bus. Sam knew it must be an attempt to cover her tears, and as he followed her slumped shoulders down the aisle, he realized that holding in his secrets was actually harder than letting them out.

No more excuses.

He sat on the seat across from her and met her eyes. "I lost her, Meredith. I was on the other side of this equation, and I lost her."

And the words were like a floodgate, opening up to let everything through.

As Meredith examined the hurt in Sam's face, she knew instinctively who he'd lost. The only other woman he'd mentioned since they met.

"Kelsey," she said.

"Kelsey," he agreed.

Meredith's heart slammed against her rib cage. She could feel the devastation rolling off him. Feel the pain and the shame.

It made sense. His drive. His single-minded dedication. The way every move spoke of true empathy. Only someone who'd experienced what she was experiencing right that second could truly understand.

"I was that hotshot," Sam told her softly. "The one every police unit seems to have. Youngest detective. Most closed cases. Mile-wide pride. So when they offered me a specialty, I jumped at the chance."

She could picture it. A younger Sam. That concerned crease in his forehead yet to make an appearance. Working just as hard for the police department as he did for his clients, his ambition dedicated to bringing down criminals. Not a stretch at all. And she knew what specialty they'd offered him, too.

"Missing persons," Meredith suggested.

Sam nodded. "I had the personality for it, they said. I played by the rules, even if it was just barely, and never missed a damned thing. Perfect, when every detail counts. Active cases only. Suspected kidnappings. They were right. I was good at it." He paused and looked out the window, and when he spoke again, his voice was hoarse. "I had this partner. Heely was his name. A real egomaniac who I hated. Never trusted him the way a partner should. I always thought something was off, so it didn't surprise me at all when I found out he and my sister were seeing each other. Lecherous son of a you-know-what. She was twelve years younger than him, so saying I lost it is an understatement. Kelsey tried to convince me otherwise, but I never accepted what she told me. I kicked her out. Asked for a transfer."

Meredith watched Sam's face, relating perfectly to the range of emotions that played across it. She squeezed his hand and Sam inhaled.

"One day I came home and found Heely on my doorstep," he said. "Told me when he showed up for their date, he found a note instead. Tucked under his plate. A ransom demand for three hundred thousand dollars."

"That's a lot of money."

"She had it. *We* had it, sweetheart. When our parents

died, they left us a generous estate. The insurance policy had a triple payout policy for sudden accidents, and the car crash fit the bill. We had enough money. For college that I didn't go to, or for a full-time caregiver that I chose not to use. Enough that we could've paid. But I insisted on doing things by the book. I forced Heely to take it to our chief, who banned us from the case. He treated us like what we were. The victim's family."

"Whatever happened, it wasn't your fault."

"What happened was that I listened, and Heely didn't. While I waited for the police to do their job, he went around the proper channels and arranged a drop. A fake exchange. Kelsey for the money. Except when he got there, they somehow knew he didn't really have the money. Or maybe they actually knew all along. Either way, Kelsey was dead already, and Heely took a bullet, too. He died on scene. And I *know* it's not my fault. I've told a hundred people in this situation the same thing. I've told *you* that. And I believe it. But with Kelsey…"

"It feels different."

"It really does." He brought his gaze back to her again. "I think about it on repeat. What if I'd broken the rules? What if I'd pursued it myself? What if I'd paid?"

"You can't think like that."

"I know that, too. But that hasn't made the last five years any different. I couldn't go back to the force. Not if I wanted to stay sane. Not if I wanted to find any kind of closure. But in the end, I couldn't stop trying to save people, either. I ask myself all the time if I do what I do to try and make up for not saving my sister. If I do it enough times, if it will give me peace."

Meredith stared at him, seeing every broken piece. Acknowledging that they hadn't been put back together properly. Yet somehow, they still made him into the beautiful, compassionate man sitting in front of her.

"Does it have to do that?" she asked softly. "Is it even what you want? To be peaceful?"

"Isn't that what everyone wants?" His reply was just shy of bitter.

"No."

"No?"

"Were you peaceful *before* all of that happened?"

He blinked at her like the question had never occurred to him before. "I don't know. I suppose not really."

"And you want to keep saving people."

"Yes."

"Even if you somehow manage to find closure."

"Yes."

"I think maybe you feel like you can't let go of the past because you're scared you *will* find peace. But saving people is who you *are*, Sam. Nothing can change that."

She watched him digest her words. He glanced away, then back again, and swallowed. His expression wasn't exactly unreadable, but it wasn't one Meredith could pinpoint, either. He seemed…relieved, almost.

"Back in the hotel, how long did you say we've known each other?" he asked.

She knew exactly which conversation he was referencing. "About five seconds."

She waited for him to toss her words back into her face. Instead, he raised an eyebrow.

"Five seconds. But somehow, you manage to see more of me than I see of myself."

She smiled. "Hearing you say that makes me feel like I should apologize."

"Funny. It makes me feel like I owe you another one."

"Oh, really?"

"Mmm-hmm."

"So what does that put the score at?"

"Let's see. I saved you from falling off a building. Saved you from getting kidnapped."

"And saved me from myself. For the half point. Wouldn't want to let that one go."

A sexy half smile made his blue eyes sparkle. "Definitely not."

"But I saved the two of us from getting shot. And I smashed that guy—a cop, no less—in the head for you."

"I got us safely out of my apartment building."

Meredith shook her head. "Only because you got us *in* to your apartment building in the first place. Negates itself."

"Fine," Sam conceded. "I'm guessing that lighting a fire to save us negates itself, too?"

"No. I'll let you have that one."

"Kind of you. So then. I'm at three and a half. And you're at three."

"Um, not quite. Don't forget to put my dragging your butt into the bus on that list, too."

He cocked his head to one side. "You want to trump my three and a half points?"

"You did say the bus was my idea."

"I did. But…"

"But what?"

"I think you have to give me double points for our ruse of a marriage."

Meredith felt heat creep up her cheeks and she fought it. "I actually think *I* should get a point for that one."

"How do you figure?"

The bus jerked around a corner, pushing her elbows into his knees. She tipped her face up and gave him her sweetest smile before righting herself.

"Because you were lucky enough to be fake-married to me, of course."

Sam chuckled. "Meredith?"

"Yes?"

"I really like you."

His statement let the heat win, and as she replied, a blush flooded her face. "I really like you, too."

"A lot."

"Me, too."

"But that doesn't mean I'm going to concede my two points."

A mechanical voice announced that the bus was about to arrive at its terminus station. As it lurched to a stop, Sam stood and offered Meredith her hand. She stared at his outstretched fingers.

"I don't think I'm taking that," she said.

"No?"

She pushed herself to her feet. "Nope. Because if I did, you'd probably try to add it to your points."

"You do realize it doesn't matter. I'm at five, you're at three, and as promised, I'm still ahead."

"I don't know if that really counts as winning."

"More points equals losing?"

Meredith moved toward the doors. "Yes. I mean, the more points you have, the safer *I* am. So technically, *I'm* the one who's winning."

"You wish."

"I know."

Sam's arms encircled her waist, and he pulled her back against her chest. "You're wrong."

"You think *you're* winning?"

"I'm sure I am." He put his mouth to her ear. "Because every point I get means you're alive and safe and still with me, and that's pretty much the only thing I need to be a winner."

The doors slid open, and a blast of cool air hit Meredith. But she couldn't feel it. Because the warmth in her heart blocked it out.

Chapter 14

Meredith didn't even bother to try and clear her head as they walked together toward Bowerville Station's ticket office. There was no *point* in trying. Sam still had his arm around her waist and his scent filled her nostrils. His presence filled all of her senses.

He likes you. You like him. But...

Like? It just didn't seem like a big enough word. And the alternative—the idea of finding a better description— scared the hell out of her. It made her head spin.

So...embrace the spin. What have you got to lose? Well. Except your dignity. And your heart. And whatever exists between those two things.

She still leaned into him a little, testing it out. And her head definitely flew straight into the clouds. Which made her have to lean into him even more. He squeezed, and her *heart* squeezed, too. So, no. *Like* was definitely not a strong enough word.

"You okay?" Sam asked.

Meredith forced a laugh. "You do realize how many times you've asked me that in the last twenty-four hours, right?"

"Don't worry. It's purely for selfish reasons. If you say yes, you're all right, I feel good. If you say no, you're not all right, then I have an excuse to hold you even tighter. And I *still* feel good. Better even."

"You're doing that good-at-being-bad thing again, aren't you?"

"Yep."

Sam held the office door open, and a fresh-faced youth greeted them from behind the ticket counter.

"Can I help you?" she asked cheerfully.

"God, I hope so," Sam replied. "I'm Derek Hall, and this is my wife."

The conversation carried on, but Meredith barely heard it. Because as they walked through the doors, she'd spotted a map on the wall, and as she studied it, her memory sprang to life, bringing forward a childhood recollection she'd all but forgotten. Hope bloomed in her heart.

"Hamish," she said.

Sam's eyes found her. "Sweetheart?"

Meredith pointed at the map. "Turtle Island."

She waited for him to examine it. Bowerville to Seattle. A connecting bus to the ferry. And from there... Turtle Island.

Sam frowned. "What about it?"

"It's a vacation we went on once when we were kids. The last summer before my mom got sick and before my dad started drinking himself to death. We spent an entire summer there. Rented a place that eventually got torn down, but...Hamish, Sam." She tried to keep her voice calm and couldn't quite manage it.

He grabbed her hand.

"Excuse us," he said to the now-puzzled ticket girl, and

then he dragged Meredith back out the door. "Tell me what Hamish and Turtle Island have in common."

"We found a dog that summer. A Scottish terrier. My sister desperately wanted to keep him, but my mom was allergic so we never even asked. Just fed him in secret. I felt guilty about it the whole summer, thinking that when we left him behind, there'd be no one to take care of him. Not Tamara, though. She said we were helping him while we could and that was all we could do." Meredith knew she was babbling and struggled to rein it in. "She named that dog, Sam. The only Scottish name she could think of."

"Hamish."

"I can't believe I didn't make the connection right away." She shook her head, annoyed with herself. "It went out of my mind completely until I saw Turtle Island there on the map. You know, Tamara stole a bag of food and got caught and cried so hard that the guy who owned the store ended up giving her the damned food. Oh, God. I wish I'd remembered all this before now."

"All that matters is that you remembered now. Do you think she went there?"

"I don't know." In spite of the gravity of the situation, a little smile tipped up her lips. "If she did, I don't think she really caught the bus."

"What, then?"

"I still think she was creating a trail. And even if she didn't go to the island, I think she wants *me* to go there."

Sam nodded. "Should we buy tickets, or steal a car?"

"Sam!"

"You said I was good at this, remember?"

"Yeah, well. Maybe I should've said *too* good. And FYI, I usually have a one-felony-per-day limit."

He shrugged. "Bus it is, then."

But as they moved to go back into the office, a familiar

navy sedan turned the corner and Meredith knew it wasn't going to be that easy.

Her eyes darted from Sam's face to the approaching car to the office behind them, then back to the car. The sedan's tires squealed as it sped up, and he tugged on her hand.

They hurried past the little office building and cut across the loop, where half a dozen buses sat waiting. Together, they headed for the road, then jumped over a knee-high chain fence in the middle of the median and hit the other side. The move gave them the only advantage they would have, Meredith thought. Running in the opposite direction that the sedan traveled, with no way for the vehicle to cross. Its driver had no choice but to keep going and turn around at the station.

But they would still be on them in two minutes.

"It really isn't right," Meredith breathed. "One tiny step ahead. One small lead. Two giant steps backward."

"Do you want to go back there and find out what happens if they *actually* catch up?"

"No."

"So stop complaining and keep moving. Whiner." His voice wasn't quite breathless.

"Are you mocking me? Now?"

"I'm motivating you. Out of affection."

In reply, Meredith increased the length of her strides until she overtook him. "Motivate this!"

"Hey!" he called out.

She ignored him, pushing as hard as she dared. As hard as she thought she could run and keep going. But the road in front of them seemed impossibly long. And it sloped up. Why hadn't she noticed how isolated the station was? How the scenery was nothing more than a stretch of pavement framed by tan-colored dirt? Hadn't there been buildings or trees or something on the way in?

"Nowhere to hide," she muttered.

"One place," Sam said from just behind her.

"Where's that?"

"Here."

One of his hands closed around her wrist and he jerked her off the road, stopping their crazy flight. Meredith shot a panicked look up the road. She couldn't see the sedan on the horizon yet, but she knew it was coming any second.

"What are we doing?"

The question barely made it from Meredith's mouth before he reached out, slipped his arms to her waist, and pulled them both sideways. As they flew from the side of the road, Sam twisted his body, protecting her from impact.

And he'd knocked her down just in time. As Meredith took a shaky breath, the roar of an approaching car engine carried through the air. It was fast. Loud. And showed no signs of stopping.

Thank God.

In seconds, the noise faded away, and the only sound left was the hard thump of her heart.

Meredith swallowed, realizing that while Sam *had* shielded her from the ground, the impact from his body was a whole different story. They were pressed together, reminding Meredith that so many parts of him were hard and rough and pleasant. And the narrowness of the dip in the ground allowed little wiggle room, emphasizing just how well they fit together.

And clearly, he felt it, too. He reached up a warm hand and brushed away a strand of hair from her face.

"Comfy?" His voice was throaty and teasing at the same time. Totally inappropriate for their precarious situation. But somehow calming, too.

"I don't know. Is comfy what you were going for?" she replied.

He grinned. "I was going for a good hiding place. But I'll take comfy, too."

"I see. So. This is your idea of a good hiding place?"

He shook his head. "Mmm-hmm. If I were alone, this would be a good hiding place. Since you're here…it's what I think of as a *great* hiding place."

"And suppose you *had* to throw me in, too?"

"Would you have climbed in quick enough if I asked you nicely?"

"I guess you'll never know."

"Don't assume that. The day is young and we still have to escape from those friends of ours."

The reminder brought Meredith back to the moment. "Speaking of which…how long should we wait?"

"Long enough that they're gone, but not so long that they've got time to turn around."

"Helpful." She sighed. "Have I mentioned that I hate waiting?"

"Oh, I'm aware."

"Are you calling me impatient?"

"Doggedly so." Sam smiled. "Makes grand-theft auto seem a little less insane, though, doesn't it? I mean, if we'd hot-wired that poor ticket agent's car, we'd be flying down the highway right now instead of lying beside it."

"You can hot-wire a car in under a minute?"

"Your dubious tone hurts my feelings."

"I'm not dubious. I'm concerned about my own mental health."

"Oh, really?"

"How could I not be? I'm lying on top of a man who burns down hotels and steals cars with remarkable efficiency."

"Is your problem with the lying-on-top part or with the predisposition toward pillaging behaviors? Because I only burn and steal in the name of justice."

Meredith laughed, wondering how he managed to make

her enjoy even the most dismal of situations. And wondering even more if he knew the effect he had on her.

"Right," she said. "Burning and stealing for justice. Mocking for affection."

"Motivating."

"You may have more issues than I initially believed."

"Guess it's a good thing that sister of yours is a marriage counselor. When we find her, she can sort us out."

Meredith's heart dipped a little at the mention of Tamara, and she forced a light reply. "I think she only takes on real married couples."

"Damn. Does this mean you're asking for a fake divorce?"

She stared down at him, and the intimacy of their position increased tenfold. The world slipped away as she absorbed the warmth of his gaze. And she knew that *he* knew her lightness wasn't genuine. That he'd just put on his own teasing tone out of respect for her feelings. Because she mattered to him.

"No," she said softly. "Definitely no fake divorces happening today."

"Good. Because it just so happens that I'm not the divorcing type." He stroked her cheek, then smiled. "Do you remember when I said I liked you?"

"An hour ago?"

"Mmm-hmm. And you said you liked me, too…" His fingers moved to her lips.

The attention made her mouth tingle. He tugged on her chin and ran his thumb over her teeth. *Good. So good. Since when are teeth so sexy?* Meredith wondered.

"So you do remember it?" Sam said teasingly as he brought his palms down to her throat, stroking gently.

"What?" She couldn't shake the all-over shiver, and she had to really work to make herself speak articulately. "Oh. Yes. I remember. Why? Are you taking it back?"

He chuckled. "I'm not taking it back. In fact, I'd like to add to it. I want more."

"More?"

"More than being trapped in a ditch," Sam joked.

"Ditch?"

Okay, Meredith decided. *Maybe I'm not all that articulate.*

"More than liking," Sam amended.

Hadn't she just been thinking that? She couldn't remember. Not with the way his oh-so-blue eyes were fixed on her. Not with the way her curves pushed into his hard planes. And her brain got even foggier when he slid his hand to the back of her neck and pulled her forward. Even less focused when he dragged his lips over each of her cheekbones, then up to her eyelids. And it stopped working altogether when he kissed every inch of her face before moving to her mouth. Then he kissed that, too. Attentively. Lovingly. Like they had all the time in the world instead of none at all.

And as he leaned back to gaze up at her, Meredith knew things had already progressed to so much more than liking. It *was* scary. Somehow—remarkably—right up there with the idea of what was happening to Tamara. Life-altering. But what had Sam said about fear?

Right. Face it. And move forward.

Could she do that? At the very least, she could try.

"Sam?"

"Yeah, sweetheart?"

I want more, too.

But what came out of her mouth was something else entirely. "I want you to promise me that if you think we're at a place where we might not get Tamara back, you'll tell me."

Surprise registered on his face. "Tell you?"

Meredith nodded. "I don't want to be living on false hope."

Sam went silent for a moment. "And that's your condition for more."

"I hadn't thought of it that way, but I guess it is. I don't want to be hanging my hopes on something I can't count on."

She didn't know if she was still talking about Tamara, or if she was talking about him directly. But it didn't matter. He was already nodding.

"All right. I can do that."

"I…" She couldn't quite finish the embarrassing sentence she'd been about to utter.

"What?"

She closed her eyes. "It might sound stupid, but I need you to say it. To make the promise out loud."

"Hey. Look at me."

Meredith forced her eyes open again.

"I promise," Sam said. "If we ever get to the point that I don't think we can do this, I'll tell you."

An unreasonable amount of relief flooded Meredith's body. But as she opened her mouth to express her gratitude, the click of a gun, followed by a wry chuckle, stopped her cold.

"Well, well," said a rough voice from above. "My friend here was right. That flash we saw was something important. I guess I owe him an apology. Hello, kids."

Complacent.

It was the first word that popped into Sam's head as he realized they were trapped. And that it was his fault. He couldn't move. Couldn't reach for his gun. Not with someone else's weapon trained on Meredith. And all because he'd been a little too damn complacent.

Their position blocked his view, but somehow Sam was certain the man above them was the redheaded thug. Which made him itch to lash out.

He made himself speak calmly. "You should be careful with that gun."

"Really? You're telling me what to do?" was the reply.

"You're lying on your back in a ditch. My gun has a hair trigger, and it's pointed at your girlfriend's very pretty head. And you still think it's a choice? You still think you stand a chance?"

"You won't shoot her," Sam replied. "She's no good to you if she's dead. So we both know you can't get what you want without her."

"That's true. But I *can* get it without you."

Somehow, the air shifted. Just a little. Just enough to let Sam know the gun's position had shifted, too.

Better on me than on her.

Except Meredith's sharp inhale told him she didn't feel the same way, even before she spoke. "If you shoot Sam, you might as well shoot yourself in the foot, too. Because if you hurt him, I'm sure as hell not going to tell you anything about where to find the Hamish file."

The conviction in her voice impressed Sam, but he knew she wouldn't sacrifice her sister's safety for his own. Even if she was considering it, he wouldn't let it happen. The man above them came to the same conclusion.

"You sure you want to take that risk?" he asked. "Your sister's life for his?"

Meredith had a firm reply at the ready. "I don't consider it a risk. For all I know, you've killed her already. Or she's escaped. I want proof of life."

"Proof of life. Hmm. Maybe. Or I could just shoot you both. Kill your sister. Then I wouldn't have to worry about the file at all anymore."

Sam wished he was close enough to punch the man in the throat. His hands curled into fists, but Meredith was already answering, her voice still impressively sure, her lie remarkably smooth. If Sam hadn't been able to feel the slight shake of her legs and known the truth, he might've bought the ruse himself.

"You could do that," she said. "But I made a copy of

the file, and I gave it to a friend. He has no clue what's in it, but he's got strict instructions to post it to my sister's blog if I don't check in every eight hours. She has a million regular visitors. But I guess what you do is up to you."

There was a pause, then a loud sigh. "Fine. Come up to your knees, Ms. Jamison, then stand. Slowly. If I see Mr. Potter reach for that gun on his side, I *will* shoot him. Maybe not to kill, but I'll be sure to hit something important. Once you're up, my associate will help you out of the ditch. Potter will follow."

"Got it," Meredith agreed, and she immediately sat up.

Sam closed his hands on her thighs. He squeezed, willing her to know that the man giving the commands couldn't be trusted.

"Got it," she repeated.

This time, she spoke in his direction, her voice soft but sure, and Sam relaxed as much as he dared. She was smart enough not to misplace her faith. He kept still as she put her arms out to the side and pushed to her feet. He reminded himself that lives were at stake and kept his ego in check when the ginger-haired thug leaned over the ditch and shot a smug smile downward. He even managed to maintain an outward calm when a pair of meaty hands clamped onto Meredith's shoulders. But when those same hands yanked her out forcibly, drawing a small cry from her lips, Sam couldn't contain his reaction anymore. He had no choice but to protect her.

He shot upright, cursing as he clawed at the side of the ditch. "Hurt her and you'll be—"

The rest of the sentence died on his lips as something heavy came down on his head.

Complacency, Sam thought. *Maybe now would've been a good time to have some.*

Then the world snapped into blackness.

Chapter 15

Awareness dawned, in slow, reluctant pieces.

A hand, soft and warm, holding his own.

A terrible ache in his body.

A feminine voice in his head.

No, not in your head. In your ear.

It was true, he realized. The murmur came from beside his face, somehow soothing and urgent at the same time.

"You're going to be okay, Sam. You are. I promise."

He tried to drag his eyes open, and for a second he succeeded. A swirl of blond hair clouded his vision, and the voice and the hand-holding connected in his mind.

Meredith.

He struggled to form her name, and at that, he failed completely.

"You're going to be okay, Sam," she said again.

Then the pressure on his palm eased, and the curtain of hair swooshed up and away.

Wake up.

Sam heard the command. Then ignored it. It came again. Louder. More insistent.

Wake up.

No, he thought. *I won't.*

Wake. Up. Now!

His head throbbed at the internal yell, and he mumbled back at it. "Go away."

A gasp greeted his words. "Sam!"

He forced his eyes open, and a flurry of movement brought a pair of gorgeous green irises down to his level. Meredith peered at him, concern evident in her pinched forehead and sucked-in lower lip. She was kneeling beside him now, her palm gently cupping his cheek.

"Are you with me again?" she asked, her voice barely more than a hoarse whisper.

"I'm here." Sam's own reply came out just as raw.

"Thank God."

"What happened?"

"You don't remember getting knocked out?"

He fought to grab a specific memory. The running. The kissing. Sharp anger and the redheaded man...but the specifics were just out of mental reach.

Sam shook his head, then winced at the responding dizziness. "I'm sure it'll come back to me in a minute or two."

"Water?" she offered, and held out a disposable bottle.

Gratefully, Sam took a small sip. The liquid cooled his throat, but when he tried to push himself up, an immediate wave of nausea sent him down again. Unsurprisingly, his temple was starting to throb, too.

He groaned. "How long was I out?"

"Not too long. Half an hour, maybe. Twenty minutes in the car, then ten in here."

Thirty minutes? It felt like days had passed. Or at least hours. Or maybe it was more like no time had gone by at all. It was a completely disturbing feeling.

"You opened your eyes a bunch of times, but you weren't really awake. Just muttering to yourself," Meredith added. "I was so worried."

Sam squeezed her hand and fought the urge to close his eyes yet again. He didn't want to scare her any more than he already had. He blinked away the sleepiness, trying to inventory both his state and his surroundings. Gray walls. Concrete floor. An industrial-sized door with a silver handle. Locked, presumably. Nothing to give away the purpose of the room.

Shoving aside new worry, Sam moved on to his body. He was stretched out on a couple of stacked-up, canvas-covered pallets, and a second piece of fabric had been balled up and tucked under his aching head. He hurt. Probably had a concussion. But he couldn't feel anything directly life-threatening.

"Sam?"

Meredith's voice shook a little, and he focused his gaze on her. "Still here. Wherever here is."

She sighed. "It's a warehouse of some kind, I think. After you jumped out of the ditch—"

Sam put up a hand, silencing her. *The ditch.* The memory came flooding in. Meredith's yell and his reaction. His own stupidity. It's what had landed them in this glorified cell. He'd let his emotions get the best of him and put Meredith at risk. His heart dropped into his stomach as the weight of his actions hit him. Disgusted with his recklessness, he shoved down his pain and forced himself to his feet.

"Sam, what're you doing? I don't think you should be moving around like that yet."

He turned her way, but couldn't meet her eyes. He didn't deserve her sympathy. He looked away again, then took enough long strides to bring himself to the sealed door. He tugged on the handle. Nothing. Next, his hands found the frame, sliding over the seams, searching desperately for weakness and finding none.

"Sam."

"I need to get you out of here."

"Sam!" She was already beside him, already putting a hand on an elbow and trying to lead him back to the pallets.

"Stop it." He yanked his arm out of her grasp.

She flinched. "I don't understand what's going on with you. Stop what?"

"Stop saying my name. Stop sounding like you care."

"I *do* care."

He flung a desperate glare her way. "I got us locked up in here. I let them get to us. I just about got you killed, Meredith."

"That's not true."

"It sure as hell *is*. Denying it won't change a damned thing." He paced the room, pretending it didn't hurt him, inside and out. "I've been keeping my emotions in check for five years. A half a decade. And now I know why. I can't do my job if I'm too busy *feeling*. You were right. It's impossible. It clouds my judgment and endangers the client and the more danger there is, the more it clouds my judgment. Vicious bloody circle."

"You're wrong."

He spun. "Wrong? How can you stand there and say that?"

"Because it's true." She looked utterly calm.

"Really? I cared about my sister. She was my whole damned life, and I couldn't save her. Now this." A bitter laugh escaped from his throat as he swept his arm through the air.

"I think your head injury is affecting your judgment."

"It's not the damned injury!"

"Sit down, Sam."

"I'm not going to—"

"Sit down before I lose it."

"I'm—"

Meredith put her hands on her hips, calmness gone. "Now!"

Startled by the vehemence of her tone, Sam backed up until his calves hit the pallets. When he didn't sit right away, Meredith took several angry, forceful steps toward him, her eyes flashing. When she reached him, she shoved a hand into his chest—not hard, but he collapsed backward anyway. His rear end thumped hard against the pallet.

"I'm not going to apologize for that," she snapped. "And not because I think you almost killed me, but because you're being an unreasonable idiot."

"There's nothing unreasonable about anything I said."

"Oh, really?" She stepped back and lifted up her shirt.

"What the hell are you doing?"

"Showing you the real meaning of the word unreasonable."

Sam tried to look away, but the color of her stomach made him stop. It made him cringe. It made him *angry*, and it made him forget—at least temporarily—about his self-loathing.

"What the hell is that?"

"That's the residual effect of being beaten with a golf club."

Sam jumped to his feet, swaying as dizziness hit him once again. "When did you get beaten with a golf club?"

"The man who pulled me out of the ditch was the detective. The one I knocked out at your apartment building. Apparently, he wasn't too happy with me."

Guilt and sickness added to the dizziness. "If I hadn't jumped in…"

"The only reason it's not worse than it is, is *because* you jumped in. He dragged me out, then knocked me down,

and the second I landed on the ground he started hitting
me with the club. I screamed. It was more the look on his
face than the pain, really. He wanted me dead. I'm sure
of it. But you jumped in. And it distracted him and he hit
you instead. You didn't almost get me killed. You saved
my life. So go ahead and add that to your IOUs if you feel
so inclined. Six and a half to three, or whatever." Meredith
paused, then shook her head and added in a far quieter
voice, "And if you did it because you let your emotions
get the better of you, then maybe you should do that a
little more often. Because it sure sounds like a good idea
from where I sit."

Sam's whole body sagged with momentary relief. He'd
done something *right*. It wasn't time to give up. Not yet.
Then his eyes drifted up and he saw that Meredith still
had her shirt lifted. And the sight of the bruising hit him
far harder than the dizziness.

"I'm going to kill that jerk," he muttered.

"I don't think you're going to have to."

"What do you mean?"

"That man with the red hair. He was furious at the cop.
He made him load you into the car at gunpoint. Then he
forced him to drive out here, too. The last thing I saw before he locked us in here was him tying the cop to a chair
while he talked to someone on the phone. I don't think the
redhead is going to let him live. Not if he's got a choice."

Sam gave himself a moment to process what that meant.
Disregard for life was one thing. Disregard for a cop's
life—and a detective, no less—was a whole other animal. Dead officers drew attention. If the person in charge
gave the redheaded man permission to kill the detective,
it meant no fear of retribution. Which filled Sam's mind
with unease. And renewed urgency.

"Not good," he said under his breath, wishing his head
would clear. "We really need to get out of this room."

Fighting the roiling of his stomach, he strode across the room and bent to look at the door handle. Standard commercial-issue. Designed to keep people out by locking on the exterior side only. A small hole decorated the center, though, and Sam was sure a narrow tool would allow him to pick it.

"You don't happen to have a bobby pin in your hair?" he asked over his shoulder.

"No."

"A lock-picking kit hidden in your bra?"

"Hardly."

"Never hurts to ask." Sam shrugged, stood up and scanned the room for an alternative.

Meredith caught on right away. "What about the pallet? The nails holding it together?"

"Good thinking."

Aided by the adrenaline rushing through his body, he moved to the wood in question, tossed aside the canvas sheet and tipped up the pallet. Flat, metal nail heads held the slats to the sides. Could he get them out? If so, would they be long enough to do the job?

"Only one way to find out," he said, then caught Meredith's eye. "You ready?"

"Ready for what?"

"This."

Straining against his overall body ache, Sam lifted the pallet to shoulder level, then slammed it to the ground. It thudded against the concrete, making the wood splinter. He lifted it a second time and smashed it once more. This time, the wood cracked open completely, exposing the nails. At least one looked promising. Sam started to work it free, speaking as he did.

"Tell me everything you know about this warehouse. What's the layout like? Where are we in terms of the exit?"

Meredith closed her eyes like she was picturing it.

"The warehouse is big and completely empty. We're on the second floor in some kind of storage room, I think. There's a walkway outside this door. It goes all the way around the perimeter and it's open to the area below. There's only one set of stairs, and beneath those is an office. That's where the redhead tied up his friend." She opened her eyes. "Does that help?"

He nodded. He could imagine the layout perfectly. He hoped like hell they'd simply be able to open the door, walk down the stairs and leave. But he knew the chances of that happening were slim to none.

He pulled away some more of the fractured wood, then wiggled the loosened nail. "Weapons?"

"He took them before we got in the car, but I don't know if he brought them in. He tossed our phones, but I can't see that he would've done that with the guns."

Sam heard the spike of worry in her voice and shot her a reassuring smile. "We'll get it all back, sweetheart."

"He never got around the proof of life, Sam. What if Tamara is…"

"She's not. They won't do anything until they have the file they're after. And I'm not going to let them get that far."

The nail finally sprung free, and he held it up triumphantly, then made his way back to the door, where he jabbed it into the hole. It scraped against the sides, but it fit, and the small victory helped ease the throb in Sam's head. Which was good, because he needed to come up with a plan.

"Do you know where we are in terms of the bus station?" he asked as he jiggled the nail. "Lots of turns on the drive out here? Or you think you could find your way back?"

"Nothing but one long road, a railroad track and a couple of hills. But it would take us hours to walk back to the station."

He met her eyes. "I have no intention of walking."

"Are you saying what I think you're saying?"

The lock clicked free and Sam grinned. "Yep. I get to steal a car after all."

But his amusement was short-lived. Because when he swung open the door, he saw that they weren't alone. At the other end of the walkway stood their redheaded friend, surprise on his face and his hand moving toward the pistol at his hip.

For a too-long moment, Meredith stared at the man across from them, her panicked thoughts tumbling on top of one another.

We don't stand a chance. We'll never get by him before he takes us out. He's going to kill us. No. Not us. He needs you alive. He'll just incapacitate you. But Sam... Oh, God.

If it came down to a choice between killing him and letting her go, she didn't think it would be a choice at all. And Sam was already moving to position himself between her and the armed man.

In slow motion, Meredith saw the redhead's mouth tip up into a smug smile. She heard the click of the handgun cocking.

No.

In a panicked flurry, she shoved Sam out of the way. He let out a yell and stumbled sideways, probably propelled as much from her push as from his recent head injury. A bullet whizzed by. It lodged into the gray wall behind them, spraying out flecks of debris. Meredith didn't give herself time to be relieved. She snapped up a piece of broken pallet from the ground, then spun back to their captor. Logically, she knew the jagged wood would be an ineffective shield against a bullet. But that didn't matter, because she only wanted to use it as a distraction. Her real shield would be her own body.

Careful to keep herself in front of Sam—who was groaning just a little—Meredith brandished the slice of pallet in front of her. The redhead snarled and dodged out of range of her wild swing. She swung again, and he cursed and lifted the gun.

"Shoot me and you'll never get that file," she reminded him. "And before you aim for an incapacitating shot rather than a lethal one, you should know I won't be holding still and you'll be taking your chances."

"I'm caring less and less about the file and more and more about the headache you two are creating for me."

"I'm sure your bosses will be happy to hear that."

He inched closer. "I'm caring less and less about that, too."

She thrust her makeshift weapon forward and made herself speak as casually as she could. "Really? You're going to go back on whatever deal you made because the job isn't easy? You're nothing like the criminals on TV."

"You're not exactly a typical damsel in distress, either."

"I never said I was."

He tipped his head to one side thoughtfully. "What is it you think is going to happen here, Ms. Jamison? That I'm just going to step aside and let you walk out of here?"

"More or less." Did she sound as falsely overconfident as she felt?

"Better stick with less. This is a standoff you can't win."

"I happen to be an optimist."

The redhead smiled a smile that made Meredith want to twitch.

"You might be a glass-half-full girl," he said, and inclined his head to indicate over her shoulder, "but I don't think Mr. Potter has the same luxury."

She refused to look. Sam *had* been awfully quiet. She'd

been too caught up in holding her ground to think about it. But she couldn't turn in his direction. She didn't dare. Because she knew the second she did, the other man would be on her.

"Mr. Potter is just as sunshine and flowers as I am, thank you very much."

"You're awfully certain of that. Especially considering the amount of blood pooling around Mr. Potter's body at the moment."

His words made Meredith's heart skip a terrified beat. And even though she fully acknowledged that it might be a ruse, she couldn't help but check. With the wood stretched out, she swiveled her head to glance toward Sam.

And her stomach dropped to her knees.

The gunman had been telling the truth. Though he still sat on the ground, Sam had pulled himself to the wall and leaned his back against the flat surface. A crimson puddle decorated the concrete floor beside his elbow, and a matching stain feathered out along the sleeve of his sweatshirt. Abruptly, Meredith realized the bullet in the wall must've grazed Sam's arm before making its final landing.

She rounded on the redhead, fear and anger mixing in her shout. "You shot him!"

"I guess I did." His smug smile was back in place.

Her gaze flew back to Sam. Every part of her wanted to help him. To attend to his wound and feel his forehead and check his pulse and *save* him. And she was sure that was exactly what her captor wanted.

"I'm guessing he might need some medical attention," the man said. "If you put down that glorified club and tell me where the file is, I'd be happy to give you some assistance with that. A hospital, maybe?"

The glint in his eyes infuriated Meredith. She was going to hurt him. Slam the piece of pallet into his stomach. Something. Anything to wipe the look off his face and punish him for hurting Sam. For making her choose between helping her sister and helping the man who'd already stolen such a large piece of her heart.

But in the end, she didn't have to. Before she could settle on a course of action, a dark-colored, Sam-shaped blur flew across the room. It slammed into the redheaded man and sent him careening backward. His gun slid from his grasp, clattered across the floor and landed at Meredith's feet.

She stared down at it for a shocked moment. Then she lifted her eyes and met Sam's pale gaze.

"You might wanna pick that up," he said. "I'm not sure how much longer I can hold this idiot down. My arm kinda hurts."

Chapter 16

Meredith's big green eyes widened. She blinked. Once. Then she dropped the wood from her hands and bent down and picked up the gun, and Sam finally let go of the breath he'd been holding. He didn't loosen his grip on the man underneath him, though. He held fast to his arms and kept his knee on his chest. No matter how badly he thrashed and no matter how much it made the gunshot wound hurt, he couldn't let go.

Oh, hell. A gunshot wound.

Three years as a cop, three more as a detective and five as a private investigator. Dozens of chases and arrests. Actually, hundreds. Yet he'd never taken a bullet.

"Dodged a few, maybe," he muttered.

"Sam?"

He looked up and realized that even though his hands remained fixed in place, he'd actually zoned out. Probably from the blood loss. Shock. Both. And he had time for neither. What he needed was adrenaline. A shot of the stuff that had helped propel him from his spot against the wall to the position he was in now. Instead, he just felt shaky and a little lost.

"Sam?" Meredith repeated.

He forced himself to focus. "Point the gun at him, sweetheart."

"Like this?" She raised it obediently.

"Exactly like that. Thank you."

"So polite," the redhead snarled, kicking up a leg. "How sweet."

"A little bit of manners go a long way," Sam agreed through clenched teeth. "Which reminds me. I'd appreciate it if you'd hold still. Make it easier for me to think about what to do with you."

The man didn't even pretend to listen. He strained against Sam's hold, lifted his head and bucked. The motion jarred the wound and jarred Sam's head and made his already short temper flare. He momentarily forgot his politeness.

"Cock the gun, Meredith!"

"I don't—"

"Black lever. Pull it back with your thumb." A second later the familiar click sounded, and Sam breathed in deeply, then exhaled and channeled as much serenity as he could. "Thank you. Again. I want you to get as close to him as possible without actually being in his reach."

Meredith looked nervous, and Sam wished he could simply take the burden off her, but the cloudiness of his head worried him. The last thing they needed was for him to take possession of the gun, then get fumble-fingered and drop it. So he just offered her a nod and a smile.

You can do this, he willed.

She nodded back and stepped forward with the weapon trained on their assailant-turned-captive. "How's this?"

"Perfect." He lifted the other man's wrists, then slammed

them down again, momentarily stunning the criminal into immobility. "In a second, I'm going to lift my knee from your chest and I'm going to let you go. You're not going to move. Not an inch. You're barely going to *breathe.* Got it?"

"She's not going to fire," the thug said.

Sam opened his mouth, but Meredith beat him to the punch, her voice quiet but steady. "I don't *want* to fire. Even though you kidnapped my sister. Even though you've been chasing us all over the city, and even though you still haven't shown me proof that Tamara's still alive. And you shot Sam. I still don't want your death on my conscience. But I will, if it's our lives or yours."

"Hear that, Red? She doesn't want to. But she will. So can I count on you to keep still?" The man grunted, and Sam chose to take it as assent. "Good. And just so you know…she's far kinder than I am. You shot me, and that pisses me off, so I'm not going to be at all unhappy if the trigger does go off. Keep that in mind."

He pulled back, positioning himself into an awkward squat and making sure that the man below him had a clear view of Meredith and the gun. He didn't want the redheaded man to forget for even a moment that his life hung in the balance. Sam knew if he sensed an inch, he'd take something worse than a mile.

"You still ready to shoot, sweetheart?" he asked.

"Ready and reluctantly willing," Meredith confirmed.

Sam eased up to his feet. He sucked in a shallow breath as dizziness threatened to overtake him. He widened his stance to stabilize himself and looked down at the redheaded man.

"All right. You're going to get to your feet. You're going to walk one step in front of me. Meredith is going to walk directly behind you with that gun of yours pointed between your shoulder blades. You're going to lead us out

that door and you're going to put us in immediate contact
with whoever has Tamara Billing."

"You have no idea who you're dealing with," the thug
retorted.

"I know they hire men like you." Sam crooked his finger. "Up."

The other man stood. "They're smart. These aren't a
bunch of clumsy, two-bit criminals who'll make a mistake
or bend over because you ask nicely."

"They're cops, Red. That doesn't make them infallible."
Sam pointed to the exit. "Like I said, lead the way. And if
you so much as stumble, I promise she'll put a bullet into
your spine. Understood?"

"Whatever."

The redhead turned and took two steps, but paused in
the doorway when Meredith spoke.

"Who are they?" she asked softly. "The men who have
her."

Her inquiry made Sam stop for a second, too, and he
cursed himself for not asking it himself. He'd been too
distracted by his own feelings. And his damned gunshot
wound and the accompanying wooziness.

The thug's head spun their way. "You don't know?
You've read the file, but you haven't figured it out?" His
gaze flicked from Meredith to Sam, then back again. "You
haven't read the file." He took a small step backward, his
eyes narrowing. "Or maybe you don't actually *have* the
file. Holy mother of—"

His words cut off with acute abruptness. His mouth
hung open for a second, like he was going to finish the
sentence. No. Not quite. More like he *wanted* to finish the
sentence, but couldn't.

Sam frowned, a question on his lips. Then the other
man's body crumbled to the floor, a bright red dot visible
on the side of his head. It only took Sam a second to rec-

ognize the dot for what it was—in fact, he knew it well. He had a matching one on his arm.

Goddamn.

And there was that kick of adrenaline he so sorely needed. With a muted growl, he reached for Meredith, then pulled her hard against the wall inside the storage room. Sam pushed his body to hers and cursed the fact that he couldn't even take the time to enjoy the close contact.

"Did he just get shot?" Meredith breathed.

"Damn right he did. The real worry is, who did it?"

"The cop."

"You think the redhead didn't kill him?"

"Or didn't get around to it yet."

Sam looked down at the body on the floor, then said grimly, "Guess it's too late now."

Another bullet flew through the air and shattered a lower section of the door frame. The hinges loosened, and the door creaked to an angle. And less than a heartbeat later, the slam of boots on metal announced that they might be out of time in a second as well.

Unless it's only too late for one of us.

Sam pulled away. "Give me the gun, sweetheart."

"What?"

The thump of feet got closer and Sam put out his hand. "Quickly."

She met his eyes. "What are you going to— No."

"There's no choice. The man attached to that weapon is going to burst through that door and I want to give us a fighting chance."

"You mean you want to give *me* a fighting chance."

"One of us has to get out of here."

"I'm not letting you sacrifice yourself for me."

Before he could argue, Meredith ducked underneath his arm and dropped to her knee, and by the time Sam realized her intention, it was already too late to stop her.

* * *

Praying that fear hadn't made her delusional—that this was an idea that could work—Meredith closed her eyes and she squeezed the trigger. A boom echoed through the warehouse, and the gun's minimal kickback managed to send her falling backward. She smacked straight into Sam's calves. Immediately, his hands closed on her shoulders, yanking her up. And as soon as she was on her feet, he tore the gun from her hands, worry evident in his pinched brow.

"What the hell are you trying to do?"

His voice sounded far away and underwater. The after-effects of firing a gun, Meredith supposed.

Her own reply sounded no better. "I'm buying us a bit more time. Giving us a chance."

"By shooting at nothing?"

"By letting whoever's out there know that we're armed, too. Did you have a better idea? I mean, other than sacrificing yourself."

Sam made an exasperated noise, but before he could speak again, the footsteps stopped and a rough voice carried through the air. "All right. I get it. You're not coming out without a fight. So I'm willing to talk about this. I'll give you two minutes to decide if that's an offer you want to take."

Meredith shot Sam a weak smile. "You're welcome."

He rolled his eyes. "Wonderful. Get behind me."

"Happy to. So long as you promise not to try and take a bullet for me."

"If I promised you that, I'd be lying."

"Then I'm not getting behind you."

"Ninety seconds!" the man outside the door yelled.

Sam sighed in Meredith's direction. "Look. I promise you I won't intentionally take a bullet for you. But if he fires on you, I can't say I'll stand idly by. That's the best I can manage."

"I guess that'll have to do, then," Meredith conceded, and she tucked herself behind his wide frame.

And truly, she was glad for his solid presence. Because in spite of her bravado, mounting fear threatened to over-whelm her. The thought that Sam might get shot again, this time on her behalf, scared her. The body at their feet hor-rified her. It made her shake. She was frightened by both the violence itself and the fact that these people they were up against—who still held her sister—would so easily kill their own. Which brought her back around to another fear. That this would be the end of the road. That they wouldn't ever even make it to Tamara.

Like he could sense her trepidation, Sam pulled one of her hands forward and secured it to his hip.

"One minute!" came the bellowing reminder.

"Ready?" Sam asked.

"If I say no, will we just keep hiding out in here?"

"And waste the chance you gave us? I don't think so."

"Then I guess I'm ready."

He squeezed her fingers, then pulled them away to grip the gun and hold it out as he called, "I don't need the last thirty seconds. I've got your dead friend's weapon. I'm prepared to come out firing."

"I'll hold if you do," the other man answered.

"I'll just assume you're lying."

"A safe assumption. Seeing as I'm the bad guy and you're the good guy, right? You really need to let go of this black-and-white thing, Potter. The world is full of gray."

"Funny. I feel like we've had this conversation before. And it wasn't fruitful the first time around, either," Sam said.

"Could be." The answer held a shrug. "I guess this means we're at an impasse."

"We're only at an impasse if we're both out of moves."

"Do you have some tricks I'm not aware of, Potter?"

"If I told you that, they wouldn't be tricks anymore, would they?"

"I just hope you're not counting on that lucky charm of yours, seeing as she's already in there with you and there's no chance she's sneaking up on me again."

"Now, now, Detective. Don't underestimate her. She's a resourceful girl."

His confident words, tendered in her defense, gave Meredith another idea. Knowing Sam couldn't protest out loud, she released her hold on his hip and slipped out from behind him. Even without checking, she could tell he'd gritted his teeth. She could all but hear him gnashing them together. For some reason, that made her smile.

You're the one who said not to underestimate me, she thought.

She bent down and snatched up the discarded piece of pallet. She slipped off her hoodie and wound it around the end, then held it out, hoping her suggestion was obvious.

Sam glanced down. His brow clouded, then cleared, and he raised an eyebrow. He got it, Meredith was sure. She nodded.

"Okay," he said, his voice so low that she had to read his lips.

Meredith jabbed the wood into the door frame. As expected, the man on the other side let loose. Three shots in quick succession. The board exploded in Meredith's hand and sent a shock wave up her arm. She shook off the pain and did a quick, mental calculation. A bullet in the redhead, another in the door frame and three in the palette board. So five bullets altogether. Did that also mean he only had one left? Even if it did, that was one too many.

But apparently Sam didn't care.

He grabbed a chunk of the shattered wood, drew his arm back and threw it—hard and upward. The second it left his hand, he did a stuntman-style tuck and roll, then came to an impressively graceful sliding stop in the very bottom of the doorway. Without missing a beat, he propped up his gun and fired. As Sam scurried back to his position inside the storage room, a pain-filled holler from the other side of the door signaled his success.

"Behind me again," he ordered as he pushed himself to his feet and glanced out.

Meredith didn't argue. She stepped to his back and tucked herself close, following as he led them onto the platform. As they moved, she snuck a glance around Sam. Midway between them and the stairs, the corrupt cop was leaning on the metal railway, clutching his shoulder with one hand. His gun hung loosely in his other hand, but the second he spotted Sam and Meredith, he fumbled to lift it.

"Sam!" As soon as his name left her mouth, she realized the warning was unnecessary.

Sam had already raised his own weapon. Already taken aim.

Thank God.

Meredith never thought she'd be so happy to see a gun at all, let alone be so pleased to see one at the ready. But her relief was short-lived. When Sam squeezed the trigger, nothing happened.

She knew what that meant. And clearly, so did the man at the other end of the platform. He smiled. He grasped the rail and took a few steps closer. Slowly. Like it no longer mattered that his arm shook as he took aim.

But Sam wasn't giving up that easily. With a wordless yell, he launched himself away from Meredith. Building up a remarkable amount of speed for such a short distance, he tore toward the other man. Then knocked straight into him. Hard enough that Meredith heard the gasp of air tear from the detective's throat.

The two men landed on the platform, a blurred roll of arms and legs, grunts and curses. Sam was bigger. Taller.

Wider. Clearly more dominant in any normal setting. But Sam had also lost a lot of blood. Suffered a head injury. And who knew how long it had been since he slept? Even though his opponent had a fresh wound, Meredith could tell it wasn't wearing him down the same way Sam's own injuries were.

Desperate to help but too afraid to look away even for a second, she inched closer, searching for some means of giving him an advantage.

The detective's gun.

But it sat on the ground on the wrong side of the struggle, and there wasn't near enough room to get past so she could retrieve it. Unless… The idea that popped into her head was sheer insanity. Totally unreasonable. But Sam let out a stifled cry as Boyd landed a blow, and Meredith knew she was going to have to do it anyway.

She slid toward the railing, took a breath and looked down. Ten to twelve feet, if she had to guess. A sheer drop would mean breaking bones at the very least. Maybe worse. She took another breath. She swallowed her fear. And she swung a leg over the railing.

Chapter 17

From the corner of his eye, Sam spied Meredith, and for a moment, he thought he was seeing things. That the trauma he'd sustained had finally got the better of him. Because her slim body was on the *wrong* side of the railing with nothing to stop her from falling down and cracking her head open on the concrete below. And no way was that possible. Except, when he blinked, she stayed put.

What the hell was she thinking?

She mouthed something at him, then pointed. He had no clue what she meant, and he didn't have time to figure it out. The man beneath him was gaining ground in the fight. He'd worked a hand free and drawn it back and— holy Lord, that hurt—slammed it into his so-tender wound. Sam bit down to keep from hollering, then fought back. He twisted his own hand into a fist and smashed it into the detective's chin. He hated the feeling of his knuckles coming in contact with someone else's face. Conflict resolution, not confrontation. He used his words and his authority.

Those had been his things as a cop, and they'd carried over just fine into his work as a PI. At least until now.

"Stop!" Meredith's voice carried through to Sam's ears, but the clang of metal drowned out everything she said after that one word.

And he didn't have time to pause and decipher it. The detective bucked up, driving a knee into Sam's thigh. Pain reverberated up to his hip. The man was damn strong. Sam needed to incapacitate him. Badly. He drew back a fist again. Then stopped short as a shot rang out.

His eyes flew up. Meredith had returned to the right side of the railing, and she stood near the stairs, her feet wide apart, the gun pointed at the ceiling. Drywall rained down on her. It coated her hair with dust, and it pinged against the metal under her Converse sneakers. Her expression looked regretful, and it took Sam a second to figure out why.

The last bullet.

She'd fired it up instead of using it on the detective. Instead of using it as a threat.

But regret was another thing Sam didn't have time for at that moment. Besides which, the shot had distracted the corrupt cop, too. The man was struggling to look toward the noise. Probably trying to discern where the bang had come from, and wondering if another bullet would be on its way. A perfect opportunity.

With a heave that made his wound burn, Sam pushed himself off Boyd and rolled the man to his back, then snapped the detective's wrists together and forced them both up. Immediately, the other man lifted a foot and slammed it backward. The kick landed sharply, making Sam stumble. His grip slipped. His knees smacked into the platform and his head swam.

For the love of all that's holy! he thought as he grabbed

for the railing and fought to regain some stability. *One little break would be nice.*

Except luck wasn't running his way. The other man was already loose, and his attention wasn't on Sam. Instead, he'd turned his furious gaze toward Meredith—who had pushed herself back against the railing and whose eyes widened with fear—and his feet were quick to follow.

Damn, damn, damn.

Sam flew up and made a hasty attempt to catch up before the other man could reach Meredith. But his efforts turned out to be unnecessary. A split second before the detective reached her, she slid sideways, avoiding the man barreling toward her. And though the cop stuck out his arms and tried to stop himself, his momentum was too great. As Sam watched, the other man's hips smacked into the railing, bending him in half. He teetered there for a moment, his body a living pendulum. Then his feet skidded against the platform, trying and failing to find purchase, and the frantic movement sent him over the edge. With a distinctly unmanly shriek, the detective toppled to the ground with a sickening thud, just as Sam reached Meredith's side.

She was staring down at the warehouse floor in horror. Sam put a hand on her elbow and tried to pull her back. She didn't budge. He reached down and peeled her fingers off the railing, then slid his arms around her shoulders.

"Hey." He kept his tone gentle. "We need to get moving again."

She met his eyes, her face ashen. "We need to… Is he… Should we… Oh, God. I couldn't shoot him. I wanted to, but I couldn't. I wanted something to just happen so I wouldn't have to, but… Oh, God. Not this. Maybe if I'd just fired. I probably would have missed, but at least…"

"If you'd fired, chances are good that you *would* have

missed. But you might've hit me, and I'm not exactly eager to experience that again so soon."

She eased out of his embrace, and Sam held still while her eyes ran over his torn and bloody shirt. He couldn't feel the wound at the moment, which probably wasn't a good thing. Trying not to show his worry, he bent to pick up a scrap of fabric—from her bullet-riddled sweatshirt, Sam thought—and used it to bind the bloody mess. When he was done, Meredith lifted her hand, then dropped it again without actually touching him.

"We really do need to go, don't we?" she asked.

"We do."

Moments later, they were moving down the stairs. As they hit the bottom, Sam turned to the side, trying to shield Meredith from having to view the man who lay crumpled on the ground. As they walked past, though, a ragged inhale made him stop and turn. Boyd's eyes were closed, his mouth open, his chest moving—but barely. Meredith pushed past, and her gaze landed on the detective.

Sam recognized the desperation in her look. The concern. It made his heart ache. And he knew how guilty she must feel about her unwanted compassion for the man on the ground. How torn. He'd experienced the same conflicting emotions on the job many times.

"Even though it feels wrong to leave him, it's what we have to do," Sam said. "Sticking around to see if there's a way we can help would just put us in more danger."

"I know."

"If it makes you feel better, it's safe to assume someone'll be looking for him."

"The same someone who's probably looking for us."

"Yes."

She shot the detective another regretful glance, and for a second Sam thought she might insist on helping the other man anyway. Then she grabbed his hand and pulled. But they barely made it two steps before another sound, far louder than Boyd's breaths, stopped them again.

A cell phone.

It came directly from the unconscious detective.

"Answer it," Meredith said.

Sam didn't have to be told twice. He strode to the man, flipped open his jacket and snapped up the phone. He smacked the answer button and waited.

The caller issued a greeting without preamble. "Did you take care of our redheaded loose end, Detective? And verify whether or not the Jamison girl's story about the file being set for release was true?"

Sam made a noncommittal noise in reply, hoping to draw out something else. But the words and their meaning were already enough to disturb Sam. Almost as much as the fact that there was something vaguely familiar about the man's voice.

"Boyd?" the caller prompted. "Answer me in a way that's going to make my life easier."

"I'm afraid I can't do that."

There was a pause. "Samuel Potter."

"You have me at a disadvantage."

The familiar-sounding man let out a chuckle. "Says the man with my number-one guy's phone in one hand and the girl I need in the other. I don't suppose you have the file handy, too?"

"Hardly had the time. Been a little busy defending ourselves from your number-one guy. And his dead friend."

"Can't blame me for trying to expedite the retrieval."

"How's that working out for you?"

"Well. Until you picked up this phone, I thought it was going just fine."

Sam struggled again to place the voice. Someone from his past? His days on the force? Likely. Who, though?

"Guess you were wrong," Sam said.

A sigh carried across the line. "Back to our previous arrangement then."

"Tamara."

"What about her?"

Sam reached out and pulled Meredith close enough that she'd be able to hear as well. "We want to know she's alive."

"She's alive."

"We want to know *firsthand* that she's alive."

"Fine. You've got twenty seconds."

There was a shuffle, and then—for the first time—Sam got to speak directly to the woman he was trying to save.

"Merri?" Her query sounded breathless and scared.

"She's safe, Tamara. I'm working with her to get the Hamish file."

"Did she hire you?"

"No. Your client did."

"Oh, thank God."

Sam frowned, thinking it was a strangely enthusiastic reaction. Before he could ask where it came from, though, the other man's voice burst onto the line.

"Time's up. I want that file, Potter."

"And I want you to call off your dogs."

"I believe you've already *put down* most of my dogs."

Sam glanced toward the fallen detective, who was still breathing shallowly. "You've got one alive here, if you're interested in saving him."

"I'm not that much of a bleeding heart, I'm afraid."

"Maybe not. But a dead cop is going to draw the wrong kind of attention."

There was a long pause. "Just bring me the damned file and keep this phone handy."

Then the line clicked to a dead silence, and Sam bent to set his hand gently on Boyd's chest. When he straightened up again, he caught Meredith staring at him, a funny look on her face.

"You did that for me, didn't you?" she asked. "Told his boss he was alive."

"He made his own bad choices, and if he does die, it's not your fault. But the conscience isn't a logical animal, sweetheart. We already established how misplaced guilt can be. How it can eat away at us." He shrugged. "This way, Detective Boyd might live and we can say rightly say we gave him a chance."

"Sam…" She met his eyes. "Thank you."

"Anytime. Now. Can we get the hell out of here?"

Meredith cast one more look at the detective, then nodded. He could see from her face that whatever was in her head wasn't over, but she'd pushed it down, and that would have to do. For now.

As Sam yanked off the cover of the steering column, then dragged out a few wires from inside, Meredith decided in spite of the hard time she'd given him before, she didn't care where he'd acquired the skill. Only that he had it. They'd found Sam's wallet in the office, and a jacket that sufficed to cover his wound. Though their own weapons were MIA, they'd snagged another gun, loaded with a single shot. But the car keys were a whole other story. And Meredith had no desire to search either the redhead or the detective to find them. She shivered involuntarily and turned her attention to what Sam was doing to distract herself from thinking about it.

He worked efficiently, stripping wires, then winding them together. The first set lit up the dash. The second kicked the sedan to life.

"One more thing," Sam said.

He placed the cover back on, then put both hands on the steering wheel. With a grunt, he twisted. And twisted.

And twisted some more. Hard enough to make his face turn an alarming shade of red. And just when Meredith was about ready to tell him to stop—not that she had a clue what he was doing—the column snapped loudly. Sam leaned against the driver's seat and drew in a deep breath.

"Okay," he said after a very long moment. "Engine's running. Steering wheel's unlocked. Let's get this show back on the road."

Meredith scrambled around the car and plopped herself in the passenger seat. As she fastened her seat belt, she kept her eyes on the side mirror, watching as the warehouse got smaller. She watched and watched until it was nothing but a dot on the horizon. But the pressure in her chest still didn't ease. In fact, now that she wasn't moving, it almost seemed worse.

"It's okay to breathe, sweetheart. We're safe."

At Sam's soft statement, Meredith jerked her gaze forward. "I'm just… I'm not scared. I'm waiting for it to feel better."

"Could be waiting awhile."

"That's not very helpful."

"You're a good person. When bad things happen, you feel bad."

"I didn't just feel bad, Sam. I was glad that detective was alive. I *am* glad." She shook her head. "I shouldn't be happy about that."

"It's okay to be glad someone's not dead."

"Even when that someone is a murderous, kidnapping cop?" She meant it to sound funny, or at least sarcastic, but it just came out bitter.

Sam didn't comment on her tone. Instead, he reached across the center console and squeezed her forearm. "Especially then."

"Seriously?"

"Yeah, sweetheart. It's easy to feel bad for the nice guys.

For the innocent ones. It's much harder to sympathize with the bad ones." He released her arm. "If that goes away, that's when you should worry."

"So I'm normal?"

"Better than normal. You're you."

Meredith exhaled, and the squeeze in her chest eased just a little. "Okay."

"Good. We should probably make a call."

"Worm?"

"Yep."

He dug into his pocket, then handed her Detective Boyd's phone. She shoved down another small stab of guilt as she clasped the device. She focused on Sam's voice instead, plugging in the number he reeled off. But when she lifted it to her ear, it only rang once before an automated voice came on the line, telling her the number wasn't in service.

She snapped the phone off. "I think I dialed wrong."

Sam smiled. "Give it a minute or two."

Sure enough, just a few clicks of the odometer later, the phone jingled to life. A blocked-call message flashed across the screen.

Meredith picked up the phone cautiously. "Hello?"

"You!" Worm's voice snapped.

"Um. Hi."

"Is Potter dead?"

"What?"

"Because if he's not dead, then why the hell didn't you stay at the hotel and why the hell are you calling me on a phone that's registered to the Bowerville Police Department?"

Meredith's hand tightened on the phone. "Sam isn't dead."

"Got shot, though!" Sam called out a little too gleefully.

"He got shot?" Worm asked.

"Yes."

"Is he dying, then?"

"I hope not."

"So. Just a death *wish*, then. Put me on Speaker."

Meredith fumbled for a minute, found the right key, then held the phone out. "Okay. You're on Speaker."

"You're an idiot, Potter."

Sam smiled. "It would've been more idiotic to stay at the hotel, Worm. We got ambushed."

"How the hell did you manage that? Your identity is virtually untraceable and as I'm sure you recall, I turned off the GPS on the princess's phone."

"I can hear you, you know," Meredith interjected.

"I'm sure he's aware of that." Sam's tone was dry. "They must be following us some other way. They tracked us out to a bus station, too."

Worm dropped a string of curses, then muttered at them to hang on. In the background, Meredith could hear the clack of keys, and she wondered if the man ever really unplugged.

When he came back on the line, he sounded no calmer. "What's she wearing?"

Sam tossed Meredith a wink. "Little inappropriate at the moment, my friend."

The other man cursed again. "I'm serious here, Potter. Something she's wearing might be bugged. I know it's not you, because you're too smart to let them get to you."

"I can *still* hear you," Meredith said.

"And yet you're still not giving me the details."

She rolled her eyes. "I've got a pink blouse on the top and jeans on the bottom. But everything I'm wearing came from the hotel."

"Everything?" Worm asked. "Socks and underwear?"

Sam interrupted again. "You really think her panties are bugged, Worm?"

"Devil's in the details. Isn't that what they say? So. Underwear. Yay or nay?"

A blush crept up Meredith's cheeks, and she raised her voice. "Yes to both. Underwear, top and bottom, provided by the hotel. Socks, too."

"Anything not given to you?"

Meredith looked down at her feet, then shifted them restlessly. "Just my sneakers."

"Take the damned things off."

The urgency in his voice made her scrunch up her legs and unlace them as quickly as she could. "Now what?"

"Throw them out the window."

"Shouldn't I try to find the bug first?"

"Simpler to toss 'em."

"But—"

"But what?"

"Shouldn't I make sure it's really there?"

Sam groaned. "Now you've done it."

"Done what?" Meredith asked.

But she didn't have to wait long; Worm launched into a tirade. "Look. I know stalking. I know it better than that our so-called PI of a mutual friend. And I guarantee you those shoes are wired. Probably with something stupidly slow and unreliable. But somewhere, somehow, they got to you. A fail-safe in case that necklace camera didn't work. It's what I would do. So you can spend all the time you want tearing them apart. But when you're doing it, remember that every second you spend doing it is another minute they can spend tracking you. And from what I can tell, *you're* not the one with the death wish."

"I don't have a death wish," Sam muttered.

"Then throw out the shoes."

And before Meredith could protest again, Sam snatched up her favorite pair of sneakers, rolled down his window and tossed them straight out. Meredith's head twisted, and she watched as they bumped along the highway. Then a car, approaching fast from the other direction, ran them over, signaling their complete demise.

Meredith spat out an annoyed breath. "Okay. Seriously. I couldn't have just dug out the sole or something? I'm going to be running from the bad guys in my socks."

"No," Worm argued. "You won't. Because now the *bad guys* won't be able to find you. Speaking of which. This phone you're on is probably pinging off every location device the cops have at their disposal. Don't suppose you're willing to throw it out the window, too?"

"No can do," Sam said. "This phone is our new default lifeline to Meredith's sister. Think you can do your thing from there?"

"Think? Uh-uh. I know I can do it."

There was a pause on the other end, and Meredith got the feeling Worm was struggling to decide if he should add something else. And after a few breaths, he did.

"Don't shoot the messenger about this next bit, okay?" he said. "Because I'm sure as hell you're not gonna like it."

Meredith's heart beat nervously in her chest.

"Spill it," Sam ordered.

"I tracked the husband, Nicholas Billing, a little more."

Now, Meredith's heart thundered. "It's not Nick."

Worm made an unintelligible noise, midway between a snort and a sigh. "Fine. But just as a reminder, the last thing he bought was a piece of luggage. Is that a coincidence?"

"He was going on a vacation."

"That he never booked."

"It. Is. Not. Him." As Meredith bit off the words, she could feel Sam's eyes on her, doing their best to bore into her thoughts.

"Shouldn't you be watching the road?" she asked.

He turned his gaze frontward. "Anything else, Worm?"

"I think you should reconsider whatever crazy course of action you're on. But I'm going to guess that's another no-can-do."

"Your guess is correct."

"Then I've got nothing. The client list isn't ready yet and it's not the husband, so—"

"We're going to hang up now, Worm." Without waiting for a reply, Sam reached up and ended the call, then flexed his hands on the steering wheel. "Meredith?"

"Yes?"

"I think it's time to tell me why you're so damned sure your brother-in-law has nothing to do with Tamara's kidnapping."

She stared out the windshield for a long moment. Then took a breath. And started talking.

Chapter 18

"Nick didn't kidnap Tamara because he didn't need to. If he wanted to hurt her, or get a hold of her money, or cover up some secret file, all he'd have to do is tell the world her secret. *Our* secret." Meredith paused to glance at Sam, trying to gauge his reaction, but aside from a barely discernible twitch of his mouth, his face betrayed nothing, so she went on. "I was twenty when I met him. He was a junior associate at the law firm where I worked as a paralegal, and I kind of thought of him as a reward for the years I spent raising Tamara. Smart. Handsome. Thoughtful. The perfect trophy boyfriend. *My* trophy boyfriend."

The label came out a little shaky, and it felt funny—unnatural—to place herself with Nick in those terms. And now Sam's mouth more than twitched. It drew into a straight, thin line.

He's jealous.

And that didn't feel funny. It felt…good. Weirdly good, tinged with a tiny bit of guilt.

She stared at him for another second and then added, "We couldn't tell anyone about our relationship because it violated company policy. It didn't last for long anyway. Ten weeks. Which was just enough time for me to introduce him to my only family."

Sam's jaw loosened a little, then tightened again. "Tamara."

"It only took them a week or two to fall in love. And a whole month to confess it to me."

"The one bad thing you were talking about was this. Nicholas Billing had an affair with your sister."

"Yes."

"But you're set on defending him."

"I'm defending him because he's innocent."

"I see." His voice was wooden.

"I was setting on hating him for a long time first. Both of them."

"And that changed why?"

Meredith remembered how much the betrayal galled. Not how much it hurt, just how angry it made her. She'd worked for so long, putting aside her personal needs, putting aside the possibility of wanting anything for herself. And then she'd found Nick, and he'd fit the mold of everything she'd being missing. Of everything she *thought* she'd been missing in life.

"But I really wasn't missing him at all," she said softly.

"Pardon me?"

Meredith cleared her throat. "It changed because I was mad at them for taking away what I thought I wanted. But eventually I realized that it—that Nick—wasn't what I wanted anyway."

"That simple?"

"Not even remotely. Before I figured it all out, I said a lot of cruel things to Tamara. I accused her of not understanding what I'd sacrificed to raise her. Of deliberately sabotaging my happiness. That she was too young. And

I told her Nick wouldn't be faithful to her, either. I *promised* her he wouldn't, actually. After that, I didn't talk to them for months. I moved away from the house our parents left us. I quit my job at the firm where Nicholas worked. Changed my phone numbers. I did everything I could to put separation between me and the humiliation."

"But you forgave her."

Meredith's heart clenched. "I didn't forgive her. Not then. In fact, the more that went right for Tamara, the less I was able to feel happy for her. The better their life seemed to be, the more I pulled away. But then Tamara came to my apartment with a ring on her finger, begging me to be her maid of honor. And I couldn't very well say no. She was still my sister. The kid I raised."

"I get it."

"I know you do." Meredith stared out the window and watched the horizon for a minute before speaking again. "They had a long engagement. Eighteen months. And that's when she started building her blog. Her perfect upcoming marriage to her perfect man with her perfect plan to make the whole thing last. Her blog gained traction quickly. And by the time the wedding day rolled around, Tamara's business was in full swing. Her advice column became a book deal. Some community college courses and a certificate made her a counselor. And all of it was documented for her fans."

"Leaving out one small detail, of course."

"Yes. Leaving that out. Because it would've destroyed her business completely before it even got off the ground."

Sam shook his head. "You don't think there might be something in the so-called Hamish file that trumps that?"

"No."

"Evidence of an affair, maybe? Or something else luridly and lawyerly that Nicholas got involved in."

"Trust me. The man's about as mundane as they come. And his lawyerly-ness is far heavier than his luridly-ness."

Meredith laughed a little. "And besides that, they have an insane prenuptial agreement."

Sam's eyes snapped her way for a second. "An insane prenup?"

Meredith nodded. "Typical Nick. His way of apologizing. Of reaching out to me to try and right the wrong he'd done, because that's just how he works. The agreement was full of crazy conditions that would void any future claim Nick had to her not-yet-existent fortune."

Sam tapped his fingers on the wheel, a frown digging a furrow in his brow. "Conditions. You're not seriously saying that included kidnapping."

"Anything that would cause Tamara harm, physical or emotional."

"That's awfully vague."

"I told you it was insane."

"I'm not sure that's a strong enough word."

"But now you see why he couldn't be involved? If it was as simple as wanting to bring her down, Nick could do it. And if he tried to get around the conditions of the prenup, he'd have to give up any stake in her business," Meredith said, then let out a raw, shame-filled breath. "I never got up the guts to tell her I forgave her. Or to admit that even though what she and Nick did to me was awful, it didn't hurt me the way I made it out to do. I left that giant rift between us. I let it grow and grow."

"I've been on the short end of this particular stick myself. Wishing I'd kept some things to myself and wishing I'd said more than a few aloud, too." He shrugged, but his face was pained. "I'm sure Kelsey would rather have had my support about her and Heely instead of my constant doubt. I could've bitten my tongue. Kept my opinion to myself. Would, if I could go back."

His expression mirrored the feelings in Meredith's heart, and she wanted desperately to soothe away his hurt.

"But at least everything you went through was to do some good. Maybe Kelsey would like that."

Sam shot her a funny look—like he'd never considered that idea before—and his mouth turned up in a half smile. "I bet you're right. She complained a lot about how dangerous my job was, but she always said it made her proud to know I was out saving lives and protecting people. That I was doing the right thing."

"Do you think it's too late for *me* to make something good out of all this?"

He reached out to squeeze her hand again. "I'm not going to let it be too late, sweetheart."

"Are you making another impossible promise?"

"I guess I am."

"You're setting a bad precedent, you know."

"Yeah, I should probably rein it in before I take it too far and accidentally stick a ring on your... Oh, wait."

Meredith glanced down. She'd all but forgotten the small diamond.

"I can give it back," she said quickly.

"Uh-uh. I think I'd like you to be my fake wife a little longer."

She leaned against the seat, almost giddy with relief. *Ridiculous relief.* But she still had to resist an urge to tuck her hand away to hide the ring in case Sam changed his mind.

"You realize this means I'm going to go ahead and take a point," she said.

"For continuing to be fake married?"

"Yes."

His lips curled up even more. "Explain to me how that's a point for you."

"Easy. I'm saving you from having to keep track of the ring, of course. So that makes it what? Five to four?"

Now Sam was full-on grinning. "So long as we agree that it's still in my favor?"

"Like you'd let it be any other way."

He chuckled. "I'm glad we're at a point in our relation- ship that you understand that."

Their relationship.

Meredith's heart did a wild flip. One part nerves. One part hope. Though maybe it meant nothing. Or maybe it was a slip of the tongue.

But maybe not.

She fixed her gaze out the window, afraid if she looked at Sam, he'd read the way her thoughts were going.

Could a relationship—a real one, that is—develop over such a short time? It seemed like a crazy leap. Sam was more or less a stranger. But he really didn't feel like one. Instead, it felt as though she'd known him for a lifetime. She'd shared more of her secrets with him, been more genuine and open with him, than she had been with anyone. She was used to distancing herself from men and keeping her guard up. And spending the last five years in temp jobs didn't give her much of an opportunity to make close friends, either.

Meredith wondered again if the frantic pace of their search had also increased the pace of the getting-to-know- you phase. She guessed it made sense. And it probably should've been at least a bit frightening. But instead of scar- ing Meredith, it comforted her. Like riding the downward slope of a roller coaster. Fast. Heart-stopping. And utterly exhilarating. So if she had to go through this, at least she could go through it with a man who made her feel like that.

And how much time had they spent together anyway? How many solid, one-on-one hours? Over a day and a half. That equaled more than thirty-six hours. The equivalent of eighteen two-hour dates. Or maybe twelve three-hour ones. What did twelve to eighteen dates equate to in the grand scheme of relationship things? Three months of dat- ing? That sounded about right. So. Not a stranger at all, if she thought of it like that. Out there, in the regular world, they might be in a coffee shop, talking about moving in together. They might be under the covers of their shared bed, talking about the future. Or they might be under those same covers, not talking at all.

And for sure, they would've shared those three little words that bubbled just under the surface of Meredith's heart and made it pound recklessly.

She was falling in love with him, and it scared her as much as it pleased her.

Sam watched Meredith from the corner of his eye, trying to figure out what was on her mind, but her expression was unreadable.

He hadn't meant to drop the *R* word. And even if he *had* planned on saying it, he wouldn't have expected her to go so suddenly quiet. To shut down. He guessed he had no one to blame but himself. He'd assumed her feelings were turning the same way as his. That she was falling as fast and hard as he was.

With as much subtlety as a freight train, he thought.

He tested out the corners of his mind where Meredith had taken up residence. Probing them in search of weak spots. All he found was solidity and warmth.

Thirty-six hours in, and he was crazy about her.

He wanted her to feel the same. He wanted her to put aside sense and reason to see how perfectly they fit together.

Hell. He just plain wanted *her*.

For himself and no one else.

Sam's jaw stiffened. He was doing his best to rein it in, but her confession about her involvement with her brother-in-law set Sam's teeth on edge. Not because Meredith had dated the man. She was a grown woman—a dating history was pretty much a given. But that wasn't what dug at him the most. It was everything else. The betrayal by both Tamara and Nick. The wild conditions of the prenuptial agreement as some kind of peace offering. The fact that Meredith had no choice but to let it slide for the sake of her family. Her fortitude about it all.

Sam's anger spiked. He wished like crazy he could go back in time and undo the hurt.

Dammit.

He didn't have time to add something else to his list of regrets. Especially not for something he had no control over. Could *never* have had control over. He needed to get past it. To let it slide the same way she had.

He glanced at her again. As much as Sam wanted to talk to her about all of this, he knew that what they really needed right that second was a bit of levity.

"Hey, sweetheart?"

She jumped like he'd pinched her, then swallowed. "Yes?"

"Do you want to play Twenty Questions?"

Her face went from nervous to puzzled. "Why?"

Sam shrugged. "Because I Spy is a little boring when all the scenery is the same color."

She smiled. "Fine. You go first."

"Perfect. I'll give you a hint. The theme is my favorite things. And the first one is smaller than a breadbox and it goes well with ice cream."

Her smile widened. "I think I'd better explain the rules to you."

Relieved that then tension was gone—at least for the moment—Sam steered the conversation to lighter topics. Middle names—hers was Charlotte after her grandmother and his was Gordon after some singer his parents liked—and favorite foods, which turned out to be Chinese for Meredith and fried anything for Sam. They compared old sports injuries—she had one twisted ankle to his two broken arms—and Sam told her stories about his time on the force, funny enough to make her laugh out loud.

He coaxed out the disastrous tale of her first high school dance and told him about his failed senior year romance. He lamented over the fact that she had an unreasonable fear of motorcycles, while he loved them and had always wanted to own one.

But if Sam was being honest with himself, even the lighthearted conversation just drove his desire for Meredith higher. The more he knew about her, the more he wanted to kiss the hell out of her and hold her close and tell her how he felt. To not let his feelings become one of those things he left unsaid. To remind her again that he wouldn't let her down. To reassure her about Tamara's safety and… Sam's brain skidded to a stop at Meredith's sister's name.

Tamara.

His mind paused there, hanging. Then it rewound to the thing that he hadn't been able to pinpoint—the thing that struck him as odd during their brief phone interaction. Clarity came rushing forward.

It's not what she said. It's how she said it.

She'd been relieved about the fact that her client had hired him. Almost excited. Sam couldn't think of a good reason for a kidnap victim to care about *who* had sought professional help. It should've been just enough to know that the help was coming. So why, then? And how could he find out? It wasn't like he could get ahold of Tamara and ask. Or even the client herself, who'd somehow disappeared. He still thought that was odd, and it nagged at him, too. Maybe related somehow. He couldn't put his finger on the how of it, though.

"Sam!"

Meredith's frightened cry brought him back to the moment, and too late, he realized he'd been distracted just long enough to lose focus on the road. The sedan slid across the shoulder, bouncing into the gravel. Frantically, Sam jerked the steering wheel hard enough to make his wounded arm ache. He dragged his foot off the gas pedal, slammed on the brakes and brought them to a skidding halt just inches from the trees lining the road. For several long moments, they sat there, their equally heavy breathing carrying over the engine's rattle.

It was Meredith who finally broke through the wordless noise. "I thought we were trying *not* to get killed."

"Sorry, sweetheart."

"What happened?"

Sam exhaled and released the steering wheel. "Can you think of any reason why your sister would be glad a client hired me to track her down?"

"Why wouldn't she be glad?"

"I don't mean because of me. I mean because of the client specifically. When the kidnapper put her on the phone with me, she asked me about the woman who hired me."

Meredith frowned. "I don't know. You never told me who the client was."

Sam hesitated, remembering the confidentiality clause of his contract. It seemed far less important now. Especially since he was pretty damn sure he wasn't even working for the woman who hired him anymore.

"Her name is Matilda Mathews."

Meredith let out a gasp. Automatically, Sam glanced over, taking in her appearance with surprise. Her eyes had gone wide. She was already shaking her head.

"Matilda Mathews hired you?" she asked. "And she said she was a client of Tamara's?"

"Yeah."

"Online? Or a real, live person? Like, an in-person person?"

"An in-person person. A professional-looking brunette. Big, fat diamond ring. Driver's license with her name on it."

Meredith shook her head again. "That's impossible."

"Why? Is she someone you know?"

"No. Matilda Mathews isn't a person at all."

Chapter 19

Sam studied Meredith's face, trying to figure out if he'd heard her wrong, or if he'd just misunderstood. "What do you mean? She's not a real person? It's a fake identity?"

"More than that," she told him. "Matilda Mathews is another Tamara thing from that summer we spent on Turtle Island."

"Another stray dog? An imaginary friend?"

"A place, actually. A spot on the island we weren't allowed to go. A little cave beside Turtle Beach. My parents thought it was too dangerous. Too close to the water, too dark, too slippery, too…everything. But Tamara and I used it as a clubhouse anyway. It was her idea to give the place a girl's name. That way, any time we wanted to hang out there, we'd just tell our parents we were going to visit Matilda."

"Okay. But that doesn't change the fact that a woman who called herself Matilda Mathews *did* hire me."

"Whoever she was, she was lying."

Sam ran a hand over his hair. "Why?"

"I don't know. But if I was going to hide something somewhere on the island—something I wanted Tamara to find—that's exactly where I'd put it."

"You think it's another clue." He posed it as a statement rather than a question.

"You don't? We're on the right track. We have to be. Hamish. Matilda. It's the only place that makes sense."

His kept his face carefully neutral, and made sure his voice matched. "There's another possibility."

"Which is?"

"Think about the sequence of events. The way everything is lining up to get you to the island."

"You think it's a trap?"

"I wouldn't rule it out."

"But there are only three people who— Oh." Meredith's face crumpled with worry.

"Three people who what?"

"Know about this island and how much it meant to me and Tamara." Her voice shook. "We kept it a secret. Except…"

Sam knew right away who the third person had to be.

"Except for Nicholas Billing," he ventured.

"Yes."

He met her eyes. "I think we need to go back and go over everything we know. And in spite of the circumstances surrounding his and Tamara's marriage, consider that he might be involved after all."

She looked like she wanted to argue, but after a second, just nodded. "Okay."

"I'm sorry, sweetheart."

"Don't be." She closed her eyes, and her chest rose and fell with several deep breaths. "Let's just do this."

"All right. We'll start with his time line. We know he left his job about a week ago, and around the same time, his credit-card purchases stopped abruptly. But Tamara's kept up, like normal, for a couple of days after that." He paused. "Are we assuming Nicholas really went on vacation?"

Meredith opened her eyes. "No."

"So he needed some time off but didn't want to draw any attention to the fact that he was going to be off. Do you think Tamara knew he was missing work?"

"If I had to make an educated guess, I'd say she knew. Nick is smart, but not creative. And if he needed to cover up being off, he would've had to find something to do, right? During the day when he should've been there. And whatever that might be, it would cost money. But he didn't use a credit card and he didn't take out any cash. If he had, Worm would've found some trace of it somewhere."

Sam nodded. "Agreed. So Nick leaves his job—at least temporarily—Tamara knows…and then what?"

"Nick uses the luggage he bought?"

"Right. That was his last purchase. But we already decided he didn't really go away."

"No," Meredith said. "We decided he didn't take a vacation. That doesn't mean he didn't go away. Maybe he went into hiding."

Sam heard the catch in her voice, and guilt made his chest twinge. He wished he hadn't had to call her brother-in-law into question. But going in unprepared had the potential to be so much worse.

He reached out to squeeze her hand. "Listen, sweetheart. Whether or not Nicholas has any responsibility only matters in that we have to be even more cautious. We have to operate under the assumption of a worst-case scenario."

"So you're not saying we shouldn't go to Turtle Island?"

"No. Just the opposite. I'm pretty damned sure we *need* to go see Matilda Mathews."

"The spot, you mean. Not the person."

Sam strummed his thigh with his fingers. "I think we need to contact the person, too."

"She's not real."

"Someone wanted me to believe she was."

"I know." Meredith sagged. "But it's not going to matter anyway, will it? Because once we have the file—if we get it and this isn't just a trap—we're going to walk straight into it. And even if it feels like we're in control, we're not, really. They have all the power."

"I promise you we're not going in blind."

"They're not going to let us just have her."

"No. They're not going to make it easy. But neither are we. This won't be my first hostage negotiation, and this is your sister we're talking about. We aren't just handing over the file and we sure as hell won't be leaving without Tamara. I have faith in our ability. In us."

"Could you spread some of that faith around? 'Cause I'm struggling over here."

He eyed her up, easily seeing the downward spiral of her thoughts. Guilty once more, he pulled out Detective Boyd's phone, dialed Worm's number and put it on Speaker.

The other man picked up immediately. "Italian takeout."

"Super. Now I'm hungry."

Worm sighed loudly, making the line crackle. "You know, Sammy, if you really wanted this relationship to work, you'd call a little less often."

"I can't help it. I need you more than you need me."

"No kidding."

"You have time to give me some help?"

"No. But I'll do it anyway."

"I guess I'll take what I can get," Sam said drily.

He reeled off his set of requests—a room on the other end of the ferry, some *real* Italian food, a laptop and, finally, a basic background check on Matilda Mathews—then hung up and faced Meredith once more.

"Does that help any?" he asked.

"Some."

Sam flexed his hands on the steering wheel, scrambling to find something that would lift her spirits. "You ever driven a stolen car in your bare feet?"

"No."

"You want to?"

"Out of pity?"

"Out of trust."

"You need trust to let someone else drive?"

"Been driven around by too many crazy cops and chased by too many crazy criminals."

Her lips turned up a tiny bit. "So you're a control freak. I guess I shouldn't be surprised."

"Not in the least. If you won't do it out of respect for my faith in you, then do it because you're the one who knows the way to the ferry."

"Aha. The truth comes out."

"Of course it does. I would never lie to you, sweetheart."

"Wouldn't you?"

He pushed open the car door and swung out his legs. "Not unless I had to."

"Seriously? *Had* to?"

"Uh-huh."

"Always a caveat."

Sam paused, brought his legs back in and turned to face her. Under his gaze, she shifted slightly in the seat. The movement drove her blouse up, just a little. Sam felt his Adam's apple bob in his throat. The tiny bit of exposed skin sent his heart pounding and made him light-headed, too. He remembered well how that velvet flesh felt under his hands. How her body felt pressed into his. He met her eyes, taking in their pretty hue. He raked his gaze over her face, admiring the pink of her skin. Her full, kissable lips. Her dark brows and wild, blond hair. She was so damn stunning.

"Sam?"

He blinked and realized he'd been sitting and staring at her for a little too long. "It's just one caveat, sweetheart. And it's that I have to keep you safe."

"Okay."

Sam blinked again, surprised at her immediate acquiescence. "Okay?"

"Yes. I'll agree to your caveat if you agree to mine."

"You have a caveat?"

"That's right."

Sam let himself grin. "All right. Tell me what it is."

"I'll drive. But only if you let me patch you up."

"I'm fine."

"You look terrible," she added.

"Thanks."

"You know what I mean. You need a doctor, but I know we can't call one. So I'll settle for some proper bandages and some painkillers." She crossed her arms. "See that? My caveat is the same as yours. I'll do what has to be done. But only if I can keep you safe, too."

His smile widened. "I'll think about it."

Sam swung his legs out of the car again, then stood and moved to the passenger side of the sedan, where he opened the door with a gallant flourish. "See? Fine."

Meredith tipped up her chin and narrowed her eyes at him. "If fine means you grimace every time you move that arm. You have to let me take care of you."

"Has anyone ever told you that when you're mad, you look like a rabid chipmunk?"

"You realize I'm almost five foot ten. And you're avoiding my caveat."

"A tall, rabid chipmunk."

She ignored his teasing. "Just so you know, I'm not driving anywhere until you agree to my terms."

Sam bent down and placed a kiss on her lips. He meant it to be brief. Teasing. But the moment their mouths fused, her arms came up, drawing him in. The burn of his wound slipped away. The dull ache in his head all but disappeared. Everything but Meredith ceased to exist as the kiss increased in intensity.

He pulled away reluctantly. "All right, sweetheart. You can patch me up the second we get to that boat. From here on out, I'll protect you and you'll protect me. We'll both be very, very safe."

Meredith guided the car along the highway, and she had to admit that it felt good to have the little bit of control it afforded. Sure, the hot-wired ignition had a mind of its own, and the thought of getting pulled over and caught with her bare feet on the pedals kept her hovering at the speed limit. And yes, she was full of bitterness at the thought that Nick might have done something terrible to Tamara. Angry at herself for defending him so vehemently. But for the moment, her hands on the wheel were enough to help her tune out the unpleasant swirl of emotions that threatened to overwhelm her.

She even turned up the radio and let herself get carried away in car karaoke, ignoring the amusement on Sam's face as she belted out her off-key accompaniment.

She managed to hold on to the cheerful mood as they paid the toll and booked themselves into a small stateroom. She kept upbeat as they grabbed an assortment of makeshift first-aid items from the gift shop, even though the ferry was crowded enough to negate any real conversation until they made their way to their tiny room.

But as they walked through the door, reality hit Meredith again. Tears formed in her eyes. She swayed on her feet. And Sam pulled her into a much-needed embrace.

Chapter 20

Sam held Meredith close. He let her cry into his chest, taking comfort in the fact that she was taking her comfort from him.

"I'm failing her," she finally whispered.

Sam shook his head. "Failing her? Sweetheart, you've been chased through the streets, shot at, knocked a guy unconscious, pretended to be married to me, got kidnapped yourself, all in the name of figuring out what the hell is going on. As far as I'm concerned, that's the complete opposite of failure."

"But I let her down. I pushed you to rule out Nick as a suspect, when maybe if we'd focused on him from the beginning, we'd be in a better position."

"We still don't know if he's behind this. And nothing would've changed, the way we came at it. We still would've followed the paper trail, we still would've found the same clues." He reached down and tipped up her chin.

"Do you know what most families do in these situations, sweetheart?"

"No."

"They fall apart. Sit staring at the clock. Rely on me to do everything. And there's nothing wrong with that. Really. It's normal to feel too desperate, normal to leave it to the professionals. But you're *not* doing that. You're here, digging in and helping and matching every stride. The exact opposite of failing."

She lifted her eyes to his. "How do I convince myself that's true?"

Sam slid his hand from her chin to her cheek. "Keep doing what you're doing. Move on to the next step. And count the small victories."

She sighed. "I'm not even sure I can remember what it is I'm supposed to be doing next."

"If it helps any, I promised you as soon as we got on the boat, you could poke and prod me."

"I think I said patch you up," she reminded him, and moved toward the supplies. "Sit down?"

Sam sank into the crisply made cot and watched as Meredith set to work at arranging the cache of items they'd purchased on their way to the room. A pair of slip-on boat shoes to replace the ones she'd lost out the window. Distilled water and a tiny bottle of hand sanitizer for cleaning the wound. A baby blanket embossed with the ferry's logo that she told him she was going to use as both a cloth and bandage. A bottle of some electrolyte-based sports drink Meredith insisted he needed to replenish his vitamins and minerals, and a travel-sized package of ibuprofen. And a nail kit, which Sam wasn't entirely clear on, but knew must have a use. And all of it made him smile, because even though the circumstances were just the opposite, there was something soothingly domestic about the flurry of activity. He couldn't help but wonder what Meredith was like in her own home. Sam tried to recall what her apartment looked like and couldn't. In spite of the fact that he'd seen it just the morning before, all he could remember was how *she* looked when she opened the door. Cautious. Guarded. Beautiful.

"You okay?" she asked, interrupting the pleasant memory.

"Do you cook?" he replied, then chuckled at his seemingly random abruptness.

A tiny frown creased her forehead as she twisted the cap off the sports drink and handed it—along with two painkillers—to him. "I'm not sure what it has to do with how you're feeling."

Sam offered her a grin. "Maybe knowing the answer will make me feel better."

She narrowed her eyes. "Well. I don't have a personal chef. And before you ask, I don't have a maid, either."

Sam popped the pills into his mouth and took a swallow of the sweet beverage. "What I meant is, are you the type to do Sunday dinners, or do you like to slap together a package of instant noodles with diet soda?"

Meredith used the nail scissors on the edge of the baby blanket to cut it into strips. "Hmm. I guess it depends. Does admitting I like roast beef and gravy condemn me to a lifetime of slaving over the stove?"

"I can think of worse things to be condemned to."

"Probably because you're on the receiving end of the mashed potatoes and I'm on the sweat-covered, peeling end."

An image of Meredith, wrapped in a kitchen apron—and not much else—flew to the forefront of Sam's mind. "I'll gladly peel."

"In exchange for what?"

"I'm not sure you want to know."

"Oh, sure. You can play Twenty Questions for two

hours, but the second I ask what you're thinking, you clam up?"

"I never said you couldn't ask. I just pointed out that you might not want to know." Then he shrugged. "Although, if this is going to be a lifetime thing…"

She colored. "I didn't mean that literally."

He grabbed her wrist and pulled her toward him. "How do two people spend a figurative lifetime together?"

She let him hold her there for a second, pressed to his knees, then shook herself free. "You need to let me look at that arm."

Sam frowned, unsure why that guarded look—the same one he'd been remembering from the previous morning—was suddenly back in place. A heartbeat later, though, his curiosity flew from his mind. Because Meredith had sat beside him and her hands were on his shoulders, pushing down his jacket. The motion seemed intensely intimate. And how could it not? She was undressing him. On a bed. Sam tried to speak, to draw out some more levity, but now she was rolling up the tattered edges of his sleeve and she kept brushing his skin and all that came out of his mouth was a light groan.

Trying to distract himself, Sam turned his attention to their modest accommodations.

Small—as the ferry guy had called it—didn't begin to describe the actual size of the room. A swatch of carpet decorated the floor in front of the tiny bed where they sat, and a fold-down table on a swinging arm rested to one side of a single armchair. A round window let in a bit of natural light. That was the room in its entirety. Nothing else to see. And Sam's attention came right back to the way Meredith's fingers felt as they unwound the makeshift bandage. Gentle. Sure. Tender. Sam groaned again.

Meredith stopped. "Am I hurting you?"

Sam managed to shake his head. "Nope."

"You sure?"

He gritted his teeth. "I'm perfect."

She went back to work, unwrapping the sticky bits of fabric, pulling on the skin and making the sore area burn. He fought a wince.

"Perfect?" she repeated dubiously.

"Aside from the gunshot wound, the various car chases and the currently cramped quarters…"

He shrugged again and her hand tightened on his arm.

"Hold still." She pulled aside the last of the fabric and inhaled sharply. "Gee, Sam. I don't know why I didn't see the relative perfection before."

"Is Worm's prediction coming true? Am I dying?"

"Ask me again in two minutes."

Meredith leaned back, then reached for a water-saturated piece of torn blanket and pressed it lightly to Sam's arm. This time he couldn't suppress his cringe.

"Sorry."

Her apology was heartfelt, but she didn't stop sponging away the grunge from his wound. She worked for several more minutes in silence, a light sheen of sweat marking her brow. Sam kept silent, too, his teeth pressed together as he attempted to block out the sting of the antiseptic. She kept working until her pieces of cloth came back clean.

She exhaled, her expression marginally relieved. "Good news. It looks better than I thought it would."

"Considering the fact that it's a gunshot wound dressed with a sweatshirt?"

"Yes. That." She sighed. "Even though my knowledge of gunshots is limited to what I've seen on TV, I think you got lucky. *Really* lucky. The bullet grazed your skin more than it dug into it, and it even cauterized the wound. You'll get a scar but—"

"But that'll be sexy," Sam ventured.

She ignored his interruption. "But I don't think it's in danger of getting infected."

"So I'm cleared for duty?"

"Hardly. If it was up to me, I'd make sure you stayed in bed for a whole week."

"Is that right?" Sam teased.

Meredith jumped back, the nervous, guarded look in her eyes once more. "Not like that."

Sam frowned. "What's going on?"

"I need to wrap up your arm again." She started to stand, but he closed a hand on her wrist and held her in place.

"Isn't the fact that I'm not dying *good* news?" he asked.

"Yes."

"Then why do you look so miserable?"

Meredith blew out a breath. "Maybe it's because every time I think things are going right, something goes horribly wrong. And you seem good, so I can only assume that your arm is actually going to fall off any second. Or maybe the boat's going to blow up."

"Fatalism doesn't suit you."

"Fatalism. Hmm. I guess that explains this horrible, tight feeling in my chest."

Sam studied her face for a second. "What else?"

"What else what?"

"What else is making you look at me like I'm going to disappear in a puff of smoke?"

Meredith stared back at Sam's concerned face. She was grateful for his presence. For his incredible perseverance. For his dedication to the case. But his question dug straight to the heart of the worry clouding her mind.

She was scared that everything she'd told him—about her and Nick and Tamara, in particular—would drive him away.

Drive him away? Since when are you so insecure?

But the answer was easy. Since she'd found something she was so scared of losing.

"Sweetheart?" Sam's face was intent and serious.

"I'm damaged goods." Meredith looked down at her hands. "And as clichéd as that might sound, it's true."

"You're…what? Where is this coming from? The fact that you have a past?"

"It's not just any past, is it?"

"Do you wish it had worked out differently?"

She knew right away what he meant. "With Nicholas?"

"Yeah."

She shook her head. "No, I don't."

"Not even a little bit?"

"He wasn't the right man for me."

"So if you know that, why are you letting him—and your past—hold you back from having a literal lifetime of a relationship?"

Heat crept up Meredith's face. "I don't want to be a disappointment."

"Sweetheart, I'm nothing but thankful for your past. Nothing but thankful for what Nick did to you."

"Thankful?"

"As mad as I am that he screwed you over, and as furious as I am that he hurt you, I can't really resent it. If things hadn't happened that way, you wouldn't be you. And when all is said and done, I have a feeling that you being you…is perfect for me."

Meredith's breath caught, but she couldn't form any words.

"Show me where that ache is," Sam commanded softly.

"What?"

"Show me where you had that tight feeling."

"Oh." She lifted her hand and placed the tips of her fingers between her breasts. "Right here."

Sam's hand closed over hers. He pressed down, flattening both of their palms.

"Here?"

"Yes. But it doesn't hurt so much right this second."

"No?"

"Mmm-mmm."

And his warmth continued to seep through, spreading out like a spider web. It felt nice. Comforting. Meredith inhaled and exhaled, enjoying the way their hands moved up and down together.

"Any better?" Sam asked.

"Much."

Meredith brought her palm to his elbow. Then down to his wrist. Then back up. He caught her hand and dragged it up, pinning it to the wall.

Sam's head tipped sideways and down, and his lips found her neck. He sucked gently, finding the sweet spot where her pulse throbbed, then trailed kisses up to her jawline. His lips followed the entire path. They brushed the sensitive skin, sending up a thrill of heat that made her gasp. His fingers weren't far behind, either. They swept away her hair, creating even more of a canvas for their artistic exploration. The nameless spot behind her ear. The arch of her cheekbone. The slope of her brow and the crease in the corner of her eyes. Meredith relished each taste Sam took.

In pursuit of more—or maybe in pursuit of giving back—she adjusted her body. And Sam seemed happy to accommodate. He released the arm he'd pinned back and lifted her sideways into his lap. She slipped her hands over his shoulders and around his neck, mindful of his wound. Her fingers dug into his hair, and it was her turn to explore.

She ran her mouth over the stubble on his chin. The pinpricks of a day and half of growth dug into her lips, each point a sharp flick of pleasure. She kissed the tip of his nose, just because she could, then peppered his face with sensual attention. Lick. Suck. Kiss. Lick again.

Her touches made him growl lightly. And through her jeans, Meredith could feel the evidence of his increasing desire. It made her want to give him even more.

Spurred by his obvious want, she shifted again. She lifted a leg and positioned herself over him, her knees hugging the outside of his thighs. His response was a throaty, animalistic noise—one she could feel as it lifted from deep in his chest and escaped from his throat, one that made her feel powerful and sexy and in control.

But then Sam brought his mouth forward, smashing it to hers. And Meredith realized her control was nothing more than an illusion. This man might be underneath her, but if he wanted the upper hand, she wouldn't even try to keep it. Whatever he wanted from her, he could have it. Meredith would gladly indulge him. Encourage him to take it, even. Like Sam could sense that, he slid forward on the cot, then lay her back against the cotton-covered mattress and positioned himself above her.

His eyes were dark with desire, but his voice was full of restraint. "I want you, sweetheart. I have since the moment you answered the door. And more every second I've known you. But you should know that I'm an all-or-nothing guy. A lifetime guy."

Meredith's heart thumped. "I want it all."

"You have to be sure."

"I'm sure."

"A lifetime."

"A lifetime," she agreed.

"Good. Because when this is done..." He trailed off and raised a suggestive eyebrow.

"When this is done, what?" She heard the eagerness in her own voice and she didn't care.

He stared at her intently, and Meredith swore the temperature in the tiny room rose several degrees just based on his look alone. The heat was palpable, reflected in Sam's stare.

"When this is done," he repeated, "I'm going to take you somewhere isolated with nowhere to go but the big, cushy bed. I'm not even going to let you get up to eat. Breakfast in bed. Lunch in bed. Dinner in bed. I'm going to spend days and days making up for the years we didn't know each other."

Her breath caught. "And in the meantime?"

"This."

He parted her thighs with his knee and exerted a small amount of pressure against her core. Meredith arched a little underneath him. She couldn't help it. Sam groaned in reply.

"I take it back. King-size and cushy would be nice," he said, his voice thick. "But it wouldn't matter if our bed was made of hot coals. Or nails. As long it's ours and we're in it together."

In reply, Meredith lifted her hands to her blouse to undo the buttons. As quickly as she could without fumbling. Sam watched, still and silent until she got to the last one. Then, like he couldn't take it anymore, he dipped his head to her exposed flesh. His mouth was hot and needy as it made its way across her collarbone and down to the lace of her bra. In a slick move that made Meredith gasp, Sam slid his hand to her back and freed her breasts. And his mouth found those, too. Teasing and tasting and making her shiver.

As he kissed her, he slid his hands to the button of her jeans. He popped it open, then dragged down the zipper. He lingered for just a moment, his palm resting above the waistband of her underwear, his mouth at her stomach. Then he grabbed the sides of the jeans and pulled them down. Meredith kicked them off the rest of the way, and the cool air hit her exposed skin. But the cold didn't last long. Sam's fingers landed on her—here, there and everywhere—and warmed her immediately. He stroked her, from thigh to throat, then back, and then he paused. For a moment, Meredith was disappointed. Then she realized he'd only stopped to draw off his own shirt, and her disappointment dissolved. Sam's chest was wide and muscled, and Meredith's hands came up of their own accord to explore it. His skin felt a little rough. A little weathered. Perfectly suited to Sam's personality. And utterly appealing.

He leaned down to kiss her again, but Meredith wanted to see more.

She dragged her hands to the waistband of his jeans, making him draw in a sharp breath. Impatiently, she undid the pants, and in moments, he was naked and poised over her. He held very still, his eyes trained on her face.

"Meredith," he said.

"Yes?"

"I need to say something."

Her heart twitched with worry. "What is it?"

"I'm telling you because I don't ever want there to be a regret between us. Nothing left unsaid. Even the crazy bits, okay?"

The butterflies in her chest beat even harder. "Okay."

"So in the never-going-to-let-it-happen-but-just-in-case-I-never-get-another-chance grand scheme of things, I should warn you…" He inhaled. "Once I have you, sweetheart, I'm never going to let go. Because I love you, Meredith."

The nervous fluttering stopped and now her heart soared. "I love you, too, Sam."

And Sam plunged into her, filling her body the way his words had filled her soul.

Chapter 21

Sam lifted a lazy finger and twirled it in Meredith's mess of blond hair. He squinted, examining the varying shades of gold in the waning light. The sky outside—just barely visible through the little window on the wall above them—had darkened rapidly, and Sam suspected a storm was on the way. As he released the curl, a loudspeaker squawked to life, confirming his suspicions.

"Good evening, ladies and gentlemen. This is a general announcement to let all our passengers know our service to Turtle Island is anticipating some rough waters for the last twenty minutes of our trip. A heavy storm front has moved into the Puget Sound area earlier than expected, and we may experience a slight delay in arrival. Thanks for your patience."

The overhead voice clicked off, and Meredith groaned. "Great."

"Feeling impatient?" Sam teased.

She propped herself up on one elbow and pursed her

lips irritably. "You aren't? I feel a bit like we've been sitting on our hands. I'm tired of waiting."

"Sitting on our hands? Is that code?"

"Code for what?"

Sam raised an eyebrow, and Meredith's cheeks went pink.

"I meant, we haven't been working on the case."

"Right. I'll just sit here and pretend not to be insulted by both your terrible short-term memory and your lack of faith."

"That isn't... I wasn't... Ack."

"Ack?"

She stuck out her tongue. "Yes, actually. Ack. It perfectly describes my current state of mind."

He ran his thumb over her mouth. "That shouldn't be attractive. But it is."

"You might be sick in the head."

He grinned, brought his hand to hers, then dragged them together to his chest. "Do you mean sick in the heart?"

She wrinkled her nose, but when she spoke, her voice was warm. "And that shouldn't be attractive, either. But it is."

"You don't like sap?" he teased.

"Maybe a little bit."

He pulled her close and gave her a slow, deep kiss. "Then I guess you only want to hear a little bit about how you make me feel?"

"I can be bought," she breathed. "With kisses like that."

"And with repeated declaration of love?"

A blush crept up her cheeks. "Yes."

"Good. Because you're going to be hearing a lot of them."

A loud chime, coming from somewhere on the floor, cut her off.

"Saved by the bell," Sam joked, and he rolled over to

rifle through their pile of clothes and yank out Detective Boyd's phone. "Text message from Worm."

"What's it say?"

"Let's have a look." He flopped back onto the bed, pulled her into the crook of his arm and held the phone above them both.

"It's a document link," Meredith said right away. "Click it."

Sam slid his thumb over to open up the file. A few simple paragraphs of text and an embedded photo of a driver's license popped onto the little screen. He recognized what it was immediately.

"This is the background check on Matilda Mathews," Sam explained. "Lists her immediate family. Her employer. A driver's license. Social media connections. Typical stuff."

"But it's all fake. It has to be."

"Yeah, but it's a pretty elaborate one."

Meredith frowned. "Just elaborate enough to make you not bother taking a second look, right?"

"Pretty much. And Worm followed up on everything, and it *still* looks good." Sam squeezed his arms around her to zoom in on the information. "The employer is a call center and they *do* have a Matilda Mathews employed there. No way to tell if it's the same woman, but I'd be surprised if it was. The parents' answering machine has a message saying they're in Florida for the season and the rest should try to enjoy the Washington weather, and the social media accounts are active. The license is the only questionable thing here. And even then, only because it's new."

"Can you crop the driver's license photo?"

"Probably."

Sam fiddled with the phone for a second, zooming and searching for the right buttons. After a minute of trying, he had a passable image isolated. He turned the screen toward Meredith.

"Someone you know?" he asked.

"No. But maybe if you copy that picture into the search engine…"

He did as she suggested, then let out a low whistle. "I'll be damned. She's an actress. Olivia Childress. Agented by Rising Star Talent."

Meredith grabbed the phone and eyed the website with obvious interest. "They're open evenings."

"You're going to call? And say what?"

She didn't answer. She just pressed the link to the number, then set the phone on speaker.

On the third ring, a crisp voice answered. "Rising Star Talent, how can I direct your call?"

"Hi, there!" Meredith greeted brightly. "I'm looking to book a particular client of yours. Olivia Childress. A friend hired her recently and I think she's perfect for an upcoming gig."

"Ah, yes. Olivia's lovely. Is this for a commercial?" The woman on the other end sounded pleased.

"It is. But it's got some particular needs and I was hoping to speak to Ms. Childress directly."

There was a brief pause on the other end. "I can get a message to her. Is the number on our display correct?"

"That's the one. Have her ask for Meredith."

"Meredith. And you're with the Bowerville PD?"

Meredith winced. "Yes. I'm in PR. We're looking for someone to be the face of the department."

"Okay. I'll pass along the message."

"Can you also let her know that our need is somewhat urgent and the pay reflects that?"

"No problem."

"Thank you." Meredith hung up the phone and turned to Sam with a triumphant grin. "See? Now all we have to do is wait for her to call back."

"Not bad."

"Not bad? It was brilliant."

Sam chuckled. "One good move and you're brilliant? I must be a genius."

She shot him a look. "I'll admit you're not bad."

"Is that right?" He grabbed her and rolled her to her back and gave her a thorough kiss.

"Okay," she breathed. "Maybe you're more than not bad…at some things."

"Admit I'm a genius," Sam ordered.

"Admit I'm brilliant," she countered.

He kissed her again, running his hand up her bare thigh as he did. She arched into the kiss.

"Brilliant," he said against her mouth. "Beautiful. Everything in between."

He felt her lips turn up under his. "I'd like to hear about the in-between in great detail."

Abruptly, the speaker above crackled again. "Once again, ladies and gentlemen, we apologize for the interruption. We've come up on that patch of rough water we mentioned earlier. We'll be taking things a little slow as we come up on our approach. This will set us back by approximately a half hour. For your information, this will also be our last sailing of the day. If you need accommodation on the island, do come and see our friendly staff at the concierge's desk. Our partners on Turtle Island will be offering a significant discount to our travelers. Our apologies for the inconvenience."

Sam pushed his palms to the cot and grinned down at Meredith.

"Still feeling impatient?" he asked.

She shook her head.

"Good. Because I've got a few ideas about what we should do while we wait."

One hundred and nine minutes. That's how long it took the ferry to get from the mainland to the island. Twenty-one more than scheduled. Twenty-one minutes Sam put to good use, getting to know every inch of Meredith's five-foot-ten frame. The best twenty-one minutes of his life. Hearing her cry his name and seeing the joy in her eyes as they gave over to the passion... Incredible.

Sam had never been so grateful for a weather-related delay. As they exited the ferry, he couldn't even resent the way the wind whipped through some of the cracks in the old sedan.

Worth the chill.

He glanced over at Meredith. She had her fingertips on her lips and a ghost of a smile turned up the corners of her mouth. As though she couldn't quite help it. He felt the same. Invigorated and satisfied. An unbreakable bubble of contentment sitting just under the surface.

So incredibly worth it.

She caught him looking and her smile widened. "You sure you're good to drive?"

"I'm sure I'm good enough to fly a plane."

She pressed her lips together like she was trying not to laugh, then opened them and let it go anyway. "Let's just stick with roads for now."

Sam shrugged. "If you insist. Ready to boss me around and tell me where to go?"

"You mean navigate?"

"Isn't that what I just said?"

She rolled her eyes, but unfolded the map they'd grabbed from the collection on the ferry. "Tell me the address."

Sam gave her the name of the road, then guided the car off the ferry and followed her instructions to the coastal road that ran around the outside of the island.

"I remember it being really pretty here. Lots of different shades of green." Meredith peered out. "But it's hard to tell now, isn't it?"

It was true. The storm had really picked up steam, and

though the headlights caught the odd flash of foliage, everything else was a blur of wet darkness. The rain pelting down on the windshield came in a slant, and it hit the road hard, too, filling any available dip with sludgy water. In the minutes it took to cover the few miles between the terminal and the turnoff to the cabin, the sky turned completely black. The conditions forced Sam to take the last few hundred feet—a dirt path that had turned to mud— at a crawl. Even then, the sedan's tires protested against every rut in the slick surface below.

"Still want to fly that plane?" Meredith joked as Sam finally put the car in Park and unhooked the wires that had been keeping the engine going.

He eyed the dimly lit wooden structure in front of them. "Still might be safer than this place."

But when they made their way through the downpour and up to the porch, then opened the front door, the interior of the cabin turned out to be warm and sturdy. One wall held a fireplace, stacked with wood. A leather couch, draped in a speckled quilt, sat opposite the hearth. The other side of the large room housed a modern kitchenette. A bench-style, corner seating area framed a squat table, and on top of that table sat a closed laptop, a stack of steaming containers and two disposable place settings. A partly opened door revealed a glimpse of a four-poster bed.

"Not bad," Sam said as he glanced around. "In fact, this may even be more romantic than the stateroom on the ferry."

Meredith shot him a dirty look, but he knew she'd be hard-pressed to deny the appeal. He grinned and moved toward the table, his stomach growling at the scent of fresh Italian food that wafted from the containers. Meredith followed behind him, but when she sat down and reached for the computer rather than a fork, Sam shot out his hand and stopped her.

"Food first," he said. "Shower second. Check out whatever lead Worm has lined up on the laptop...third."

"You really expect me to eat and get clean *before* looking at whatever's on that computer?

Sam shrugged. "We can't go anywhere until the storm passes, anyway. Or at least until it calms enough that we won't be driving blind. We need food and rest and we have the perfect opportunity to do both. Putting off looking at whatever Worm sent us for another hour isn't going to slow us down. And while succumbing to exhaustion won't help us, refreshing our bodies *will*. Eat, shower, work. Trust me."

He opened the lid of the first container and scooped out a generous helping of lasagna onto each plate. Then he moved on to the next plastic tub. Caesar salad. He dished out two spoons worth, and Meredith's eyes followed the movement.

"If you're trying to distract me," she said, "it's not working."

"Liar."

"That's not very nice."

Sam popped open a third container, dug out a piece of parmesan-crusted broccoli with his fingers and tossed it into his mouth. "You know what *is* nice? This food."

Meredith reached for the laptop again, and for the second time, Sam stopped her. When she attempted to squirm away, he spun her around and—in a tried-and-true throwback to his days on the force—pinned her hands behind her back.

"I've captured hardened criminals who can't escape this hold," he informed her.

She lifted a foot and stomped. Her ferry-bought slip-on hit his steel-toed boot with all the effectiveness of a feather.

Sam chuckled. "I guess I can't blame you for trying."

She sighed and leaned back, settling against his chest

as best she could with their hands locked between them. Her curves begged to be flush with his body. Sam couldn't help but loosen his hold to draw her closer. And she took immediate advantage, wriggling free and dancing away.

"I'm guessing most of those hardened criminals weren't women?"

"Some of them were."

"Oh, really?"

"Yep." He lunged toward her, and she moved out of his way easily.

"Not smart women, then."

He lunged again—this time with a feint to one side, then a jump in the other direction—and caught one of her arms. She let out a surprisingly girlie squeal as Sam pulled her close, lifted her from the ground and set her down on table beside the food. He flattened her hands to the smooth wood and looked her straight in the eyes.

"Some were smart. Some were pretty. A few were both. And I promise you...lots of them batted their eyelashes at me."

Meredith snorted. "I don't know how you managed to hold on to any of them."

Sam shrugged. "Easily. Because I wasn't in love with any of them."

Her chest rose and fell a little quicker. "Oh."

"Oh, indeed."

He gave her a light kiss, then let her go to grab a chunk of garlic bread. He tore it in half and offered her one of the pieces. She took it, but her eyes strayed to the laptop once again.

Sam sighed. "Fine. We'll open it. But we'll eat at the same time, and you have to promise to finish the whole plate."

She jumped off the table and went for the laptop eagerly. "Okay."

Sam slid the computer back out of her reach. "I want you to take a nap, too."

"Sure."

"And you have to agree to the shower."

"Fine, whatever."

"With me."

"All right."

She's not listening.

"While we're in there…together… I want you to wash my feet," Sam added.

"I said fine."

Covering his chuckle with a cough, he relented his hold on the computer. She grabbed it from him and opened it immediately, but after just a second of fiddling with the keyboard, she lifted her eyes to his face.

"You do realize I'm crazy about you, too," she said. "So if you want to get me naked in a tub, there's really no need to try and manipulate me into doing it."

He studied her face for a second. "Worm encrypted the computer, didn't he?"

She pursed her lips irritably. "Yes."

With another laugh—this time fully on display—Sam sat down beside her and angled the laptop so they could both see. He followed the trail of virtual bread crumbs his friend had left behind in the form of personal questions. After typing in the sixth answer, a swirling icon popped up on the screen. Sam clicked it, and it prompted him to log in to the email account he and Worm used for trading their most sensitive information. After another series of verification questions, he was finally in.

"Seriously, Worm," he said to the computer. "You're happy to text me links to whatever, but you make me jump through hoops for this? You'd better be about to show me something good."

He opened up the solitary email in his in-box and stared

down in puzzlement. It was nothing but a long list of women's names. And before he could even speculate on what it meant, the air sizzled and the whole cabin plunged into darkness.

Chapter 22

Sam jumped to his feet, automatically taking a defensive stance. He positioned himself between Meredith and the door. And waited. There was no sound but the thick pounding of rain on the roof above.

"Sweetheart," he said, careful to keep his voice low, "I want you to get behind the sofa."

"You want me to hide?" she replied, her voice equally muted.

"Yes. And now isn't the time to be a pain in the butt about your own safety, either."

"You realize that every time someone comes after us, you want me to run for cover, right? I *can* be helpful."

Sam exhaled. "I know you can. But I'd never forgive myself if you got hurt. And I left our gun in the car."

"Well. That wasn't smart."

"I did say *not* to be a pain in the butt, didn't—" A clatter from the porch cut him off. "Behind the couch, Meredith. Now!"

At the snap in his voice, she jumped to comply. He knew he'd likely hear about it later, but for the time being, he didn't care. She was slightly safer. Out of the sight lines of whoever stood on the other side of the door.

As stealthily as he could, Sam slunk low across the room. He paused at the kitchen counter, slid open a drawer and dug around until he found a steak knife.

It's not much. But it's better than nothing.

It didn't matter. Surprise was going to be a better weapon anyway.

Still crouched down, Sam moved to the door and pressed his ear to the wood. On the other side, he could hear the rattle of someone on the porch. Just barely, but there nonetheless.

He leaned forward and gripped the handle. And—hoping that the person outside stood just as close to the door as he did—Sam twisted and pushed as hard as he could. It flew open and flapped wildly.

Sam braced himself for an attack. For someone to jump at him. For a gunshot. What he got instead was nothing. Well. Almost nothing. Just the howl of wind, the rain whipping into him and a very perturbed-looking raccoon with a paper towel in its paws, sitting on the top step. The oversize animal seemed to glare, with beady eyes, at the knife in Sam's hand. It chittered furiously, tossed aside the already soggy paper towel and scampered away.

For a stunned second, Sam stood staring at the place the furry beast had been. Then a deep chuckle overtook him. Then another. In moments, laughter wracked his whole body. He shook with it so hard that his stomach hurt and he could barely acknowledge Meredith as she tiptoed out beside him.

"Sam? What happened?"

He waved a hand, unable to form an answer. Her palm landed on his arm, and the concerned look on her face made Sam laugh even harder. He was soaked. Freezing. Probably getting pneumonia. And wielding a kitchen knife against a glorified rodent.

"I take it there was no one out here?" Meredith asked, a touch of amusement overriding the worry in her voice.

Sam wheezed in, trying to steady himself enough to talk. "A bandit in a mask."

Understanding showed in the narrowing of her eyes. "Perfect. I'm inside cowering behind a sofa and my hero is out here laughing hysterically. At a raccoon. Why didn't you just invite him in for some lasagna and a shower while you were at it?"

"No way. The thing had a paper towel and I'm pretty sure he knew how to use it."

"Ha-ha."

"Seriously. Who knows what else he was capable of?" Sam grinned. "And besides that, I don't want to share my lasagna with anyone. Not even my furry friend with the non-opposable thumbs."

Meredith crossed her arms over her chest, drawing attention to her increasingly damp shirt, which prompted Sam to forget his amusement. He ran his gaze over her body. Slowly. Every curve was highlighted. Not exactly on display, but definitely shown to an advantage.

"Speaking of things I don't want to share…" His voice was thick.

She took a small step backward, a dot of color on each cheek. "Stop looking at me like that."

Sam took a step of his own—wide enough to put him within touching distance. "Like what?"

"Like you're going to beat your chest like a deranged gorilla and toss me over your shoulder."

"Maybe that raccoon brought out the animal in me."

"Don't you dare."

"Too late."

Sam dropped the kitchen knife, crouched down and closed his arms around her knees. Then stopped as something far off and down the road caught his eye.

"What?" Meredith said from above him. "Am I too heavy? Because that'll kind of take away some of that romance you seem so set on."

"No, I—"

There it was again. A flash of light in the otherwise dark woods. He released Meredith immediately and stood. The flash had already become a beam, and the crunch of tires on the road could already be heard above the rain. Before Sam could speak, a marked SUV turned up the muddy road and pulled in and came to a stop. His eyes flicked to the cabin door, an order on his lips. But the driver had already swung open his door and it was too late to send Meredith back into the house in any inconspicuous kind of way.

This isn't Bowerville, Sam reminded himself. *And this man isn't Bowerville PD.*

In fact, as he approached—a tentative smile on his face—Sam realized his tan uniform wasn't even standard police issue, and the man's greeting confirmed it.

"Sorry about the bells and whistles," he said. "The security car I normally use can't handle the mud. Local police lent me theirs. I'm Jimmy."

Sam relaxed. "You're private security?"

The other man nodded. "Yep. We take care of most of the blocks of cabins around here, yours included. Keep it all in line. Which brings me to the first and foremost point of my visit. Everything okay out here?"

Sam fixed an easy smile onto his face. "Aside from a close encounter with a raccoon and a power outage, we're pretty much perfect."

Jimmy laughed. "Little buggers are everywhere out here. Night, day. Rain, shine. They're not picky."

"So we're finding out. Nothing we can't handle, I guess."

Jimmy nodded again. "Glad to hear. And it brings me to the second point of my visit. Passing along a message from the PD—all two of 'em."

"All two of them?" Meredith repeated.

"Yep again, ma'am. We've got a total of five responders on the island. Two cops, two paramedics and one official firefighter. Our part-time dispatcher is working like crazy at the moment, and the lines are tied up something fierce, so we're trying to minimize all the calls in. Power's out all over the place. So we're stressing that if you call in, make sure it's an emergency and expect a delay in getting through. Police don't want anyone to panic, but the non-emergency line is shut down completely."

"No problem. The power outage and the storm just give us newlyweds an excuse to stay indoors," Sam stated.

"Glad to hear it. Because everything out there's pretty much unpassable at the moment. Brings me to my third point, as a matter of fact. Friends over at the PD want everyone to stay off the roads. Reduces the potential for unnecessarily dangerous situations."

"Sounds pretty much perfect. No excuse to leave, no excuse for anyone to disturb us."

Sam deliberately widened his smile and slung his arm around Meredith. He pulled her close and ran his hand up and down her arm with exaggerated intimacy, then leaned down to place a slow, firm kiss on her forehead.

The security guy cleared his throat. "Well. I'll take that as my cue to go."

Sam pretended to be too engrossed in pulling Meredith's hair away from her face to hear him. He stared into her eyes, his smile now affectionate. He waited until Jimmy was already back at his borrowed SUV before he turned his attention back to the other man.

He issued a little wave. "Thanks for stopping by."

"Stay safe," Jimmy called back.

"Will do!"

He continued to hold Meredith tight until the vehicle disappeared into the dark, but the second it was out of sight, she wriggled away. She rounded on him and put her hands on her hips.

"All right," she said. "You want to tell me what that overly dramatic PDA was about? Because I know a put-on when I see it."

Sam smiled—this time far more genuinely. "I'll do you one better. Grab us the flashlight that's hanging just inside the door and I'll show you."

With her pulse jumping around nervously, Meredith followed Sam to the side of the driveway, then down a sloped path. He held the flashlight out, its beam on the ground in front of them. Even though they moved slowly over the sticky terrain, the mud below was as thick as the rain above. And just a few steps in, Meredith hit a dip in the path and lost her footing.

Right away, Sam's hand came out to steady her. But he was about five seconds too late. Before she could grab hold of his outstretched fingers, Meredith's knee slammed to the ground. She skidded forward, spraying dirt all the way up her body. And the momentum didn't stop there. She stumbled sideways, then over the path edge. She face-planted right into a bush.

"Meredith?" Sam's worried voice accompanied the frantic rustle just to the left of the spot where she'd landed.

"I'm here," she replied, spitting out a mouthful of dirt and leaves.

"You okay?"

"Okay-ish."

The flashlight flickered above her, illuminating a wooden post. Meredith reached out and used it pull herself up, and as she did, her breath caught in her throat and she fell back to the ground. She stared up. A small, rusted metal sign was fastened to the top of the post. And in faded letters, it announced that Turtle Beach was just one mile away.

"Sam?"

His hand appeared at her head. With shaking fingers, she grabbed ahold of it and let him yank her to her feet.

"Turtle Beach," she said. "Is this what you wanted to show me?"

In the dark, he nodded. "I was pretty sure I read it right when the headlights hit the sign. That's the place, isn't it? The one where the cave is?"

"Yes."

"Walking distance. In normal weather, anyway."

Meredith's eyes lifted to the sky. Not even a sliver of moonlight found its way through the wild clouds above.

"We're so close." She heard the wistfulness in her voice, and judging by the loud sigh from Sam, he heard it, too.

He turned the flashlight and held it out. "You okay here for a few seconds?"

"Sure. Why?"

He sighed again. "Don't ask, or I might change my mind. I'm already thinking I must be crazy."

"Okay."

"And Meredith?"

"What?"

He handed her the flashlight, then jogged lightly back up the path. Meredith stared after him for a moment—if it had been light out, he wouldn't even really have been out of sight—then turned to shine the beam in the other direction. She only got visibility for another five or so feet before the landscape plunged into darkness again. At the other end of that black space, they'd find the Hamish file.

Which is what you want. What you need. The whole reason you're here.

But she couldn't shake a sudden feeling of foreboding.

She glanced from the Turtle Beach sign to the path once more. She knew she was right about the location. Every bit of her gut told her it would turn out to be true. So why did she have such strong reservations about what else they might find at their childhood hideout? Meredith couldn't pinpoint an answer.

The squish of Sam's boots hitting the muddy path had already come close again. And within a couple of seconds, he was behind her, draping an oversize coat across her shoulders.

"I'm probably going to regret this," he said. "But let's go."

"Go?"

He nodded to the path, past the sign. "To see Matilda Mathews."

"Now?"

The sense of foreboding increased. Almost, Meredith wanted to tell Sam they could wait until morning. As he'd already pointed out, they wouldn't be allowed to leave the island—or even the general area of the cabin—until the storm had cleared, and she doubted that would be this evening. They still had to go over whatever Worm had sent their way, too. And at least that could be done inside.

But then Sam squeezed her arm and said, "If Nick is setting a trap for us, this storm is probably our best chance to get around it. And if you're right, and the file is there, we'll have enough time to have a look at it before the battery on our laptop runs out. Maybe even get it over to Worm if we need to. And if you're wrong and it's not there, we can plan our next move."

And his statement reminded Meredith that a precious amount of their forty-eight hours had already been eaten up. What little time they had left couldn't be wasted on procrastination and nerves.

"I'm not wrong," she said.

And she started down the path, not looking back to see if Sam was keeping up. She was sure he would be.

They traipsed through the woods, then out to a more open area. Sam knew they'd hit part of the beach—even though he couldn't see it—because the sound of the ocean smacking the shore had grown so loud that it almost drowned out the rain. Meredith seemed indifferent to either form of water, though. She pushed along the farthest edge of the pebbled beach, bringing them closer to the trees again. She only paused once, to stare at the woods, then started moving again, slower than before, picking her way into the foliage.

Sam couldn't help but admire the determined set of Meredith's shoulders as she trudged along. Though she now led their movement, he'd sensed a hesitation to head out immediately, but she'd pushed past it. Not that he could blame her for the reluctance, either. The conditions were all but treacherous, and this was a potential turning point in their case.

Their case.

Sam almost stumbled. When had it become *their* case instead of just *his*?

He studied her back a little harder and realized he'd been thinking of it that way nearly the whole time. In all but name, anyway. And it made sense. He trusted Meredith absolutely. He had no doubt about where her loyalties lay. In that way, she was the perfect partner.

Except for the part where you feel the need to protect her 24/7. Sam frowned. *But that could work, too, couldn't it?*

Because he *should* want to protect the person he worked alongside. He ought to be willing to put his life on the line to do it. Knowing that his partner wanted to protect him just as much was equally important. Besides that…everything about working with her just plain felt right.

"Probably too right," he muttered.

Meredith stopped. "What?"

"Nothing." Sam shook his head. "We can keep going."

She didn't move. Instead, she held out the flashlight and shone its narrow arc on a pile of stones.

"We don't have to keep going," she said. "We're here."

Above them, three flashes of lightning illuminated the sky. In the brief moments of brightness, Sam saw that the rocks extended out from a bush-covered hill. At their highest point, the stones were large, and stacked as high as five feet tall. At their lowest position, they were small and peppered the muddy ground, leading to a drop-off of dirt and slick grass that led to the beach again. He stared out. Presumably, no one would be able to see the arrangement from down near the water, and unless someone happened to be right there in the woods, it probably remained hidden from the casual hiker as well.

As the thunder rolled through the air, Sam turned back to find that Meredith had made it halfway up the side already. He had to scramble to catch up, and his first step on the rain-drenched stone nearly sent him flying.

"Be careful!" Meredith called from up top.

Sam started to growl out something about irony, but as he glanced up, Meredith slipped down suddenly, sliding out of sight. His heart dropped. Had she fallen? Hurt herself? She hadn't screamed, but if she'd hit her head, maybe she hadn't had a chance to.

Sam put aside his need for caution and took the rest of the rocks quickly. He crested the top, frantically searching the raised, uneven ground in front of him. He saw nothing. Even the rocks themselves were barely discernable from one another.

Another flash of lightning lit the sky temporarily, and

Sam looked around again, even more urgently. He still didn't see her.

"Meredith!"

The resounding thunder drowned out his voice, but as the sky darkened again, he did catch a flash of dim light. Oddly, it seemed to come from just ahead and *below* the rocks.

"Meredith?" he called again, this time uncertainly.

"Down here." Her reply came from below, too.

Sam moved forward, a few inches at a time. The light increased—just marginally—and as he peered at it, his eyes adjusted enough to see that Meredith *was* underneath the rocks. She held the flashlight pointed up, and it issued just enough visibility to show a smooth curve leading to a naturally formed nook.

"I slipped in," she said. "But if you look over there, you can get in without actually falling."

The light swung to the side, revealing a jagged, stairlike set of rocks. Sam took them, two at a time, and as his feet met the ground, Meredith's hand snaked out to grab his.

"When we hit the beach back there, I knew exactly how to find it," she told him, her eyes flicking around the cave. "It's almost the same as I remember it. Except the size. It seemed a lot bigger when we were kids."

Sam nodded. His head almost fully stuck out the top, but anyone under five feet tall would be well covered. He could easily imagine the appeal of the secret hideout to a couple of kids.

"Very cool. And I can see why your parents would be worried about you hanging out here," he said. "Any sign of the file?"

"Not yet. But somewhere by our feet, there's a long, narrow opening. When we were kids, we used to climb in together and dare each other to slide back farther and farther. If it were me, hiding it for Tamara to find, that's where I would put it." She held out the flashlight. "Can you shine this down there while I look for it? It was always hard to find, even when it was right in front of us in the daylight."

"You got it."

Sam grasped the light in his hand and aimed it toward the ground as Meredith bent down. He moved it along slowly, shining it over mud and rocks and moss. A flash of color caught his eye, and clearly Meredith saw it, too.

"What was that?" she asked right away.

"Not sure."

Sam brought the beam back. Then immediately wished he hadn't. He tried to pull the light away, but he wasn't quick enough. With a cry, Meredith flew up from her crouch and pressed herself into his chest, shaking.

Chapter 23

Meredith stifled a sob and tried to focus on Sam. To concentrate on the way he smoothed her hair and whispered wordless comfort into her ear. To un-see what had flashed in the beam of light. Because the limp, plaid-covered arm jutting out from their secret hiding spot belonged to Nicholas Billing. She knew it was him.

Oh, God.

What would this mean for her sister? Meredith's heart ached for the loss of life. For the loss of a future.

In spite of her resolve to not look, her head swiveled back again.

His hand. His jacket. His body. Her brother-in-law.

She didn't even realize she'd spoken aloud until Sam answered.

"You're sure it's him?"

Meredith lifted her gaze and nodded. "I'm sure. He's dead, isn't he?"

"I think so, sweetheart."

She took a breath. "Check."

"Check?"

"We have to *know*, right?"

"Meredith, we shouldn't disturb—"

"Please."

She sensed his reluctance as he pulled away, and she had to force herself to keep from holding on to him. She let him go and balled her hands into fists at her sides, watching with as much stoicism as she could muster as Sam squatted down. He set the flashlight on the ground and reached for Nicholas's lifeless wrist.

"No pulse," he confirmed, his voice full of genuine regret.

Meredith's chest wanted to collapse in on itself as she struggled to find a way to ask what she wanted to know. "Can you tell what— How he— What—"

She closed her eyes as Sam bent to do a more thorough examination, but flew open as he spoke.

"Gunshot wound in the gut."

"Someone shot him?"

"Afraid so." Sam stood, then held out something small and rectangular. "He had this in his hand."

Meredith took the object and turned it over. "A USB stick?"

"The Hamish file, maybe?"

"But…if someone killed him for the file, why would they leave the file behind?"

Sam met her eyes. "You don't have to hear this if you don't want to."

Meredith shook her head. "I need to know."

"The wound looks like hell. He's been gone a few days, and the shot must've happened a day or two before that, even. And I think he self-treated the whole thing. Wrapped it with gauze, but not much else. Probably didn't even realize how bad it was until it was too late and he was already down here."

"Oh, God."

"But it means you were right, sweetheart. Nicholas had nothing to do with Tamara's kidnapping. He was trying to help her."

She looked toward Nicholas's still form, a thick lump in her throat. "I'd almost rather have been wrong. At least he'd still be alive."

"I'm sorry it turned out like this." Sam reached out and enveloped her in his arms. "And I wish I had something more comforting to say."

Meredith sunk into him for a long moment. The storm raged above, but she ignored it, digging herself deeper against Sam's chest, driving away its violence. She inhaled and exhaled slowly and willed herself to rally. She knew she'd have to grieve. For both her and Tamara. But for now, her sister still needed her in control of her faculties. She worked to gather her thoughts.

"I feel like we shouldn't just leave him here. Like we should call the police," she said, not able to cover her worry at how much doing it would slow them down and how much it would jeopardize the case and maybe even tie their hands completely.

Sam's reply confirmed it. "It's the right thing to do. For his sake and to cover our own rear ends. But doing it will bog us down in red tape and keep us from Tamara."

The lump in her throat seemed to double in size. "Why do I feel like this is just me, having to pick the lesser of two evils?"

"This is you, prioritizing for the living, sweetheart. Besides that…you heard what the security guard said. The lines are tied up like crazy. Chances are, we wouldn't even be able to get through."

Meredith shifted from foot to foot. She squeezed the

USB stick in her palm so hard it hurt. Sam was right, but that didn't mean she had to feel good about leaving Nick behind.

Not Nick, she told herself. *Nick's body.*

She opened her mouth to tell Sam they should go, but before she could speak, Detective Boyd's phone rang from inside Sam's pocket.

"You should get that," she said.

"It's probably Worm. He can wait."

Meredith met his eyes. "He can. But Tamara can't."

He slid the phone from his pocket, then held it out to her. "Caller ID says it's Olivia Childress."

She breathed in, then pressed the button to answer. "Meredith Jamison speaking."

"Hello!" came the cheerful reply. "You called about an audition?"

Meredith forced herself to speak with a matching amount of enthusiasm. "Hi, Ms. Childress. That's right. You were referred to me in regards to your work in the role of Matilda Mathews."

The woman let out a tinkling laugh. "Really? That was the strangest job I've ever done. If I didn't know better, I'd think the guy playing the PI was the real deal."

"Yes, I can see that."

"Do you know him?"

Meredith glanced toward Sam. "We've done a bit of work together."

"If you get a chance, tell him he does an amazing job. I'm sure the husband would've been thrilled with the performance."

"The husband?"

"Nicholas Billing." There was a pause. "Tamara Billing's husband?"

Meredith swayed. "Right. Tamara and Nicholas."

"At first when Mrs. Billing came to me, I thought she

was trying to set up her husband on a cheating sting or something. And I admit I've gotta eat, but that's not my kinda thing. But Mrs. Billing explained she was actually leaving clues for a birthday gift. Some kind of elaborate treasure trail and my role was just a hint along the way. Still not my usual gig, but it was supersweet and she was paying up front, to…"

Meredith could hear the shrug at the end of the explanation. "You did it anyway."

"And since you're calling, it sounds like maybe I should put it on my résumé." Olivia laughed. "The agency said you were with the police PR department?"

"Right. But I'm afraid the role's already been filled."

"But you—"

"I'm sorry, Ms. Childress." Meredith ended the call and looked at Sam. "We should go."

The wind picked up and whipped through the cave. It drove the rain in, too, puffing out Meredith's coat and making her shiver. Sam tried to draw her close, but she pretended not to notice, and she pushed her way up and out of the cave, glad that the noise from the storm drowned out any chance at conversation.

A heavy silence weighted the walk back to the cabin. Meredith could feel it hanging between them. Loss of life was never easy. Loss of family was even harder. And the loss of someone you'd kind of rather not have had in your family…

Guilt hit her even harder.

She'd spent the last five years resenting Nick. Over the last few hours, she'd been ready to lay the blame for Tamara's kidnapping at his feet. But he'd actually been trying to save her. And now he was dead.

She held in a whimper.

When they reached the wooden porch at the cabin, Sam

held open the door to let her enter first, but she stopped on the threshold and turned his way.

"It was Tamara who hired her. For *Nicholas* to find. The clues were all for him. She didn't even want my help, Sam. Was the wedge between us that big?"

Sam shook his head. "Of course not."

"You really believe that?"

"I told you I'd never lie to you, sweetheart. She *does* need you. And even if she thought she didn't, when all of this started, somewhere inside she must've known it anyway."

She didn't move. "You said you *would* lie, if it was to protect me."

"Sweetheart…"

She shook her head. "I don't need protection right now, Sam. I need a reason to believe there's a light at the end of this."

"Meredith, she wouldn't have chosen *this* place if she didn't think there was a chance she might need you."

A small amount of the pressure in her chest lifted. "Thank you."

"For?"

"Being a person I can trust."

"Always."

She brushed her lips over his softly, then moved past him to get into the cabin, where she discarded her jacket and headed for the laptop. She grabbed it, sat on the couch and plugged in the USB stick, then gestured for Sam to join her.

Together, with hands laced, they watched as the master file popped up. Only two subheadings were listed below.

Meredith read them allowed them aloud. "Deleted files. Corrupted files. Sam…there's nothing here. These are just Tamara's trash."

Disappointment washed over her, but Sam stared at

the computer for a second, a frown creasing his forehead hard enough that Meredith thought it must hurt. "Open the second one."

"What?"

"Do you know anyone who *keeps* corrupted files?" He didn't wait for her to answer, he just reached across and double clicked.

"It's a list of names," Meredith said. "But why are they in here under corrupted files?"

"Because," Sam replied. "These aren't corrupted files at all. They're files *about* corruption."

He clicked on the third name from the top, and a new list formed underneath it. Dates. File numbers. And ranks.

"Boyd, Brody. Detective." Meredith lifted her eyes to Sam's face. "These are police?"

"Not just police."

She glanced down again. "Right. Detective Boyd... This isn't Tamara's USB stick at all. Why does she have it? How did she get a list of corrupt cops?"

"I don't know. But I recognize nearly every name in here. Most worked in missing persons in Bowerville. A few are from other cities. And this is more than just a list, sweetheart. This is a paper trail with traceable illegal activity. Look."

She watched as he clicked again, this time on one of the numbered files. It showed two witness statements, nearly identical. But one placed Boyd and three others at the scene of a murder *before* it happened, and the other had clearly been modified to put them there after. Sam clicked and clicked and clicked again. And even Meredith could tell that the pages contained irrefutable evidence of cops on the take, cops covering for drug dealers and cops killing to cover up their misdeeds.

Sam strummed his fingers on the table. "So now we know why our friends on the Bowerville PD want this."

"But why would someone even make a set of files like this one? Wouldn't they just risk exposing themselves?"

"Not as much as they'd risk by *not* having the files. These are for blackmail, plain and simple. Perfect records so no one can turn in whoever's running the operation. The real question is, why would your sister have it?"

Meredith stared down at the computer for a silent moment, then asked, "Can you pull up that other list? The one Worm sent over?"

"Yep." He minimized the USB file and pulled up the email instead.

Meredith tapped the screen. "These are Tamara's clients. The list Worm said he could create from her credit-card files. Can you go back to the main list of cops, then line them up, side by side?"

"Sure."

When he was done, Meredith scanned down, then sighed. "Nothing."

"What about the other folder, then?"

Meredith leaned over, minimized the two windows, then opened up the folder labeled Deleted Files. A trail of information, very similar to the stuff attached to the list of corrupt officers, appeared on the screen. But under each name, there was a date. And a single word in all caps. *DELETED.* Frowning as a name caught her eye, Meredith shuffled until she had all three in a narrow row.

Then she tapped the screen. "There. Look. Sergeant Daniel Barovitz is on the list in the deleted files and Mrs. Trina Tyler-Barovitz on the credit-card-holders list. There's no way they're anything but husband and wife."

"What're you thinking?"

"Well. My sister is pretty tight-lipped about her clients, and it'd be breaking the law for her to release privileged information. But if she knew someone was in danger…"

Meredith trailed off as she realized Sam had stopped

listening. His eyes were glued to the screen and his expression had grown dark. Stormier than the exterior of the cabin. Meredith followed his gaze. And it only took her a second to figure out what had taken his attention. The top name of the deleted files screen.

Heely, Abel.

His old partner.

"Click on it," he ordered.

Meredith didn't hesitate, or even balk at the roughness of his tone. She just put one hand over top of Sam's, squeezed, then used the other hand to obey his command.

And suddenly it wasn't hard for Meredith to put the appropriate meaning to the word *deleted*.

Sam's heart was in his throat. The five-year-old memory, the five-year-old devastation…it all came rushing back.

When he spoke, his voice came out hoarse. "That date there. It's the day they died. The day they tossed Kelsey's body from the car and killed Heely. And these connections here are proof that I was right. Heely was no good. But…"

"But they killed him."

"Yes."

"Why?"

"Damned good question."

Sam pulled the computer away from her and went back through the names on the list of deleted files. He clicked and read and clicked and read some more. Then he leaned back and met her eyes.

"I don't think they just killed Heely. I think they executed him. And all of the other corrupt cops on this list."

As Sam walked Meredith through it, showing her the common threads, he was utterly sure he was right. Nearly every one of deleted names had, at some point, met with someone from Internal Affairs. Sam suspected that the ones without a concrete connection had done the same.

And each of them had died just after, assuming the dates corresponded.

Deleted.

The euphemism made his lip curl in disgust. Regardless of their involvement in criminal activities, they'd been murdered, plain and simple. Sam's teeth clenched together hard enough to make his jaw ache.

What did that make Kelsey's death? Collateral damage? Whoever made the file hadn't even bothered to note her name. How many other innocent people had been killed in the process of self-preservation? And not just that, but preservation of the worst kind of villain—those who were sworn to protect and serve, and instead subverted justice.

And that brought back another, harsher, forcefully buried feeling—utter helplessness. The thing Sam railed against most for the years without his sister. The driving force behind almost every one of his actions since she'd been murdered. And all this time...

"Sam?"

He jerked his eyes toward Meredith. "I'm sorry. It's just that whoever killed my sister and my ex-partner walked away without ever giving me a reason. They didn't get the money, and they never asked for more. They didn't leave a clue, and I'm damned good with clues. So I've never stopped wondering why and I've always thought somehow it was my fault. But this... I was *right* about Heely. And whether or not he decided to do the right thing in the end doesn't matter. The responsibility for Kelsey's death lies at his feet, not mine."

"You see what this else means, right?"

"I see a lot of things." Sam knew his voice was rough. "Scumbag cops. Senseless death."

"I'm talking about for *us*. For *you*. Sam, the men who killed your sister...they're the same ones who took mine. When we get to Tamara, we'll get to them, too."

He stared at her for a long moment, startled that he hadn't immediately connected those particular dots. For a moment, he was elated. The end of this case could mean the end to a half a decade of wondering. Then he remembered that they were stuck. On Turtle Island, and on the case. Their next move was to hand over the file, and in spite of what he'd said earlier about not going in blind, they still didn't know where Tamara was being held. Sam exhaled heavily and ran a frustrated hand through his hair.

"We need another clue," he said. "Or we're just going to be sitting here on our hands—and no, I'm not using that as code for anything."

"What about that other file?" Meredith replied.

"What other file?"

She pointed. "The actual trash file. It won't hurt to look, right?"

Sam leaned forward and clicked. The folder only contained one thing. A link to a video site, labeled with a date and Tamara's name.

Echoing his earlier command, her voice tinged with worry, Meredith said, "Click on it."

"Chances are good that we won't even be able to get an internet connection," Sam replied.

But Worm had clearly thought ahead. When Sam clicked, a free, mobile hot-spot log-in appeared on the screen. He hit the enter key, and immediately a picture of a woman's face popped onto the screen.

"Tamara?" Sam asked.

She nodded. "This looks like one of her weekly video posts. Every Friday, she puts up a snippet of advice."

Sam studied the date stamp. "Except this was posted on Wednesday."

"I know. Press Play."

Sam did, and the picture faded to a title—Tamara's Two

Cents—and then to a live shot of the same girl. She sat at a rustic desk, her hands folded and her eyes on the camera.

Sam examined her face as she issued what he assumed to be her standard greeting. The woman didn't look much like Meredith. Her hair was dark, her skin more tanned and her face made up. Even though she was seated, she gave the impression of being petite. Her narrow chin rested on a delicate hand with painted nails. Only the eyes gave away their shared parentage. Brilliantly green with an undisguisable hint of sass. Under any normal circumstance, that would've made Sam smile. Right that second, though, all he cared about was what the video had to do with their case.

"All right," Tamara said with a little smile. "Today we're going to talk about timing. About finding what you seek. Because those two things, combined with keen observation, will help you find happiness."

She continued on for a bit, her spiel just vague enough to apply to almost any situation, and just banal enough to make Sam wonder how she'd gained such popularity. The video was also clearly recorded on a lower quality device—even he could tell that.

At the end, Tamara smiled again and the camera panned out just enough to show a wood shelf behind her. "I'm Tamara Billing. On location. And that's this week's two cents."

Sam turned to Meredith, a puzzled question on his lips. Her eyes had gone wide with excitement.

"If you're trying to figure out how *that* sells anything," she said, "you can stop. Because that wasn't a real piece. It was another clue. When Tamara does her on-location shoots, she always announces where she is. She calls them her two-and-a-*half*-cent pieces. She does a little bit on why she chose the spot. Like, a lingerie store for a clip about spicing it up in the bedroom. Or a restaurant to talk about date nights. She shows the viewer everything. Plus, her narrative is always smooth. Snappy. Funny but sensitive. None of this…choppiness with weird words standing out. Timing? Finding and seeking? That's not directed at her subscribers. That's directed at us. It has to be. We should watch it again."

Sam hit the replay button. As the video started up for the second time, Meredith leaned forward eagerly. At the forty-second mark, she reached over and froze it.

Her gaze found his. "I know exactly where Tamara is, Sam. She's *here* on Turtle Island. In the cabin where we stayed when we were kids."

"I thought you told me it got torn down."

Her visible excitement didn't diminish in the slightest. "It did. All of the houses along that side of the beach were declared unsafe and demolished. But somehow, she's there anyway. I'm a hundred-percent sure of it. See that window behind her, just to the left of the bookcase?"

"Yeah."

"Look at the sill."

Sam brought the still to full screen mode. In worn, blurred letters, he could just barely make out two words. *Tami* and *Merri*. It was far more than he needed to convince him Meredith was right.

He looked up and gave her a single nod. "Keen observation."

"Just like my sister said."

Sam pushed back the laptop. "Do you know where the cabins were in relation to this one?"

"A couple of miles from the other side of my and Tamara's cave. If you were standing on the part of the beach that touches that outcrop of rock, you would just be able to see the curve where they used to be. Or where that particular one still is, I guess. All we need to do is get there."

The roof above the cabin shuddered. Like a warning.

"I guess going on foot is out of the question, and…" Sam trailed off as an idea came to mind, and under his breath, he added, "But will it work?"

"Will what work?"

"Hang on." He pulled the laptop across the table again. "Let me just send these files over to Worm. Maybe he'll have something to add. At the very least he'll make a backup copy."

Meredith waited in silence as Sam drafted an email, attached the files and sent everything off. When he was done, he stood, grabbed her jacket and tossed it to her.

"Just so you know," he said. "If, by some miracle, this works, I'm going to go ahead and take two more full points."

She met his eyes, and he waited for her to argue. Or smile. Instead, her gaze stayed steady and serious.

"I'll gladly concede those points now," she told him. "Because I know if you say something will work, it will."

She snagged the coat from his hands, moved toward the door and tossed him an expectant look. And Sam was more than happy to follow her out into the storm.

Chapter 24

Meredith gripped the seat beneath her with both hands, her lips pressed together to keep from squeaking at each jagged turn. Even though they were traveling at no more than twenty miles an hour, the going was rough. Every few hundred feet, the snow chains—Sam's big, two-point idea—caught in the mud beneath them. There was zero visibility beyond the light of the sedan's high beams. Not that Meredith wanted to see what was out the windshield anyway. The rain had reached torrential status, and Sam's hands, tight on the wheel, were evidence enough that their journey bordered on insanity.

They jerked and they bumped. But they didn't skid or slide. Not quite, anyway. Once, the tied-together wires under the steering column came loose, and Sam had to reattach them. But thankfully, they didn't stray from the road.

The farther they got from their cabin, the worse the conditions became. And when they reached the turnoff that led to the beachfront, Meredith's arms ached from holding on. She breathed in and out, and she squeezed her lids shut. So it took her by surprise when the car bucked underneath them, then swept violently to one side. And she couldn't quite hold in the responding shriek as her body slid, too. The sedan came to a stop so abruptly that the seat belt dug into her throat.

Sam reached across the console and grabbed her hand. "Sorry, sweetheart. Log in the way."

Meredith peeled her reluctant eyes open and followed the glow of the headlights. *Log* was an understatement. An entire tree had come down, exposed roots and all. It completely blocked the road.

"We can turn around," Sam offered. "Try a different way?"

Meredith shook her head. "There *is* no other way. This is the only road that goes down to the beachfront properties."

"The morning, then?"

"No. The longer we take to get to her, the more likely they are to expect us, right? The fewer hours we have left and..." She swallowed and peered out the windshield, and tried again. "And I think I might even recognize this spot. We're not that far. We can walk."

"Meredith—"

"We walk."

She grabbed the flashlight, opened the door and climbed out. Then she slammed it behind her so he couldn't talk her out of it.

And seconds later, she heard the other car door slam, too, followed by the sound of Sam's feet hitting the soggy ground. He caught up to her, threaded his fingers through hers and pulled her to a stop.

She tried to yank her hand away, and failed. "You're not going to change my mind. I don't care if you think it's crazy or not. We're five hundred feet from my sister and I'm not about to turn around now."

"I'm not trying to stop you," Sam replied.

"You're not?"

"We couldn't have driven the car in much farther anyway. It would attract too much attention." He let out a small laugh. "And besides that, if I *did* try, you'd kick me in the shins and run in the other direction."

"I would," Meredith agreed, relieved he understood. "So why are we stopping?"

"So I can give you a speech."

"Now?"

"Yes, now." Sam let her fingers go so he could lift a sopping wet curl from her cheek. "I love you, sweetheart. If you get hurt, I get hurt. So I want to be clear. Our odds suck. These guys aren't going to negotiate nicely. They might even have a shoot-first mentality. And our own gun only has one bullet left. So we need to make sure we go in smart. We take our time. We assess. We don't take any unnecessary risks. Okay?"

Meredith lifted her chin, knowing she might sound childish and not caring at all. "I'll risk whatever I have to, to save Tamara."

Sam lifted an eyebrow at her. "Unless it's unnecessary."

She started to protest, but before she could get a word out, he tipped up her face and planted a soft kiss on her lips. Meredith thought she should probably protest against that, too—the unfair use of his perfect mouth to get what he wanted—but the kiss made her pulse race. It drove away the chill in the air. And she couldn't find a reason to ask him to stop. In fact, when he did pull away, she had to force herself not to drag him back again.

"Remember that kiss," he said, his voice husky. Then he grabbed her hand, pressed it to his lips and released her completely. "Lead away."

Meredith moved slowly, careful to keep to the edge of the road, where the mud was least thick, and where they were most hidden. It was funny to her, how well she remembered the path. Fifteen years had gone by, and she hadn't thought much about the trip to Turtle Island at all. But now that she was back, that summer of walking up and down with Tamara in tow seemed to have brought back some buried recollection.

Partway down, they reached a long, flat patch of grass. Overgrown hedges lined the space, and Meredith recognized it, too.

She pointed. "There used to be a store here. They sold candy by the bag. Tamara and I weren't allowed to go any higher up the road than that."

"Let me guess. You went anyway."

"All the time. We'd dare each other to get closer and closer to the main road. The first one to chicken out had to give the other all her candy."

"How often did you win?"

Meredith smiled. "Never. Tamara would've cried. And then she would've ratted us both out."

"Typical Tamara and Meredith?" Sam teased.

"Pretty much."

They started walking again, and just below the now-gone store's site, the road grew abruptly steep, and in several places, the foliage grew out into the middle of it. It was obvious, though, that a least one vehicle had come through recently. The flashlight showed broken branches and tire tracks leading straight down.

And knowing what that meant made Meredith was afraid to breathe. In fact, she was unsure if she *could*. The next curve in the road would put them in sight of the line of cabins.

Number eight. The last house. That was the one where they'd stayed as kids. While the rest of the summer homes

all touched the sandy shore, number eight had been built a
ways up, nestled into its own little evergreen grove. Like
an afterthought. Their dad had told them it was the least
desirable spot on the beach, and that's why they'd received
such a steal of a deal on the rent. Both Meredith and Tamara disagreed with whoever had given it the label. Because even though the cabin required a bit more of a walk
to actually tuck their feet into the ocean, it had charm and
privacy and a uniqueness that appealed to the two sisters.
Meredith wondered if that uniqueness was what saved it.

As they rounded the bend, she held tightly to Sam's
hand. "Here we go."

Even in the dark, it was easy to see why the cabins had
been torn down. The ocean had taken over, eroding the
shore all the way up to what little of the foundations remained.

Mother Nature's reclamation, Meredith thought.

But up the beach, she could see that the central, concrete parking lot still sat in one piece. And three vehicles
dotted its surface. She pulled Sam along, studying the
cars and straining to place them. Finally, they got close
enough to see.

The first, she didn't recognize.

The second made her heart flood with relief, because
it was Tamara's small SUV.

And the third made her heart want to *stop*. There was
no mistaking the flat-black, raised-up truck.

"Worm." Sam uttered the name like a curse.

And the reply that followed—unexpected and from behind them—was just as dark. "Didn't see that one coming, did you?"

Meredith dropped Sam's hand and whipped around. The
ponytailed man stood on the road just above them, looking
far bigger and far more menacing than she remembered. A
second man—who Meredith was sure was the same uni-

formed cop from Sam's building—stood beside him. And he held a gun in one hand, pointed casually at Meredith.

"Hola, señorita," he greeted them with a wide grin that chilled her.

Even as stunned as Sam was by the betrayal, his instincts still took over and he lunged forward, his hand reaching for the weapon at his waist. He wasn't quite quick enough.

"Stop." The cocking of the weapon emphasized Worm's one-word command.

Sam lifted his hands. "What the hell's going on here, Worm?"

"You're smart enough to figure it out."

"For God's sake. I helped you. I kept you out of jail."

"Put me in league with the enemy," Worm countered.

"Saving people's lives? Explain to me how that's bad."

"Not the damned PI work, Potter. The cops who always come calling. You think I want to be working with guys like Randy?" He tossed a disparaging look toward the cop with the gun, who seemed indifferent to the disdain. "Because I don't. Since the day you decided to trade my services for my freedom, I haven't had a moment's peace. And every one of my less-than-upstanding friends—which includes everyone in my business circle—has blackballed me."

"And that's worth killing for?"

Sam knew he sounded as incredulous as he felt. But Worm just offered a shrug.

"I liked my life on the periphery," he said. "So when a mutual friend of ours offered me this job, I found it hard to say no."

"A mutual friend?" Sam repeated.

"Yeah. It was supposed to be an easy job," Worm said. "Track Tamara Billing. Figure out what the hell she did with all that sensitive information. But the girl was damned hard to pin down. Smarter than I thought. Got her husband involved. All that 'til-death-do-us-part garbage. It was almost easier when you showed up. Gave me a little family insight."

Behind him, Meredith let out a little cry. Sam wished like hell he could reach for her, but he didn't dare.

Worm smiled. "Now hand over that gun you've got shoved down your pants."

Sam started to reach for it, but then Randy the cop finally spoke.

"Not you," he ordered. "Her."

Meredith inched toward Sam, and he knew she must be wondering if she stood a chance of somehow disarming Randy. Sam shook his head, just enough to warn her that she shouldn't even try.

Her mouth turned down and he knew she understood. With shaking hands, she drew out the weapon and handed it over to Worm.

"All right," his former friend said. "Both of you in front. Walk slowly toward the cabin. And you might want to keep in mind that Randy's a little trigger-happy."

As they began their descent toward the beach, the only thing keeping Sam from turning around and slamming his fist into Worm's throat was Meredith. He'd told her no unnecessary risks. Throttling the other man would definitely fall into that category. So he had to hold it in.

You'll get a chance, he assured himself. *Worm is smart. A genius, maybe. But for the years you've known him, he's always hidden behind a computer. Just like he's hiding behind that cop and his gun.*

They hit the almost nonexistent shore, and finally their destination became visible. Way back from the beach, a dim glow flickered from somewhere inside a dilapidated building. The closer they got, the worse it looked. A broken window. A rotted porch and beams. Missing stairs. Even the door barely hung on by its rusty hinges.

Beside him, Sam felt Meredith slow. He knew the state of repair would concern her. How long had her sister been held there? Under what kind of conditions? They didn't have time to wonder. And they didn't need to anyway—in moments, they'd find out for real.

Sam pressed his hand to the small of her back and urged her silently to keep going. Her pace increased right away, and together, they took the poorly spaced stairs to the hole-filled deck.

"Open the door," Worm ordered.

With gritted teeth, Sam reached up to push the cracked wood, and what he saw inside surprised him.

A second door in near perfect shape.

"That one, too," Worm added.

Sam found the knob, turned it, then stepped back, disbelief making him blink. The outside of the cabin was nothing more than a shell. A disguise. The inside had been refurbished into a studio office. The desk and the bookshelf from Tamara's video sat in front of the same wide window that had the name-carved sill. A couch rested against another wall, and a kitchenette took up a corner space. In the center of it all sat Tamara Billing. Eyes wide. Bound, gagged and tied to a computer chair, and guarded by a tall, wire-thin man wielding a gun.

Meredith hissed in a breath, but when she moved forward, Randy yanked her back roughly. Automatically, Sam stepped in to protect her. But before he could follow through, the man with the gun turned to face them and froze Sam to the spot.

He knew him. Knew now why the voice on the phone had been familiar.

Abel. Goddamned. Heely.

For some reason, thinking the name once wasn't enough. Sam had to do it again.

Abel.

Goddamned.

Heely.

A bit older. A lot more gray at the temples. But the same cold, calculating eyes that hid something dark and uncomfortable. That intangible thing that filled Sam with distrust five years earlier and filled him with sickness now.

"You're supposed to be dead." He spat out the words.

"Apparently I'm not," the other man said back.

"I saw your goddamned body."

"You saw what I wanted you to see. Your sister. And the man who told you he loved her." Heely shrugged. "You were just too damned straight to pick up on the feint."

"You were dirty. The whole time."

"Yes."

So stupidly nonchalant. Disgustingly arrogant.

"Did you kill her, Heely? Did you kill Kelsey?" Sam wished he didn't have to ask, but he had no choice—he had to know.

"Not because I wanted to."

"What the hell does that mean?"

Heely sighed. "I dropped enough hints, Potter, trying to let you in. Trying to encourage you to see the good thing we had going, skimming funds from the ransom, setting up the false drops. You never seemed to get it. Took me a long while to figure out you didn't *want* to understand."

Furious, Sam took a step forward. But Worm grabbed his collar, stopping him.

"Easy now," his former friend cautioned. "You're out-numbered and out-armed, too."

"Shut up, you traitor," Sam replied without taking his eyes off his ex-partner. "A good thing, Heely? Ripping off people experiencing the most traumatic time of their lives. On what planet would I *ever* have agreed to be involved in that?"

"In the one that kept me away from Kelsey."

The words were another shot in the gut. "You used her to get to me."

"Tried to. Failed." The other man shrugged again. "She was a smart girl, Sam. But she had a big, giant heart, too. Loved me for real and still believed I loved her, even when she knew what I was involved in. Thought maybe she could *fix* me. Begged me to go straight. Said we could trust you to help us."

"I would've done whatever she needed." Sam's voice had grown thick.

Heely smiled slowly. "That's what I told her when I turned it around on her. Told her she should be convincing you to get in on the deal. I think that's when she figured out I was in it for the long haul."

"So you faked her kidnapping, then killed her."

"Other way around, actually." Heely appeared unfazed by the admission. "It's funny, actually. I always assumed she'd told you. It was one of the main reasons I made myself disappear. Added my name to the list of deleted files to create a paper trail. Had a friend on the inside alter my fingerprints in the system for identifying *my* body, then left someone else in charge. Went off to enjoy my retirement."

Sickened by the other man's indifference toward his actions, Sam lunged again, but Worm held tightly.

Heely waited for Sam to stop struggling before he went on. "I spent the first bit of time waiting for you to do something. At the very least, to alert the rest of the PD. When that didn't happen, I thought maybe you'd figured out I was alive. That you were biding your time. Making it personal. Always assumed it would be you, not the damned file that came back to haunt me. When my contact on the force called me up and told me the USB stick had gone missing, I agreed to help get it back, but I wasn't worried. We traced it from one of our deleted friends to his wife to Tamara Billing."

Sam recalled the names from the files. "Mr. and Mrs. Barovitz."

"Barovitz had become a liability. Too much transparency with his wife." Heely smiled darkly. "Still. We thought it would be an easy recovery. Get in, get the file. Get out."

"Delete the witness," Sam added.

"Exactly." Far too impassive.

"But she was ready for you."

Heely's gaze strayed to Tamara for a second. "Expecting us, at the very least. Smart. Like your sister. Hid the file and had her husband lead us on some wild-goose chase. Took us a few days to figure out what the hell was going on, and by the time we did, you were already involved. Damned if I thought that was how it would pan out."

"Guess it's your lucky week."

Heely's jaw twitched. "Sam?"

"What?"

The twitch became a smile. "You realize if you'd just been a little less by-the-book—if you'd been even the slightest bit willing to look the other way—Kelsey'd still be alive. You're just as much to blame for her death as I am."

For a second, the familiar guilt hit Sam again, and the emotion ruled him. Then Meredith's voice—gentle and sure and just at his shoulder—carried up to him.

"He's a liar. Kelsey wouldn't have let you help them. She was proud that you were a cop and proud of all the good you were doing. You told me that yourself."

Her words rang true, and Sam saw Kelsey's kidnapping and death for what it really was. Not his fault. Not his responsibility. Just cold-blooded murder. And her killer stood just five feet away.

"Meredith," he growled, very, very softly.

"Necessary action," she murmured back.

Together, they moved.

Intuitively, Meredith knew what Sam expected. What he'd trusted her with.

As he charged forward, she drew back her elbow and slammed it back as hard as she could, straight into Randy's stomach. Surprised, the cop grunted and stumbled. He shot out an arm, knocking Meredith to the ground. But the flailing motion made him lose his grip on his gun. The weapon landed on the ground. It slid across the floor and stopped just in front of Tamara's chair. Her sister met her eyes, nodded, then lifted her bound feet and covered the gun.

Meredith struggled to right herself, and noticed that Randy was already moving toward Tamara. With a gasp, she went after him. Her sister saw him coming, too, and she kicked the weapon in Meredith's direction, then slammed her feet into the corrupt cop's knee. He buckled, but his eyes stayed on the gun as it skittered along, then bounced under the desk.

Meredith scrambled across the floor after it, ignoring the scrape of wood on her knees. From the corner of her eye, she could see that Sam was still grappling with Heely.

Heely.

Sam's dead partner. When he'd addressed the man by that name, she thought she'd misheard. But no. The conversation that followed confirmed it. Heely was alive. And he was the one who'd taken her sister.

He'll pay for both things, Meredith thought as she reached a little farther under the desk.

Her hands closed on the cool metal just as Randy reached her. She tried to turn the gun on him. But he was too quick. Too strong. Before she could even get her fingers in the right place, he tore it from her grip, pushed himself to his knees and took aim at Meredith.

She didn't have time to react. A bullet flew past from the other direction, grazing the shoulder of the man who threatened her.

"Get down!" Sam barked.

Meredith's head whipped to the side. Worm was against the wall, wheezing. Sam stood in front of the big man, Heely's gun in one hand and the man himself in the other.

"Get down," he repeated. "Put the weapon on the ground."

Thank God.

But her relief was short-lived. Heely wasn't ready to give up. With a wild twist, he spun and drove a fist into Sam's injured arm. Sam let out a holler, and the gun slipped from his hand. Faster than seemed possible, the other man reached down, stood up again and then lifted the gun.

"Guess I'll take you out one at time on my own," he said grimly. "Starting with the girl who couldn't mind her own damned business."

He pointed the weapon at Tamara, and Meredith was near enough to see his finger tighten on the trigger. Near enough that she swore she could hear the tiny squeak as he squeezed. But she wasn't near enough to get there. It wasn't enough to stop her from trying. As she dove forward, though, a familiar, solid blur beat her to it.

Sam slammed straight into Tamara, then toppled down beside her, fresh blood soaking in just above the old wound. Meredith glanced back to Heely. He was smiling smugly, and Randy had regained control of his gun, too. Worm was already pushing himself away from the wall toward Tamara.

Meredith tried to move, but Sam lifted a hand and groaned, "Hamish," and she knew her best bet for saving them lay elsewhere.

As Heely raised his gun again, Meredith stood. She jammed her hand into her pocket and dug through until her hands closed on the USB stick. Then she yanked it out and lifted it up.

"You can't kill us," she gasped. "If you do, you'll never get the Hamish file. Or find out where the copy is."

The salt-and-pepper-haired man didn't move the weapon. "It'll be easy enough to take it when you're dead. And as far as the copy is concerned… I have my doubts about its existence."

"Ask Worm," Sam interjected from the ground. "We downloaded what's on that stick and we sent it to him. Is it so hard to believe we made a backup?"

Heely's eyes flicked toward him. "Worm?"

The ponytail bobbed up, then down. "Could be true. They sent one over to me."

Heely sighed. "Get me that hard copy. I'm going to shoot the hell out of it so no one can make a damned copy ever again. Then we'll figure out whose death is most likely to motivate Ms. Jamison to tell us exactly who else she sent a copy to."

Randy took a step toward Meredith, and she backed up automatically.

Heely growled and switched his aim to Tamara, who had started to cry. "Just give me the damned thing."

Meredith took one step toward him. Then another. On the third, Worm gave her an unexpected shove, and she fell forward, smacked straight into the cop and lost her grip on the thumb drive. She cried out as her back slammed into the wood wall.

For a second after she hit, she was winded enough that she couldn't move. She saw Sam try to stand, and Worm's foot land on his back. She saw Tamara's shoulders move up and down in a near silent sob. She heard Heely bark something angrily at Worm, who was staring at the USB stick near his feet.

He lifted his gaze to Meredith. "Get it."

"What?"

"You dropped it. Pick it up."

Confused, aching and sure she was just going to wind up dead anyway, Meredith bent down to grab the file. Then froze. Above her, slim red beams filled the room. Two trained on Heely. Two trained on Randy.

"Took them bloody long enough," Worm said as he lifted his foot off Sam's back and reached down to help him up. "Please don't hit me."

As a half a dozen armed men filed into the tiny cabin, Meredith's head spun. Vaguely, she was aware of what was happening, what was being said as Heely and Randy were being taken into custody. She heard someone explain that the arresting officers had been delayed by the storm, but arrived—almost too late—via helicopter. Worm was telling Sam he'd been acting as a triple agent. And someone had started to untie Tamara.

You should be doing that, said a little voice in her head.

She tried to take a step across the room, but she swayed and had to grab the edge of the desk to hold herself up. Immediately, Sam was at her side, pushing aside the protesting paramedic who'd been dealing with his gunshot wound.

His hand landed on her shoulder. "Sweetheart? You okay?"

"We did it," she responded, barely able to talk.

"I promised you we would."

He leaned down and gave her a quick kiss before the lead officer tapped him on the shoulder.

"I'm fine," Meredith assured him, and turned her attention back to her sister.

A lump formed in her throat. Over the last two days, a whole lifetime had somehow managed to go by. She'd al-

most died. Fallen in love. Realized what her sister meant
to her. But none of that stopped those old feelings—the
insecurities and the rift between them—from resurfac-
ing. Even though she wanted to put it aside, even though
she knew how insignificant it all was, she found herself
unable to move.

But in the end, she didn't have to. The second the last of
the ropes came off, Tamara launched herself from the chair
and barreled straight into her arms, and Meredith didn't
hesitate. She wrapped her sister—her living, breathing,
safe sister—in as tight an embrace as she could.

Epilogue

"It's so quiet in here," Tamara said.

It was true. The hospital that they'd been airlifted to had been train-station noisy the last few hours. But since things had settled down—with Tamara in bed and hooked up to an IV and Meredith in a lounge chair—it seemed very empty.

Meredith offered her sister a smile. "You want me to call the cavalry back in?"

"No." Tamara sighed. "It just feels funny to be peaceful. My client brought me that USB stick a week ago, and my head has been buzzing ever since. And then today with all the police and the doctors, and..."

Meredith saw the way she trailed off and swallowed, and she knew where her mind had gone. "Nicholas. I'm so sorry, Tami."

"I knew he was dead before they told me. We were supposed to meet. To take the USB stick and figure out who to give it to. We knew we couldn't trust anyone in Bowerville, so we were going to go all the way to Seattle. I waited for two days, worried sick. Then Nick called me and told me the plans had to change. He sounded…funny. He said it wasn't safe for us anymore and he'd hide the file somewhere only we would know about. He told me if anything happened, to call you. Our fail-safe, he called you. And he said to remember Hamish and Matilda and to tell you to remember, too."

"So it was him leaving the clues."

"Yes. And when I didn't hear from him again, I knew they'd got to him." She paused, her face crumbling, then inhaled raggedly and continued. "I followed Nick's clues, trying to find him and the file. I didn't want to call you, even though he told me to. I got Sam's name from my client. She said her husband had told her he was the best in the business. And trustworthy. But I didn't want my name attached to the request, so I hired an actress to do it."

"We found her," Meredith confirmed. "But you could've come to me, Tami. I would've helped."

"I know. But I didn't want to put you in danger. And I didn't want you to know how badly I needed you."

Meredith reached over to take her sister's hand. "It's what older siblings do."

Tamara looked down at their clasped palms. "I've never felt like I measured up, Merri."

"I didn't mean to make you feel like that."

"It wasn't that I didn't measure up to your expectations. It's just…you. Everything you did was so perfect. So good. It all mattered. I could never be that way."

The revelation startled Meredith. "You think *I'm* the more successful sister?"

"You are. You're a paralegal. You're completely self-reliant. You—"

"You run a million-dollar business!"

"Giving my opinion to sad couples."

"Helping people."

"Sad people."

Meredith stared at her sister, dumbfounded for a long moment. Then a small giggle escaped her mouth. And another. After a few seconds, her sister joined her. They laughed together until Tamara grabbed Meredith's hand and twisted it to look at the ring that still sparkled there.

"Is this real?" she asked.

"It's not from a cereal box."

"You know that's not what I mean."

Meredith stared down at the pretty stones. "I want it to be real."

"After two days? That's crazy!"

Surprised, Meredith brought her gaze back up. "What?"

But her sister was grinning impishly. "You should go tell him."

"I did."

Tamara's eyes went wide. "You did?"

"Yes."

"What did he say?"

"Well. Actually, he said it first."

"So why are you in here with me?"

"I just got you back. I'm not going to leave." Meredith twisted the ring on her finger and eyed the door uncertainly. "Besides that…what if it was just a heat-of-the-moment thing?"

Tamara shook her head. "I've been counseling couples for five years. I know that look on your face. You love him for real. And you should go tell him before your head explodes."

"You'll be fine for a few minutes?"

"Yes."

"You're sure?"

"Go!"

Meredith took a breath, hugged her sister and stood.

* * *

Sam tried—and failed—to roll over into a more comfortable position. The doctors had insisted on hooking him up to so many tubes that he felt like he was literally tied to the bed. Every move was a struggle. He flipped to his side, set off an alarm on the oxygen monitor, then let out a curse.

"Not the greeting I was hoping for."

Sam stopped struggling immediately, restlessness disappearing at the sight of Meredith's tall silhouette in the doorway. "Hi, sweetheart."

She stepped into the room, looking far more nervous than he had since meeting her.

"Are you okay?" she asked.

He cracked a half smile. "Isn't that my line?"

"Only when you're not the one who got shot twice in one day." She took another step, then stopped.

Sam lifted his injured arm up. "The drugs seem to be working."

Meredith winced. "I don't think you should be doing that."

He raised it higher, triggering another alarm. "This?"

"Stop that! You're going to hurt yourself even worse."

"Make me."

The beeping got louder, and Meredith hurried over. As she put her fingers on his forearm and tried to push it down, Sam grabbed her with both hands and yanked her into the bed. She fought him, but the movement just made the alarm blare, and after a moment, she gave up and settled against him.

"Do I win?" Sam asked, inhaling the sweet scent of her hair.

"It's hard to tell."

"Not from here. I've got the girl I love in my bed. I saved the day. And I'm guaranteed at least a few days of free meals. Points for me."

For a second, silence hung between them. Then she exhaled and spoke in a small voice. "So you meant it."

"Did you think I didn't?"

"I think I made you break all your rules. And there was a lot happening, and I'd understand if you said some things you didn't mean."

Sam leaned back to look down at her face. "Do you know what happened right before you came in here?"

"What?"

"My old boss from the Bowerville PD came in and offered me my job back."

"Did you accept it?"

"No. I told him I couldn't leave my new partner."

"Your... Oh."

He lifted a golden curl and twisted it around his finger. "Don't you think Potter and Jamison, Inc., has a nice ring to it?"

"I hope you mean Jamison and Potter."

She reached up to yank the curl away, and Sam grabbed her hand and pulled it to his cheek. He could feel the pulse in her wrist, thrumming against his skin.

"I've got an even better idea," he said, his voice husky.

"What's that?"

"Potter and Potter." His forefinger found the familiar, diamond-studded band and slid over it. "What do you think?"

"I won't make your life easy," she warned.

Sam chuckled. "I'm sure the risk will be worth the reward."

And he leaned down to kiss her as thoroughly as he knew how.

* * * * *

*Look for Melinda Di Lorenzo's
next thrilling tale
available from
Harlequin Romantic Suspense
in March 2017!*

*And don't miss her previous books
TRUSTING A STRANGER
available now from Harlequin Intrigue
and
PINUPS AND POSSIBILITIES
and DECEPTIONS AND DESIRES
available now from Harlequin Intrigue Noir*

ROMANTIC suspense

Available November 8, 2016

#1919 RUNAWAY COLTON
The Coltons of Texas • by Karen Whiddon

After Piper Colton is framed for her adoptive father's murder, she takes off in an effort to clear her name. Her brother sends bounty hunter Cord Maxwell after her. Their unexpected attraction leads them to strike a dangerous bargain that has them both walking a fine line between truth and deception.

#1920 OPERATION SOLDIER NEXT DOOR
Cutter's Code • by Justine Davis

Former soldier Tate McLaughlin just wants to be left alone and find peace, but Lacey Steele is detemined to bring him into the community fold. When a series of accidents escalates, Tate digs deep into forgotten memories of his time overseas to find the culprit and keep Lacey safe.

#1921 THE BODYGUARD'S BRIDE-TO-BE
Man on a Mission • by Amelia Autin

Tahra Edwards saved a schoolyard full of children from a bomb and lost all memory of the past eighteen months of her life—including Captain Marek Zale, who claims to be her fiancé. Now Marek must save Tahra from the ruthless terrorist organization that wants to silence her.

#1922 MORE THAN A LAWMAN
Honor Bound • by Anna J. Stewart

When she's targeted by a serial killer, Eden St. Claire turns to her brother's best friend, police detective Cole Delaney, for protection. Cole spent years fighting his feelings for Eden, and this time, with her life on the line and a ticking clock, he must convince Eden he wants far more than friendship.

ROMANTIC suspense

*When Piper Colton is accused of murdering her
adoptive father, she sets out to prove her innocence with
a little help from PI Cord Maxwell. Too bad her brother
hired him first—to bring her in for skipping bail...*

*Read on for a sneak preview of
RUNAWAY COLTON,
the penultimate book in
THE COLTONS OF TEXAS miniseries.*

Whatever Piper's intention, her words coaxed a reluctant smile from him. "It's the truth," Cord insisted, merely because he wanted to see what she'd do next. "I never lie."

"Never?"

"Never."

She circled him, keeping several feet between them.

"That must make life difficult for you sometimes."

Thoroughly entertained, he acknowledged her comment with a nod.

"Do you like me?" No coquettishness in either her voice or her expression, just simple curiosity.

"Yes. Actually, I'm beginning to," he amended, still smiling. "Why do you want to know?"

She shrugged. "Just testing to see if you really won't lie. Are you attracted to me?"

A jolt went through him. "Are you flirting?"

Though she colored, she didn't look away. "Maybe. Maybe not. I'm trying to find out where we stand with each other. I also noticed you didn't answer the question."

He laughed; he couldn't help it. "I'd have to be dead not to find you attractive," he told her. "But don't worry, I won't let it get in the way of the job I have to do. Or finding Renee. Both are too important to me."

Color still high, she finally smiled back. "Fair enough. Now how about we call it a night and regroup in the morning."

Though it was still early, he nodded. "Okay. Good night."

She sighed. "I'm probably going to regret this, but…"

Before he could ask what she meant, she crossed the space between them, grabbed him and pulled him down for a kiss. Her mouth moved across his, nothing tentative about it. A wave of lust swamped him. Damn if it wasn't the most erotic kiss he'd ever shared.

Standing stock-still, he let her nibble and explore, until he couldn't take it any longer. Finally, he seized control, needing to claim her. He tasted her, skimmed his fingers over her soft, soft skin, outlining her lush curves. He couldn't get enough, craving more, breathing her in until the force of his arousal told him he needed to break it off right now or they'd be in trouble.

He'd be in trouble, he amended silently. Despite the fact that he physically shook with desire, he stepped back, trying to slow his heartbeat and the way he inhaled short gasps of air. Drowning—that's what this had been like. Drowning in her.

Don't miss
RUNAWAY COLTON by Karen Whiddon,
available November 2016 wherever
Harlequin® Romantic Suspense
books and ebooks are sold.

www.Harlequin.com

HARLEQUIN®

A *Romance* FOR EVERY MOOD™

JUST CAN'T GET ENOUGH?

Join our social communities
and talk to us online.

You will have access to the latest
news on upcoming titles and special
promotions, but most importantly,
you can talk to other fans about your
favorite Harlequin reads.

Harlequin.com/Community

Facebook.com/HarlequinBooks

Twitter.com/HarlequinBooks

Pinterest.com/HarlequinBooks

HSOCIAL

THE WORLD IS BETTER WITH

Romance

Harlequin has everything from contemporary, passionate and heartwarming to suspenseful and inspirational stories.

Whatever your mood, we have a romance just for you!

Connect with us to find your next great read, special offers and more.

 /HarlequinBooks

@HarlequinBooks

www.HarlequinBlog.com

www.Harlequin.com/Newsletters

⬥ HARLEQUIN®

A *Romance* FOR EVERY MOOD™

www.Harlequin.com

SERIESHALOAD2015